GEESE TO A POOR MARKET

By L.D. Whitaker

GEESE TO A POOR MARKET

By L.D. Whitaker

High Hill Press, USA

This is a work of fiction. Names, characters, and incidents are products of the author's imagination or are used fictitiously and are not to be construed as real. Any resemblance to actual events, locales, organizations, or persons, living or dead, is entirely coincidental.

Published by High Hill Press, Missouri

HighHillPress@aol.com
www.highhillpress.com

First High Hill edition:
10 9 8 7 6 5 4 3 2 1

Cover designed by High Hill Press Art Division
ISBN: 978-1-60653-024-5
Library of Congress Number in publication data.

Acknowledgements

I owe thanks to many folks for their encouragement and support of my efforts in writing this novel and will mention a few.

To my publisher, Louella Turner at High Hill Press, for reading my manuscript and believing that *Geese to a Poor Market* was worthy to meet the world.

To Linda Wendling, my mentor and friend, whose early and continued encouragement and instruction made this book possible.

To novelist and teacher John Dalton for sharing his knowledge of the craft of writing and instilling the importance of revising.

To my goddaughter Sally Powers, a fine writer and journalist, for reading early drafts and sharing her insights and making valuable suggestions.

To Gina Keckritz, copy editor par excellent, who went above and beyond and turned an otherwise tedious job into a learning adventure.

To Mark S. Schreiber, co-author of *Somewhere in Time*, for providing historical information about the Missouri State Penitentiary.

To the directors, staff, and special friends at The Writers Colony at Dairy Hollow, where much of the manuscript was written, for providing the perfect retreat.

To Dr. Fred Pfister at *The Ozark Mountaineer* for publishing some of my articles that were a prelude to this work.

To *Missouri Life* for my first paying writing gig.

To Jama Bigger and the late Karl Largent of the Midwest Writers Workshop for jump-starting my writing.

To Denise Bogard for starting St. Louis Writers Workshop, where the manuscript got its start.

To Paul Faulkenberry and the Out of the Ozarks Literary Guild for publishing my short stories that inspired this novel.

To the late Chloe M. Briggs, Ozark novelist and poet, for her accomplishments that set a bar for me.

To my friends at the Ozark Writers League and Saturday Writers for their fellowship.

To my friend Mike Perry for being in my corner.

To my brother Jack for marking the trail for me.

To my wife Mary Ellen for her love, patience, and proofreading skills during the long haul and countless drafts of this novel.

FOR MARY ELLEN

Rarely does the devil appear patently evil—more likely he comes silver-tongued and reasonable appealing to the vain natures of the unsuspecting.

Chapter One

Home Again

*T*he boy, barely four feet tall with a sprinkling of freckles across his nose, watched as the orange semi trailer rig turned onto his street a block away. "It's Daddy!"

The truck's windshield reflected the afternoon sun like a mirror. The truck completed the turn and the reflection dulled as a cloud passed overhead. The boy turned his gaze toward his mother standing a few feet away next to their car parked in the driveway. "Mommy, who's that lady in the truck with Daddy?"

"That's no *lady*. Get in the car, Wesley; we should have been on the road by now.

From inside the car Wesley waived as the truck passed without slowing, but the woman on the passenger side looked straight ahead.

Rita Sanders strained to see through the rain-streaked windshield at the headlights of oncoming traffic. She was heading south from Iowa, and the hilly roads of the southern Missouri Ozarks made passing difficult. Fifty more miles and they would be at her parents' farm and, she hoped, in time for supper. Her seven-year-old boy in the back seat was hungry.

The radio faded out and blared static and she turned it off. She was tired of it anyway. It seemed every station she was able to pick up droned on about spring training and the chances for the 1955 St. Louis Cardinals to win the National League pennant.

"Wesley, don't eat any more root beer barrels—you'll get sick. Grandma will have something good to eat when we get there. It won't be long."

11

"OK, Mama," he said, as he put two more in his mouth and continued reading his comic book. Donald Duck and Mickey Mouse were in Alaska on a dogsled.

"Mama, do you know what an Es-ki-mo says when he wants his dogs to go?"

She looked in the rearview mirror to make eye contact. "Mush!"

"How did you know that?" He sounded disappointed.

"I've seen Sergeant Preston of the Royal Canadian Mounted Police on television, too."

"OK, do you know what they say when they want them to stop?"

"No, Wesley, what?"

"You're supposed to guess, Mama."

"All right. Raspberries?"

"No! Oatmeal!" The boy began a spontaneous staccato giggle that reminded Rita of another cartoon character— Woody Woodpecker.

"That's pretty funny, Wesley." He kept giggling, obviously proud of his joke, and for a moment, Rita forgot her troubles.

But in the next instance, she saw her reflection in the rearview mirror and was struck by how old she looked. She hoped it was just from lack of sleep. When she was a girl, people often said she looked like Elizabeth Taylor in *National Velvet*. This memory spawned some hope. After all, she was only twenty-seven, her hair was still black, and the men still looked at her. She smiled at the mirror. *And, I have pretty teeth.*

She tried the radio again. Hank Williams' nasal voice came through crooning *Your Cheating Heart*, and she thought of her estranged husband, Ray. Yeah, he had a cheating heart, too. He had met up with that truck stop waitress and cheated all the way across Texas.

12

Six months before, Rita had found a letter in Ray's shirt pocket from Betty somebody and confronted him. A series of ugly fights had followed—fights that she was ashamed to admit, Wesley had seen. Now here she was, pulling a trailer with their belongings behind a 1950 Ford to her parents' farm in the Ozark hills.

A few miles back, she had exited Route 66 and headed south on Highway 63, a winding blacktop road that went all the way to Arkansas. Along the roadside she passed shacks and farms with woodpiles stacked high and smoke coming from the chimneys. It was still chilly in March, but even in summer, many folks in the Ozarks cooked on wood-burning stoves. The smell of the smoke took her back in time.

The dense hardwood forests were beginning to show early signs of spring. Dogwoods would be blooming in a few weeks. It was still winter in Iowa. Winter, that was how she thought about Iowa—never the summers—just barren winter fields with corn stobs poking through the snow.

She should have used the restroom at the truck stop in Rolla. She had made Wesley go, but the door to the women's room wouldn't shut completely, and the room smelled awful. Somebody had thrown up, and she was afraid she would throw up, too, if she stayed inside. Now, the truck stop coffee had made its way through her system, and she felt a sense of urgency. She would have to pull off to the side of the road.

From experience Rita knew one advantage of a four-door sedan was that, in a pee stop, both doors on the passenger side could be opened, and a woman could hunker down between them out of the view of passing traffic. She told Wesley to walk down the road a short ways, to turn his head, and to watch for cars.

With her jeans and panties below her knees, she squatted and began to feel, along with a cold breeze, the sense of relief that comes with urination too long postponed. A car was coming . . . no, it was slowing. She heard the crunch of

13

tires on the gravel shoulder and peeked over the door. A man was getting out of a green Buick, three car lengths away. Wesley stood between the Buick and Rita's car.

She grimaced, and with effort, stopped the flow and jerked her pants and underwear up at the same time, letting her blouse hang on the outside.

"Is everything all right here?" the man asked, standing beside his car.

"Everything is fine," Rita called back, as she stood up behind the door. "Wesley, come over here with Mama." Wesley, showing no sense of alarm, sauntered toward her.

"I saw the boy standing by the road and both doors open and thought there might be some trouble."

The man's eyes shifted to the ground below the car door where the ground was wet, and Rita thought she saw the hint of a smile on his lips. "I just dumped out some coffee," she said.

In a conversational tone, the man asked, "Where are you headed?"

"To my parents' farm in Henderson County." She paused before adding, "My husband is a truck driver, and he's following behind me. I got ahead, and I'm waiting for him to catch up."

"Henderson County? That's where *I'm* headed." He moved forward a few steps from his car and stopped. "My name is Sam Rockford. I run a little tavern called Club 60 in Birch View."

"Wait a second," Rita said, "I remember you. You run that honky-tonk the other side of Birch View that we went to last summer. You offered me a job."

Sam's face registered a faint recollection. "Yeah," he said, pausing in thought, "you were there with your girlfriend and her sister." Then, with a laugh, he said, "Well, the job is still open. Guess, I'll be going, now. Drop in and see me."

"I might just do that."

14

Sam turned toward his car. When he got to the door, he looked over his shoulder at Rita and said, "Don't drink too much coffee."

Under her breath, Rita said, "You son of a bitch."

An hour later the bridge that spanned the Jack's Fork River at Cedar Bluff came into view. The location got its name from a gnarled ancient cedar that grew out of the forty-foot bluff that shadowed a popular swimming hole.

"Look, Mama. There are people swimming in that river."

Swimming in March? Rita peered through the bridge structure at the spring-fed river. "Oh my. They're not swimming—they're being baptized. It must be forty degrees outside."

The wide gravel bar below looked like a parking lot with a dozen or so pickups and cars aligned in rows. Men wearing overalls and long-sleeved shirts stood as a group facing the river, while women at the water's edge wrapped blankets around three or four drenched and shivering grade-school-aged children.

A preacher man, standing waist-deep in the water, covered a young girl's mouth with her hand and leaned her backwards until she was submerged. The girl arose from the water, flailing her arms to gain a footing and fought her way back to shore and the waiting arms of a woman holding a blanket.

"I'll bet they're cold," Wesley said.

"I expect they are," Rita said. "I was baptized in that same creek in *February.*"

Her mind, again, went back in time. She had just turned twelve years old, still a child, really, when she was submerged in the name of the Father, Son, and Holy Ghost one Sunday afternoon. Rita thought, *What happened to that girl?*

"Mama . . . Mama, are you listening?"

15

"Yes, Wesley. What?"

"Why were they doing that back at the river?"

"Son, when you go south of the Jack's Fork River, you go into a different world."

Wesley scrunched up his face as if he wanted to ask a question, but didn't know what question to ask, and just said, "Oh."

Twenty minutes later they came to a "T" intersection with U.S. Highway 60 and turned eastward through a string of filling stations and small businesses at the edge of Pine Grove.

"Mama, what's that man got?" Wesley asked, pointing out the window toward a motel with a sign that read "Krazy Kabins."

Rita looked through the passenger side window. In the parking lot, standing at the rear of a newer model Oldsmobile convertible, a man was either removing or loading something in the trunk. He glanced to the left and right as if to make sure no one was looking.

With an eye open, always, to the beauty in every man, Rita slowed even more to watch. She noticed that although he was a big man, tall and broad, something about him seemed almost dainty. Maybe it was because he was so well dressed.

Again, the impeccably dressed man looked furtively up and down the highway and then removed his classy sport coat and threw it over the cargo in the trunk of his car.

Rita slowed nearly to a crawl, but kept moving, watching the man in her side mirror, then switching to her rearview mirror. The man had removed the cargo from the trunk and was now carrying it, trying to keep it covered with the sport coat. Poking out from under the jacket was what looked like an animal's head, but with too many horns.

Wesley was now on his knees staring out the back window. "Mama, it looks like a woman with horns."

What a good-looking man, Rita thought.

16

Rita turned south off Highway 60 at the Tremont General Store and onto the gravel road that led to the O'Dell farm. A mile later, when the Ford bumped over the tracks at Railroad Hill, Wesley awoke from a nap. "Are we there yet? I'm hungry."

"It's less than a half-mile; we'll be there in a minute."

At the top of the hill, Rita said, "There it is." Wesley put his hands on the back of the front seat and leaned forward. "I can see it, too."

The two-story house had a square-hipped roof with two front dormers and a mansard covered with faded green asphalt shingles. The shiplap exterior was unpainted and weathered gray. The closest neighboring houses were barely visible in either direction.

In her mind's eye, Rita could see the rough-hewn floorboards on the second floor where she and Wesley would be staying. It was an unfinished attic that was frigid in the winter and stifling hot in the summer, but it would be home . . . again.

Rita turned in at the gravel driveway, stopped the car, and shut down the engine. Three dogs trotted toward the car barking.

"Wait a minute, Wesley." He was opening the door and about to get out. "Let the dogs settle down. Grandma and Grandpa will be out in a second."

Rita's father, Will, came through the door first, waving his arms at the dogs in a reversed breaststroke, which they ignored. But they stopped their barking and scattered when Will bellowed, "You dogs get out of here."

"You can get out now, Wesley," Rita said.

Wesley opened the door and ran to his grandpa. Will bent over and hugged the boy, and Wesley wrapped both arms tightly around Will's waist.

"Hi Grandpa! We drove in the middle of the night and saw a man with something in his trunk and saw another man on the road and—"

"Hold on son, you'll have plenty of time to tell me about your trip. Let me say hello to your mama."

"OK, Grandpa."

Will removed his engineer-style cap, revealing his mostly bald head, and put the cap on Wesley. It went down over Wesley's ears, but it produced a big smile on the boy's face, and a grin on Will's.

Rita closed the car door and raised both arms straight up in a full body stretch. Her back ached, her feelings were on edge, and she was at a point of exhaustion, where she knew she could teeter either toward laughter or tears. But seeing her dad's cap on Wesley made her smile.

Rita and her dad met each other walking and embraced, neither speaking for a moment. Will kissed the top of her head and said, "Welcome home. Let's go see Mom." They separated and turned toward the house.

Beulah, stout and formidable, wearing a blue gingham dress and apron, appeared at the doorway. "You all come on in, now; I've got supper on the stove." She opened the screen door. "Wesley, come and give your grandma a hug."

After supper Will took Wesley to the barnyard to show him Charley the pig and the old mare, Dolly. Rita and Beulah began the after-dinner clean up.

The smell of the fried chicken they had for dinner lingered in the air. The kitchen was sultry in defiance of the slight breeze that drifted through the open window. The room got even warmer after Beulah added dried corncobs and oak planer mill scraps to the cook stove firebox to heat dishwater.

After an extended period of silence that suggested neither knew what to say, Beulah asked Rita, "Well, have you heard from Ray?"

"Not for several weeks. The last time he was in town, he stayed with a friend. He said he was going to come and see Wesley, but he never showed up."

"I'm sorry to hear that. Maybe he just didn't want to see you."

"You think it's my fault?"

"No, I'm just surprised he didn't see Wesley, that's all."

Rita sighed. "He could have . . . why do you always take his side?"

"I'm not taking sides. I'm just worried about Wesley."

"Don't worry, we'll be all right."

Beulah lifted the metal dishpan to the stove and looked back at Rita. "How are you going to support yourself? Where are you going to get a job around here?"

"I've got some money from the house. We sold it to another trucker. I'll be fine for a few months. I thought I could help you and daddy around here and then find something. When we were here last summer, that guy who runs the tavern in Birch View said he'd give me a job if I lived around here."

Beulah's face became dour. "I hoped you wouldn't go to bars anymore when you moved down here . . . and maybe be more like you used to be when you taught Sunday school."

"Mama, that was a long time ago—before the war—things have changed."

"Well, they haven't changed that much around here."

Chapter Two

Out of the Garden

*F*rom the front porch swing, Rita watched Will without focusing as he tilled the acre garden plot with a mare and a single-shovel plow. She inhaled the freshness of the April morning, hoping the deep breath would ease the growing anxiety she felt. A half-full cup of coffee, now cold, sat next to her.

Will's left arm had been amputated above the wrist in a blacksmith shop accident when Rita was a child. When he worked he wore a prosthesis with a mechanical hook that he could operate by manipulating its leather shoulder harness. The technique was barely noticeable. With a simple shrug of his shoulder he could open and close the steel grasping hook.

With his hook clamped on one handle of the plow and his right hand gripped on the other, Will struggled to keep plow and horse going in a straight line. He would call to the horse, "Gee, Dolly" or "Haw, Dolly," and the horse would respond to the traditional language of muleskinners and go right or left.

As Will called to the horse, Rita's attention centered on her father. He was remarkably gentle working with the horse. He had the same considerate manner with animals as he did with people, and they responded in kind.

But a sure way to provoke the anger of this generally peaceful man was to abuse an animal or child. Rita recalled her father grabbing a bullwhip from the hands of a man who was beating a terrified horse and then slapping the man across the back with it and asking him how he liked it . . . and would he like some more. Only seven years old at the time,

21

but proud as a banty, little Rita had nudged a stranger and said, "That's my daddy."

Will and Dolly had been at it for thirty minutes and only had two fifty-yard furrows to show for their efforts. The April ground was still wet, but the radio weatherman had forecasted rain, and Will wanted to get the garden ready.

Rita turned her head to the distinctive whine of a tractor coming down the gravel road. Moments later, Chester Caldwell drove his row-crop Farmall, with a two-bottom plow attached and elevated like a scorpion's tail, onto the driveway. Without slowing, he proceeded across the yard to the garden and turned off the engine.

Chester was a stout, burly man with forearms like fence posts that didn't taper at the wrist. Everyone aptly called him "Stout." His voice matched his stature as he boomed out to Will, "You trying to wear out that hay burner, Will? Give her a rest. I'll have that garden turned over in thirty minutes."

Rita knew intuitively neither Beulah nor Will had asked for Stout's assistance. Most likely, a casual remark that Will intended to plow his garden had made its way by word of mouth to Stout. She knew also that Stout wouldn't accept money, but Beulah would send Wesley with a freshly baked pie to Stout's house the next day. Neighbors helped neighbors in Tremont.

The memory of this culture of safety and warmth had drawn Rita back from Iowa; it was the atmosphere she wanted for Wesley. For the moment, the restlessness that had been growing inside her for several days was calmed.

When he finished plowing, Stout stopped the tractor at the edge of the yard where Will stood waiting, and throttled back the engine.

"Stout, you better come in for a cup of coffee."

"No thanks, Will, I've got to get back to the house, but I'll be back this afternoon to disc."

22

With a beefy arm extended and a wry smile on his face, Stout pointed toward a contraption on the ground at the side of the garden. It was the size and shape of a set of bed springs with rows of railroad spikes pointed to the ground. "After I disc, are you going to use that thing over there to smooth the soil for planting?"

"You mean my spring-tooth scratcher?" Will smiled back with the pride of an inventor.

"I suppose I could hook my tractor up to it," Stout said.

"No, Stout, Dolly will do just fine."

Stout engaged the tractor's power take-off, raising the plow, and then headed back to his place to change implements. He stopped at the edge of the driveway as the RFD letter carrier slowed for the O'Dell mailbox.

The flag on the box wasn't up, which meant the carrier was delivering mail. As Will led Dolly to the barn lot, he pointed his hook toward the mailbox, as if Rita hadn't noticed or was too slow in reacting, which irritated her. Before she could catch herself, she had frowned at him but stopped short of compounding the moment with a smart comment. She felt like a churlish teenager.

The tin mailbox sat atop a split-rail post in the ditch and cantilevered toward the edge of the road. She returned the mailman's wave as he drove away and approached the mailbox with caution. Years before, she had seen a copperhead in the weeds not more than two feet from the box and hadn't forgotten the experience.

The carrier had left two pieces of mail: an electric bill from REA and a letter for Beulah with no return address—in Ray's handwriting. She raised the letter to the sun but couldn't see through the envelope. If Beulah hadn't been in the kitchen, Rita would have steamed it open over the tea kettle.

It had been over a month since Rita had heard from Ray. Ray's handwriting made her think of money—she used to sign his paychecks when he was on the road. Now her money was dwindling. She had bought a power saw for Will, shingles for the hen house, school clothes for Wesley, and brakes for the car. The money and her sense of security had gone so quickly.

Inside the house she handed the mail to Beulah with indifference that she did not feel. "The letter is from Ray, but it's addressed to you."

Beulah's lips tightened as if she had just been reminded of an unpleasant situation. She glanced at the electric bill, sat it on the table, and then held the envelope at arm's length toward the light from the window, squinting her eyes to make out the contents.

Rita's indifference turned to impatience. "Just open it, Mama."

Beulah shot a warning scowl at Rita. "If you don't mind, I'm going to open it with the scissors. I don't want to cut anything important. It feels like it might have a photograph."

Rita's eyebrows rose with suspicion. Her mind formed an image of a truck stop waitress with pouty lips and her arms around Ray.

Beulah snipped off the end of the envelope and shook out the contents. "Well, I'll swan. It's a money order for forty dollars, and it's made out to me."

"What's the letter say?" Rita asked with undisguised annoyance.

Beulah unfolded the letter and read it silently. After a moment, she said, "He says that the money is for me to take care of Wesley . . . that he doesn't trust you not to waste it. That's about it." She handed the letter back to Rita.

On Saturday Rita didn't go to Pine Grove with the rest of the family—she had a plan. After they left, she bathed in the galvanized metal bath tub that she brought to the kitchen from where it hung behind the smoke house.

God, she missed indoor plumbing, but the rain water from the cistern did wonders for her hair. It made it soft and full of body. After her bath she pinned up her hair with bobby pins and curlers and sat on the front porch in the sun.

Later, she brushed out her hair and applied makeup. She appraised what she saw in the mirror and smiled at the reflection. From a plastic toiletry bag she pulled a small bottle that had been carefully wrapped in tissue. Chanel No. 5. Ray had given it to her Christmas before last. She dabbed herself behind both ears and at the cleavage of her breasts that were slightly exposed beneath the open collar of her blouse.

Rita arrived at Club 60 around noon and parked near the front door among several cars and pickups. Her plan, which had seemed so plausible, was now riddled with doubt. What would this man think—a woman walking into a tavern alone? Do these slacks make me look fat? I wonder if he heard me call him an old son of a bitch.

Through the window, Rita could see him behind the bar and thought he was looking at her. *Rockford, Sam Rockford*, she rehearsed in her mind. She took a deep breath, let it out, and opened the car door.

She paused at the entrance before opening the screen door, turned right, and with determined steps, made her way to the end of the bar and sat on a stool. She sat her purse on the vacant stool next to her.

A half-dozen men sat at the other end of the bar, and about the same number were scattered in booths along the dance floor beyond. One man, not much older than Rita, was bent intently over the pinball machine by the front window to her left. He had a can of Budweiser sitting on the glass top.

Sam had watched Rita get out of her car. It wasn't often that a woman visited his tavern alone. It wasn't a car he recognized, at first, and then he remembered it and the woman with the little boy.

When she paused at the front doorway, Sam's back was to her as he rang up a sale on the cash register, but their eyes had met when he glanced up at the mirror over the back bar.

Sam handed change to the customer and moved to the end of the bar where Rita sat. "Well, I see you made it to Henderson County. What can I do for you?"

"Mr. Rockford—"

"The name is Sam, and I never caught your name."

"It's Rita, Rita Sanders."

"Well, Mrs. Sanders—"

"Call me Rita."

Sam smiled. "OK, Rita, what can I do for you?"

"Is your offer of a job still open?"

Sam didn't respond, but his eyes didn't leave hers for several moments. If he was surprised, he didn't show it. He broke eye contact when he pulled a pack of Chesterfields from his left shirt pocket and lit one.

Rita reached for her purse and started to get up from the barstool.

"As a matter of fact, it is," Sam said. "My waitress quit two days ago and went to work for my thieving cousin down the road. You ever waitressed?"

"No, but I worked as a riveter during the war, and then in a factory assembling brakes until I moved back here. I mean, I'm used to hard work."

"This job doesn't pay like a factory job in the city. I pay a dollar an hour, plus tips, which won't be much except on Friday and Saturday nights."

"That's more than I'm making now. When can I start?"

"Whoa, now. What's your husband think about this?" Sam took a drag from his cigarette.

"We're separated."

"Then you can start tonight."

26

"What do I wear?

"Well, for starters you ought to wear a shirt that is a little less revealing. After a few brews on Saturday night, these old boys can get a little too friendly."

Rita's face blushed, and she knew it. Defensively, she said, "I can wear a dress."

"What you have on is fine—slacks and a blouse—just button up. Get here around 5:30, and I'll show you the ropes."

Rita nodded and said, "I'll see you then." But before she turned to leave, she thought, *There is something very attractive about this man.*

Calling over to the man at the pinball machine, Sam said, "Hey, J. Bob, you're off the hook. Come over here and meet your replacement."

When the O'Dell's Mercury turned in the driveway of the farm, Rita was in the front yard, car keys in hand. As soon as it stopped, Wesley hustled over to his mother.

"Where are you going, Mama?" His yellow shirt, which Beulah had made from a feed sack, was wrinkled and more pulled out than tucked in his jeans.

"From the looks of your shirt, son, you've been wrestling with a goat."

"Ah, my new friend and I were climbing in the rafters at the sale barn."

Will nodded at Rita as he got out of car but turned to the trunk to unload groceries.

Beulah, carrying only her pocketbook, went directly toward Rita. "Wesley, help your grandpa." Wesley trotted back to the car.

Beulah looked Rita up and down suspiciously. "Where are you off to?"

"I've got a job as a waitress, Mama."

Beulah's suspicion deepened into a frown. "Where?"

"At Club 60 in Birch View."

Beulah made a dry spitting sound. "You mean that honky-tonk. Girl, you're driving your geese to a poor market."

"What's that supposed to mean?"

"It means you're making bad choices."

28

Chapter Three
Club 60

*E*ven with the windows open, Club 60 had a sour smell from the hundreds of beers that had been swilled and spilled over the years. The surface of the mahogany bar had lost its varnished luster, and countless scrubbings had turned the wooden floor to punk.

From behind the bar, Sam Rockford filled the beer cooler underneath with cans of Falstaff. It was ninety degrees outside his tavern, and not much better inside. The draft from the cooler fan felt good on his face.

Leaning over as he stacked the cans, Sam's gray hair fell over his forehead. He pushed it straight back, which was how he wore it, revealing a prominent widow's peak. For a man in his forties, he still had a fairly full head of hair.

Sam's appearance seldom changed: khaki work trousers and a patterned cotton shirt with two pockets. He insisted on two pockets. One pocket served as a filing cabinet for bills, receipts, and his glasses, and the other for a pack of Chesterfields.

It was the middle of the afternoon, and Harry Caray's voice came through the Philco on the back bar announcing the St. Louis Cardinals' game. The All-Star break was approaching and their World Series chances might be slim, but according to Harry, the Cards' Bill Virdon could follow teammate Wally Moon as rookie of the year.

The lunch crowd had left, although it was a stretch to describe what his customers ate as *lunch*: pickled eggs from the gallon jar that sat at one end of the bar, Vienna sausages (which they pronounced *viney*), and crackers—all washed down with beer.

It was also a stretch to call Club 60 a *club*. More aptly put, it was a southern Missouri beer joint on U.S. Highway 60, just outside the city limits of Birch View, a roll-up-the-streets-after-sundown village of 432 residents, according to the road sign.

In another life, the building had been a farm implement and feed store constructed of concrete blocks with a flat tar roof. When it was converted to a tavern, the previous owner added a pitched-roof attic changing the roofline and a coat of pink paint to the concrete blocks, which were faded and chalky by the time Sam bought it. Still, Sam thought the place was beautiful; he said it was a cross between a chicken coop and a gold mine.

During the week, Club 60 was an oasis for bib overall working men from the logwoods and sawmills, but on Friday and Saturday nights, it was a honky-tonk where people danced to the jukebox or, occasionally, a live country western band.

The only customer currently present was J. Robert Dalton, known by most folks as J. Bob. A regular customer at Club 60, he was one of only two lawyers in the county, the other being Chester Martin, the prosecuting attorney. J. Bob had come in twenty minutes before and already had a second can of Budweiser sitting on the pinball machine he was playing.

Sam finished loading the last flat of beer and closed the cooler. He lit a cigarette, and as he exhaled, he looked over at J. Bob.

"Hey, counselor, did you lose a case today?"

"You might say that."

"When I was in the navy, you could always tell when one of the sea lawyers lost a court-martial. He'd be in the Officers' Club drowning his sorrows," Sam said.

"I wouldn't say I'm drowning my sorrows. More like trying to get un-pissed off. Good ol' Judge Elliot denied my bail reduction motion for a client. He said his philosophy on setting a bond was not to ensure that the defendant would appear in court, but to make sure he was sufficiently punished in the interim."

"Hell, J. Bob, if anybody would run against that old bastard, he wouldn't stand a chance next election."

"There's nobody to run against him, unless it would be Chester Martin, but he likes prosecuting too much—he's such a horse's ass. Plus, he has a civil practice on the side and probably makes more money than the judge. I actually wish another lawyer would move in."

"Wouldn't that make the pickings a little thin?"

"You know, Sam, there's an old saying: A town that's too small to support one lawyer can certainly support two."

Sam laughed. "You're probably right about that—one to stir up lawsuits, and another to defend them."

Outside, a car pulled onto the parking lot. A few moments later, a man who appeared to be in his forties opened the screen door and walked in. About six feet tall, unshaven, haggard, and looking like he needed sleep, the man went straight to a barstool and sat down opposite Sam. Sam did not recognize him.

"What can I get you?" Sam asked.

The man stifled a belch and then swallowed with difficulty as if he were trying to keep the contents of his stomach down. "Give me a Falstaff." His speech was slurred.

The man's breath was stale and smelled of booze. Sam could see the outline of a half-pint bottle in the breast pocket of the man's overalls.

"Look pal, I think you've already had enough," Sam said.

"You mean you're not going to sell me a Falstaff?" The voice was louder and the tone was aggressive.

Sam's face turned expressionless, but intensity radiated from his blue eyes. "No, and I'm not going to take any lip from you, either. So just get out of here." Sam reached under the bar and felt for the leather blackjack he kept for such occasions.

J. Bob had only glanced up momentarily from the pinball machine when the man he knew as Elvin Collier had traipsed in, but now he turned his full attention to the scene developing at the bar. He knew Sam's patience could be thin, and right now he looked menacing.

Sam was nearly as tall as Collier, and at a shade over two hundred, he outweighed him by twenty pounds, although some of those were in his waistline. But Sam knew how to fight. On the back bar, an autographed photograph of the heavyweight boxing champion of the navy bore the inscription: "To Sam Rockford, my pal and trainer."

Sam pulled the blackjack from underneath the bar, held it in plain view, and stared directly into Collier's eyes.

Collier stood up. "All right, I'm leaving . . . for now." He turned around and retreated out the front door.

"Who the hell was that?" Sam asked J. Bob.

"That example of rude behavior was Elvin Collier. He's part of the Collier clan that lives between here and Wisdom. He hasn't been around in years."

As J. Bob was providing background information, Collier yelled from the parking lot, "Come out here, you son of a bitch, I'm going to whip your ass."

Almost casually, Sam said, "I guess I better see what he wants."

"Sam, you better be careful. He might be armed, and I've heard he's mean," J. Bob said.

"He's got a knife or a gun, or he wouldn't be acting so tough," Sam said, as he moved to the other end of the bar and pulled a .38 Colt revolver from underneath.

He checked the cylinder; it was loaded with six rounds of police-special ammunition. He snapped it shut with a flick of his wrist, darted to the side of the front door, and pushed open the screen door with his foot.

He eased his head from behind the doorway. A shot cracked, hitting the doorjamb just above his head. Another shot hit the lintel to his right. Sam dove through the doorway and hit the ground behind his Buick, which was parked between him and Collier.

Aiming under the car, Sam fired a shot that hit in front of Collier's feet. Collier jumped in the air like a startled rooster. When he landed, his ankle turned and he fell forward. The pistol flew from his hand as he tried to break his fall.

Sam fired another round that hit in front of Collier, scattering gravel and humming as it ricocheted from the ground. Collier struggled to his feet and hobbled to his car, yanked open the door, and dove in.

Sam advanced with the .38 pointed at Collier. He glanced at the abandoned weapon on the ground, and noticed that Collier had dropped something else . . . his car keys.

Sam sidled toward the car and watched as Collier frantically searched for his keys. He looked on the floor, on the seat, and felt under his hips. With Sam just a few feet away, Collier rolled up his window. At arm's length, Sam dangled the keys back and forth in front of the window. Collier's face blanched and his eyes got wide.

"Roll down the window."

Collier shook his head.

Sam raised the .38 level with Collier's nose and pulled back the hammer. The window came down.

"Don't shoot, man." His face was ashen.

"What the hell do you think you're doing? Get your ass out of the car," Sam said.

"Why don't you uncock that thing, man."

Sam eased the hammer down, but the double-action revolver could still be fired by simply pulling the trigger.

Sam marched his prisoner back into the tavern. He saw J. Bob crawling from underneath the pinball machine.

"Sit down," Sam said to Collier, pointing to the barstool where he had been sitting. With the pistol still pointed at Collier, Sam went behind the bar, pulled out a can of Falstaff, and slid it to the end of the bar where J. Bob was standing. "Counselor, open that and scoot it up to Mr. Collier, here. I believe he placed an order I haven't filled yet."

The expression on J. Bob's face changed from fear to astonishment, but he punctured two holes in the top of the can with a beer opener and pushed the can within the reach of Collier.

"What's this?" Collier's face was that of a condemned man being offered a cigarette before execution.

"What's it look like, stupid?" Sam said. "Drink it. And as soon as you finish it, I never want to see your sorry ass around here again, or I'll blow it off."

Collier's hand shook as he brought the can to his mouth, and he spilled beer on the bib of his overalls. In less than a minute, he finished the beer. "Can I go now?"

Sam slid the car keys to him.

Collier stood up and started backing out. When he got to the door, he said, "You going to give me my gun back?"

Sam bellowed a laugh. "You're lucky to get your keys back. Get out of here."

For the second time that afternoon, Elvin Collier left the Club 60. He started his car and stomped on the accelerator. The tires spun, throwing gravel and squealing as the car pulled onto Highway 60 headed toward town.

"Look at this, J. Bob." Sam held the confiscated handgun in front of him. "It's a nine-shot H&R .22. Maybe I'll give it to Rita when she comes in tonight?"

"So, is Rita a pretty good shot?" J. Bob asked.

"No, she's a terrible shot, but she's dangerous."

"What do you mean?"

"Hell, she might be aiming at your leg and hit you in the heart."

"That's funny, Sam . . . good old Rita. How long have you been going with her now?"

The smile left Sam's face. "Counselor, I don't need to remind you that Rita is a married woman, and a few words here and there lead to rumors and a ruined reputation. Loose lips sink ships."

"Excuse me, Sam, I didn't mean to be presumptuous."

Sam pulled two cans of Budweiser out of the cooler, opened one for J. Bob and the other for himself. "But Counselor, I know you'll keep this confidential. Rita and I have had a quiet understanding for a couple months, I suppose."

"Sam, my lips are sealed. But back to this afternoon's main event, just tell me one thing. Why did you bring Collier back inside and give him a beer?"

"I had to do something," Sam said. "I just couldn't stand out there in the parking lot with my pistol pointed at him. After he dropped his gun, I couldn't shoot him, but I wanted to scare him so he wouldn't ever come back."

"Why didn't you just call the sheriff and have him arrested. You had an eye-witness to the crime."

"By the time the sheriff got here, he could have shot us both."

"But after you had him inside, you could have—"

"You don't get it do you, J. Bob. Some hayshaker comes into my place and shoots at me; I'm not waiting on the sheriff. And I'm not going to have him stinking up my place for a half hour waiting on the sheriff. It's bad for business."

J. Bob's instinct was to ask a follow-up question, but, instead, he nodded without speaking and pushed his empty toward Sam. He suspected even if he could read Sam's mind, he would be no closer to a logical answer—it was just the way Sam was wired.

Sam set up a second round for J. Bob and himself, and they continued to relive the episode.

Shortly after five o'clock, a couple sawmill workers came in. Sam had just collected for their beers when the telephone rang. Sam picked up the receiver. "J. Bob, it's for you."

"Who is it?"

"Your secretary."

J. Bob took the call and came back to his barstool. "Well, Sam, it looks like I've got a new client."

"Who?"

"Elvin Collier. Got any coffee?"

J. Bob had grown up in Birch View. He was always the smallest, smartest, and "prettiest" boy in his class. That was until he was a freshman in high school, and he was assaulted by a virulent case of acne. He was still the smallest and the smartest, but the acne became chronic and was resistant to all attempted remedies.

The persistence of the acne kept his face inflamed and caused visible scars by the time he was a sophomore. It also caused painful scars that were not visible: shame and depression made him feel like a pariah, and he knew what the word meant. It was in high school that he discovered alcohol. It didn't help his complexion, but it made him feel like he fit in.

Over time, alcohol became his panacea—and his problem—but still there were those that said they'd rather have J. Bob, half-drunk, representing them than one of those high-priced lawyers from Poplar Bluff or White Plains.

It wasn't unusual for those in need of his services to pay him with produce from their gardens or other home-produced goods. When he saw shame in their faces, he would insist that he was getting the better end of the deal, saying something

36

like, "Jessie, you can't get eggs and butter like this at the store."

Helping others allowed J. Bob to get outside of himself and to feel bigger than his physical stature. Even in high school this quality had been evident. On the Birch View High class of '43 senior trip to Memphis, it was J. Bob that had stood up to a drunken soldier on the train who was trying to paw one of the girls in his class. During the entire episode, the principal had sat at the back of the train car staring out the window.

By six-thirty on the afternoon of the gunfight, J. Bob had driven twenty miles east and arrived at the county jail in Hendersonville. Speedo Green, the sheriff, met him at the door.

"We don't have the police report written up yet," Speedo said, "but here's a copy of the ticket. DWI with property damage. I'll let you in to see him; he's fairly sober, now."

J. Bob entered the cell.

"Are you lawyer Dalton?" Elvin asked.

"We meet again," J. Bob said.

"What are you talking about?"

"I was over by the pinball machine when you tried to shoot up the Club 60. And, by the way, if the sheriff or the prosecuting attorney gets wind of 'The Gunfight at the O.K. Corral,' I can't represent you because I'd be a material witness."

J. Bob held up a copy of the ticket. "And if I represent you on this little matter, and then the gunfight comes up, I'll have to withdraw as your attorney. However, even as an officer of the court, I don't consider it my duty to bring it to anybody's attention. And, frankly, I don't think Sam is going to press any charges either. He'd have some explaining to do about taking the law into his own hands, and I doubt he would want to appear in court."

"Well, I ain't telling anybody," Elvin said.

After the fee arrangements were made, J. Bob said, "Tell me what happened . . . as much as you remember, anyway."

"Oh, I remember all right. Somebody points a cocked .38 at your head you sober up pretty fast. I left Club 60 and headed to my brother's house on the other side of town. I knew he'd have some beer. We had a few while I was telling him what happened. Then, we ran out of smokes and decided to drive into town to get some.

"Well, I was pulling off the highway onto Main Street, and I must have hit some gravel. I wasn't going that fast, but I slid sideways and hit the culvert in front of Rose's Café, and busted a front wheel. I didn't have a spare so my brother took off to Al's Garage to try and get a loaner. Boy, people came out of Rose's like the circus was in town. I just left them looking and went inside and got me a cup of coffee.

"The next thing you know, I look outside and see the deputy pull up. So I go out, and he says, 'Who was driving this car?' I say, 'I was,' and he handcuffs me and hauls me off to jail."

"All right, I think I've got the picture," J. Bob said. "One more question, though . . . was your brother around when the deputy arrested you?"

"Nah, we were gone before he got back."

"OK. I'll see if I can work something out with Chester Martin, but if we have to try this, make sure your brother isn't at the courthouse."

The day Elvin's case came to trial, J. Bob was at the courthouse trying without success to plea bargain with the prosecutor when the judge entered the courtroom.

"All rise, the Magistrate Court for Henderson County is called to order, the Honorable Gerald T. Elliot presiding," the bailiff said.

The judge entered the courtroom. "Please be seated. The only case on this docket is *State v. Collier*. Are the parties ready to proceed?"

"Chester Martin for the State of Missouri, ready, Your honor."

"J. Robert Dalton representing the defendant, Elvin Collier. The defense is ready, Your Honor."

"Very well, proceed, Mr. Martin."

"The state calls Deputy Sheriff Archie Woods to the stand." The deputy was sworn in. "Deputy Woods, directing your attention to the seventh day of July 1955 at approximately 3:30 p.m., did you have occasion to witness the defendant, Mr. Collier, engaged in the operation of a motor vehicle or involved in a motor vehicle accident of any kind?"

J. Bob rose to his feet. "Your Honor, I'll object to the form of that question. Counsel has asked two questions. It was also leading and suggestive."

"Sustained."

Changing the question, the prosecutor said, "Deputy, would you tell the court what you observed when you arrived at the scene of the accident."

"When I arrived at the scene, there were approximately eight people standing around the vehicle that had collided with a culvert."

"Did you make any determination as to whom the driver or the owner of the vehicle involved in this accident was?"

"Yes, sir, I did. As I approached the group at the scene, I asked, 'Who was driving this car?' and the defendant said—"

J. Bob stood up. "Your Honor, may I ask a question for the purpose of an objection?

"Sure," the judge said.

39

"Is the prosecutor attempting to show by testimony of this witness who was driving the car?"

"That's exactly what I intend to show Your Honor."

"Judge, I am going to object to any testimony from this witness concerning who was driving the car, until the prosecutor proves the *corpus delicti*."

"Counselor, would you care to elaborate?" the judge asked.

"Yes, Your Honor. Under Missouri case law, and I have citations, the prosecution may not use the statement of the defendant until they prove all the elements of the crime—the *corpus delicti*. In this case, there are three elements: *Driving, while,* and *intoxicated*. The state might be able to prove my client was intoxicated, but it can't use his statement to prove that he was driving."

"Mr. Martin, your response," the judge said.

"On the contrary, Your Honor, we have established the elements of the crime—the *corpus delicti*."

"No, you haven't," the judge said. "Officer, did you see the defendant behind the wheel of the car?"

"No, sir, I did not."

"May it please the Court, I move for a dismissal," J. Bob said.

"Mr. Martin, do you have any other witnesses?"

"No, Your Honor."

"The case will be dismissed, then. Court is adjourned."

J. Bob thought his victory called for a celebration at Club 60, but it could wait until Saturday night.

Chapter Four
Take a Little, Leave a Little

"*W*ell, did you get that son of a bitch off?" Sam asked as J. Bob came through the door.

J. Bob sat down on a barstool. "Yes, I did. Didn't even have to conduct a cross-examination. Let me buy us a couple of beers."

"I'll be damned," Sam said, "that son of a bitch tries to kill me, and you get him off a drunk driving charge. The *least* you can do is buy me a beer—you ought to buy me a case."

"Hell, Sam, look at it like this, if you'd shot Collier, I'd be representing you, and you might be looking at doing time. This way we're both winners."

Glancing at the door, Sam said, "J. Bob, don't look now, but here comes trouble.."

Big John Crawford filled the doorway as he paused at the entrance to Club 60. In spite of his 6-foot-5-inch, 260-pound frame, he was dapper, wearing tan gabardine slacks and a light blue short-sleeve shirt with the collar unbuttoned.

John was particular about his appearance. Several times a year, when he was in St. Louis or Memphis, he frequented fashionable men's clothing stores that carried brands he favored and sizes that were accommodating.

As he surveyed the inside of the tavern, Sam watched him. With the happy smile of a child, John yelled over at Sam, "Hey, Cuz, I need one of your watered-down beers and a couple of those horsemeat burgers you serve here."

Sam returned the smile but thought, *That vain bastard always has to make an entrance.* Then he said, "It's Friday, why aren't you at your place? Did you run off all the customers?" Sam turned and called out John's order through the service window to Rita in the kitchen.

John glanced at the 14-carat Longines watch on his wrist. "It's only 6:30—the shank of the evening. Anyway, Marge is holding down the fort for a few hours."

John sauntered across the room and took a barstool next to J. Bob. "Evening, counselor."

J. Bob returned the pleasantry. "Hey, Big John."

Sam sat a can of Budweiser in front of John. "I thought you were going to break it off with Marge. The last I heard, Thelma's been about ready to divorce you since you hired Marge away from me."

As if *divorce* was his cue to speak, J. Bob interjected himself into the conversation. "John, if Marge is construed as a paramour, that will give Thelma grounds."

"Don't worry, counselor, if it comes to that, old Big John is going to rely on you to find him a loophole."

A sardonic smile formed on Sam's lips. "You'll end up with a loop, all right, but it'll be around your neck."

"Maybe so," John said, "but right now I've got to go to the pisser."

John left for the toilet and returned to his barstool a few minutes later. "Sam," he said, "I was just thinking, your problem is that you have a sense of propriety when it comes to women, and the idea of having more than one woman at a time offends you."

Sam fixed his eyes on John's. "No, I just know better than to get involved in a triangle. Something bad always happens."

"What's this about more than one woman?" Rita had arrived from the kitchen with John's order. She slid a plate with two hamburgers in front of him.

"Well, hi darling," John said smiling at Rita. "Ah . . . we were just saying that with a woman like you, a man didn't need more than one."

42

Rita flashed a smile. "It's getting deep in here, I'm going back to the kitchen."

John bit off half of one of the burgers, chewed a couple times, and with his mouth still full, said, "Ah, hell, I forgot the catsup." He grabbed a bottle of catsup from the bar, unscrewed the cap, and began drinking from it as if it were a bottle of beer. He kept tapping the bottle to keep the flow going and didn't stop gulping until the bottle was two-thirds empty. Then he took a long draw from his beer. He saw J. Bob staring at him in amazement, and said, "Poor man's Bloody Mary."

John looked to the other end of the bar. "Hey, Sam, come over here, I need to talk to you about something."

Sam was waiting on a customer and showed no sign of responding. As first cousins, Sam and John had squabbled as kids, argued as sailors in the navy, and now operated competing taverns twelve miles apart on Highway 60. Sam would take his time.

Moseying over, Sam picked up a couple of empties and wiped the counter with a bar towel. "Yeah, what do you want, John?"

"Got something I want to show you at my place. Why don't you and Rita come over Sunday morning around ten, and I'll fix some steak and eggs."

"How much is this going to cost me?"

"Cuz, you break my heart. This is completely social . . . well, mostly social, but I've got something to show you that you'll appreciate."

"I'll check with Rita, but I suppose we can make it."

The rest of the evening had been uneventful. The Falstaff clock on the back bar indicated it was twenty minutes to midnight. Sam stepped from behind the bar and yelled, "Last call. We're closing in fifteen minutes. And nobody leaves with an open can."

Rita repeated the warning in the dance area and pulled the plug on the jukebox as soon as Webb Pierce's "There Stands the Glass" was finished.

"Hey, I had two more songs paid for," a voice said.

"Ben, I'll give you a quarter the next time you're in," Rita said.

The last of the customers straggled out shortly after midnight and Sam locked the door and turned off the outside lights. The light from the vending machines and advertising signs gave the place a florescent glow inside.

Rita was next to him as he turned around from the door. Sam wrapped his arms around her shoulders and kissed the top of her head. "Do you want coffee or something to eat?"

"No, I don't think so. If we're going to Big John's tomorrow for breakfast, I better go home. Anyway, I'm tired."

He opened the door and walked to her car. She got in and closed the door, and Sam leaned through the open window and kissed her lightly on the lips. "You're the best, baby."

"That's sweet, Sam. You're not bad yourself."

As she drove away, he watched the tail lights get smaller and thought, *Big John is right about Rita . . . with her, a man doesn't need anyone else.* He walked back inside and locked the door.

On weekends Sam slept in the storage room. He closed up late and didn't want to drive thirty miles with the evening's proceeds over a dark winding road to Ridgeview. There, in the back of the tavern, he had a cot surrounded by brooms, beer cartons, mops, and old advertising displays.

Tonight, he wasn't sleepy so he sat on the edge of the cot in his wrinkled, white boxer shorts and a T-shirt dealing five-card stud to three imaginary players.

He was not simply passing time, as one might play solitaire. For Sam, this was disciplined practice. He devised

44

strategies as he played each hand against the others, trying to anticipate the next card to be dealt by keeping a running count in his head.

A hundred-watt bulb hung from the ceiling by an electrical cord illuminating the small table in front of the cot. The light formed shadows over the odd shapes in the rest of the room and created a wavy reflection in the window glass on the back wall.

Outside, at the edge of the light cast from inside, a man stepped from the darkness. Chappy, Sam's coon dog, started barking as if he were trying to get out of his pen.

Sam looked up and thought he saw the flicker of a shadow dart out of the light. He grabbed his pistol from under the pillow and turned off the light. Crouching, he stepped to the side of the window and looked out. A half-moon, intermittently blocked by clouds, provided a dim landscape, but Sam saw nothing. Chappy continued to bark. *Probably a raccoon,* Sam thought, but he left the light off and lay down on the cot, listening, until he saw it was dawn.

He lit a cigarette and sucked in the first puff before his feet hit the deck. With the cigarette dangling from his lips, he put on his shoes and grabbed his .38. In shoes and underwear, he stalked from window to window gazing outside. Nothing. At any rate, nothing that he could see.

Feeling more at ease, he finished dressing, put the revolver in his pocket, and went outside to investigate. In the coolness of the morning, Chappy, usually a slow-moving blue-tick mix, greeted him with a hound dog warble and jumped on the hog wire fence surrounding his doghouse. Sam scratched Chappy behind the ears as he surveyed the premises.

"Chappy, I'll feed you in a minute. First let me finish looking around and make some coffee."

Near the back window of the storage room, he noticed a flattened patch of jimson weed. There, a metallic reflection from the ground caught his attention—a brass cartridge from a pistol or rifle.

Later that morning Rita arrived back at Club 60 around nine o'clock, and Sam let her in the front door. "Hi sweetie," she said. She raised on her toes and kissed him. With closer examination, she said, "You don't look so good." Sam had shaved and combed his hair, but his complexion was sallow and his eyes bloodshot. "Do you need some of the hair of the dog that bit you?"

"I don't have a hangover. I just didn't get much sleep last night, but a shot of whiskey might help."

Sam went to the back room, and Rita poured herself a cup of coffee and topped off the cup Sam had left on the bar. He returned with a bottle of Jim Beam, and they went to a booth and sat down. Sam poured a shot in her cup and one for himself in a shot glass. After a swallow from the glass, he told Rita about Chappy barking during the night.

Rita's eyes widened. She took a sip from her cup without looking at it. "How do you know it wasn't a coon? That would certainly make Chappy bark."

"It wasn't the kind of bark he makes with the scent of a coon, or the kind of bark he makes when I come to feed him. It was the sound he makes when another dog comes on his territory or an intruder."

"I see," Rita said.

Sam took another sip from the shot glass. "Plus, this morning I saw where weeds had been tramped down like somebody had been walking in back, and I found this." He showed her the bullet.

"That looks like the bullets that go in the pistol you gave me, but longer."

"You're right—it's a long-rifle shell. It carries a bigger powder charge, but it can be used in a pistol or a rifle. It wasn't near the toilets, so it's not likely one of the customers would have dropped it there. Someone may have dropped it trying to load a pistol or clearing the chamber on a rifle."

"My God, Sam. Do you think it was that guy who shot at you?"

"I don't know."

"Sam, you have a lot of cash on hand after you close on Saturday nights. I think you ought to call the sheriff."

"I might give Speedo a call, but meanwhile, I'm going to make up an *Oscar*."

With a furrowed brow, Rita's face posed the question without her saying a word, and Sam responded. "An *Oscar* is a dummy. Remember in western movies, the cowboy would use his hat and bedroll as a decoy to fool the bad guys."

"I think you should tell Speedo."

Thirty minutes later, Sam and Rita arrived at Big John's tavern in Wisdom, an unremarkable town about the size of Birch View. From the highway, it could have been mistaken for a one-story log house, but the sign on the roof with the caricature of a pipe-smoking hillbilly proclaimed "Big John's Roadhouse."

Sam thought John's place was a dump compared to Club 60, and he told Rita so as his Buick came to a stop.

"You know, Sam, that's odd since he is so particular about the way he dresses."

Sam turned his head to Rita with an expression of one about to say something clever. "Hell, he probably thinks of himself as a gentleman farmer slopping hogs."

Sam had just turned off the ignition when John appeared at the front door. He gave a big salute and walked directly to the passenger side, opened the door, and extended his hand to assist Rita out. He pulled her up to a hug and kissed her on the side of the mouth, only because Rita had turned her cheek to avoid a direct smack on the lips.

"Now, Big John, don't get smoochy," Rita said. Her experience tending bar had given her good reflexes.

Sam walked over to their side of the car, scowling and shaking his head. John held up both arms in feigned protest of his innocence, then extended his right hand to Sam and said, "Good morning, Cuz," as they shook hands.

When customers entered the rustic interior of Big John's Roadhouse, their eyes were drawn to Rosie, hanging from the ceiling over the center of the rough-sawn oak bar.

Rosie was a lighting fixture, and one of Big John's proudest possessions. Carved from wood, she was lifelike, with raven windswept hair and a faded blue Grecian gown that draped from one shoulder, partially exposing her right breast. She looked as if she once may have been the figurehead on the bow of some unknown frigate. John was sure that was the case.

Rosie emerged at the waist from the hub of a wooden wagon wheel surrounded by a wreath of elk antlers, as she gazed into the distance over the dance floor, illuminating the bar with a soft glow. God help the drunk who disparaged Rosie's beauty in front of Big John.

John claimed to have acquired Rosie when he was on a hunting trip in Wyoming. According to him, after an unsuccessful day hunting, he ended up in a bar in Jackson Hole where Rosie adorned the entrance foyer. A long poker game later, John marched out carrying Rosie. He put her in the passenger's seat of his Olds and headed back to Missouri.

Inside, Rita cheerfully said, "Good morning, Rosie." The first time she saw Rosie hanging there, she recalled her trip from Iowa, and finally understood what Wesley had seen: *a woman with horns*. Yet Rita never mentioned it to Big John.

John ushered them past the bar to a 30 by 15-foot room partitioned from the dance floor by a waist-high wall with jalousie windows to the ceiling. With the louvers up, it was an alcove for couples who wanted to be cozier. They could sit in the flickering light of candles stuck like stalagmites in empty whiskey bottles layered with multi-colored wax, and still see the dance floor. With the louvers shut, it was a venue for after-hours gambling.

As they came through the door, Rita and Sam's eyes were drawn to the far end of the room. A red glass lampshade hung from the ceiling illuminating the stretched green felt and polished mahogany sides of a pool table. In the contrasting light, it looked like a religious shrine. With votive candles, it could have been an altar in the grotto of some Gnostic cult.

"What do you think of this baby?" John asked, his pride apparent.

"It's beautiful," Rita said.

"John, I didn't know you cared that much about shooting pool," Sam said.

John picked up three ten-penny nails from a window ledge and laid them flat on the playing surface of the pool table. "Watch this," John said. The three nails snapped straight up to a vertical position. A big grin came to John's face.

Rita looked at Sam. "How did he do that?"

"OK, John, where's the button?" Sam asked.

John showed them how he had moved his foot against a button that was disguised as a decorative knob. "That turns on the magnet."

Rita narrowed her eyes with suspicion. "Big John, what are you up to with a magnet in a pool table?"

"It's for shooting craps with loaded dice," Sam said.

John could barely contain his enthusiasm. "Sam, the slick thing about this is that suckers think they're smart and check out the dice, but they would never figure out the table. And the dice that came with this baby are undetectable. You can hold them to a light and see right through and tell there's no load in them. The secret's in the metallic paint in the dots."

Sam pondered Big John's elaboration. "What if they want to use their own dice?"

John looked indignant. "What establishment allows you to use your own dice? You use house dice. Hell, you tell them they're welcome to give the dice all the practice rolls they want. Nothing will happen unless you turn on the magnet. It beats the hell out of switching dice."

Sam saw Rita's puzzled look. "Rita, John has always prided himself on how good he is at switching from straight dice to loaded ones. I've seen him and he *is* good. He'd be cussing and sweating and then reach in his pocket for a handkerchief to wipe his face, or cough, or create some diversion, and then change to the loaded dice."

"Cuz, let me tell you, that's dangerous. I'm in my forties now, which is too old for that stuff. Rita, one time I dropped the dice making the switch and some bastard had a knife on me before I could get to my pen. He stole the kitty and robbed me, too. Actually, I suppose I was lucky."

"What do you mean 'get to your pen'?" Rita asked.

Big John pulled a fountain pen from his shirt pocket that appeared to be a silver Esterbrook. He unscrewed the cap revealing a .32-caliber cartridge without a bullet. The end of the cartridge was filled with wax. "It's a tear-gas pen."

"Does Speedo know about the table?" Sam asked.

"No, and I'm not going to tell him. Speedo doesn't mind a little poker or craps, as long as he gets a C-note once in awhile, but the idea of a *gaming table* probably wouldn't fly."

Sam gave him a knowing look. "It's like J. Bob says, 'a little bit of larceny is all right.'"

"Sam, here's the deal. I've got some old boys coming in from St. Louis to check out my place. If they like it, they'll come back in the fall for deer season. They'll stay at the motel in town, but I'll serve them dinner here. Afterwards, I'll close

50

this room for *parlor* games. I told them I could get a little action for them. You interested in playing a few rounds next week?"

"I guess. We'll need a patsy to lose a little money."

They looked at each other, and at the same time, both said, "J. Bob."

The following Thursday, three men from St. Louis arrived: Mack Thompson, who had made the arrangements, Eddie Potts, and Joe Barnes. Mack was the only one with any hunting experience. The rest were more interested in getting away from their wives, drinking, and gambling.

The thought of relieving dumb hillbillies from some of their money added to their amusement. On the way down, they had rehearsed various signals they would use to communicate with each other when they were playing.

By six o'clock they were at Big John's. John came from behind the bar and shook their hands like a Baptist preacher after a Sunday sermon. He introduced J. Bob, who was sitting at the bar, and Marge, who was behind the bar. The out-of-towners all took long looks at the curvaceous redhead.

Their attention to Marge's details was not missed by John. He said nothing, but the grin on his face said *look all you want boys, but she's all mine.*

By the time Sam arrived twenty minutes later, the men had already left the barroom. He made eye-contact with Marge, who was sitting on a stool behind the bar talking to a lone patron. Marge averted her eyes, but pointed toward the back room, and returned to her conversation with the customer.

A sign on the game room door indicated that it was reserved for a private party. Sam let himself in. Big John, J. Bob, and the three St. Louis men were gathered around the pool table.

When the men looked over at Sam, John said, "Fellows, that's my cousin, Sam—the one I told you about. I'm going to make one more pass with the bones, and then we can start playing some poker.

Big John shook the dice in one hand above his head. "Come on seven." He let the dice fly. They rolled across the pool table and stopped, showing a five and a two.

"I'll be damned," Mack said. "John, you are one hell of a craps shooter. That's three sevens in a row. If I didn't know better, I'd say those dice were loaded, but I checked them myself."

"Just lucky," John said, and picked up twenty dollars from the pool table.

A round table was set up for cards: poker chips, ashtrays, an ice bucket, glasses, and a quart bottle of bourbon in the center. The agreed-upon game was five-card stud. John explained the house rules: the ante was five dollars, the first card would be dealt facedown, the next three faceup, and the last card would be dealt facedown.

As they played, Sam conducted a subtle examination of the strangers. He watched how they held their cards, how they sat, how much they were drinking and, mostly, the look in their eyes. He was looking for a *tell*: something that gave away the hands they held. Was it good, or were they bluffing? He paid little attention to what they said; that was generally hogwash.

Mack is the player of the bunch, Sam thought. *The other two are lightweights, with their obvious signals.*

All right, Sam, take a little, leave a little. We want these boys to come back.

After several hours, the group was about ready to call it quits for the evening. Sam was up fifty bucks; Big John and Mack were about even; and Eddie and Joe were elated that each was ahead about seventy-five. J. Bob was two drinks ahead, and a hundred dollars behind.

Sam dealt the final hand. Before the last card was dealt, Joe had the best hand showing with a pair of tens. The rest had mixed hands with lower pairs or nothing showing. Sam had no face cards up, but he had an eight in the hole that gave him a pair. It didn't concern him. He had an easy fifty to lose.

Sam said, "The bet goes to Joe with the pair of tens."

"Pair of tens bets ten."

In turn, the players matched the bet. Sam dealt the last cards facedown. "OK, boys, read 'em and weep," he said, and then gave a running commentary. "Did Joe pick up his third ten? Ah, Mack has a possible straight; did he pick up the cowboy?" Sam looked at his card and thought, *Damn it, the third eight.*

"Pair of tens bets another ten," Joe said.

"Sounds like Joe picked up that third ten," Sam said. Sam hoped he had.

J. Bob said, "I've lost enough tonight. I'm out."

"Too rich for my blood," John said.

Eddie, out of turn, said, "I'm in." He had six, seven, and eight showing—a possible straight.

Sam's facial expression did not change, but he thought, *Old Ed is too anxious—he's bluffing. Amateur.*

Mack said, "I'll see that, and raise it twenty."

Sam mentally calculated that Mack had a king and a nine facedown. He also figured—because there was only one king and one nine showing on the table—that Mack wasn't bluffing and had a straight. Sam felt good; the big guy needed to go home a winner.

Sam said, "I shouldn't do it, but I'm willing to pay to see some cards. The dealer sees the bet and the raise."

Eddie's face was no longer exuberant, and he said, "I'm out." Joe stayed in.

Mack said, "Call."

Joe showed three tens.

Sam said, "Mack, it's up to you, I've only got three eights," as he turned over his cards.

Mack flipped over his two down cards, revealing a nine and a king to complete the straight, then raked over the pile of cash from the center of the table.

The St. Louis boys went home winners, just as Big John had planned.

Chapter Five

Come Saturday Morning

By the end of the summer, life had become settled for Wesley. Living in the country held endless possibilities of adventure for a boy: riding old Dolly, making forts in the hayloft, fishing with his grandpa, making friends with neighboring farm kids. And he was anxious for classes to start at the two-room school a mile down the road.

But to Wesley the smack dab best part of his life was Saturday morning. This was the day when Will, Beulah, and Wesley would make the ten-mile trip from their farm to Pine Grove. Like most folks in the area, they did their weekly shopping at this small community of less than a thousand inhabitants. They bought provisions that weren't available at Morgan's store in Tremont, and they spent the rest of the day visiting with neighbors.

Although Wesley loved the Saturday adventures in Pine Grove, the trip itself seemed to take hours. Will never drove faster than forty miles an hour on the winding blacktop road, and he was suspicious of anyone who did. And this morning, when a pickup truck was about to pass them, Will said, "Look at him, he's in a hurry . . . in a hurry to get to the undertaker's."

Preparing for possible evasive action, Will's large hand gripped the turning knob on the steering wheel, causing the sinew in his right forearm to form ridges. This arm had done the work of two ever since his left arm had been amputated in the blacksmith shop accident twenty years before. The remaining limb had nearly doubled in size and strength, yet with this right hand he could gently scoop up a baby chick and return it to a brooder cage without the slightest harm.

If you can imagine a hen's egg that someone had drawn a man's face on, with bushy eyebrows and a fringe of hair around the top, leaving the cone-shaped end bare, except for a few drawn-on sprigs, this would be a caricature of William Henry O'Dell at sixty-three. With bags under his eyes and large ear lobes, his face also looked something like a sad-eyed hound dog.

Will's pronouncement concerning the fate of the speeder seemed to put the world back in order for him, and he was able to drive on with his previous level of contentment.

Beulah, a stout five-footer who could barely see over the dashboard, sat calmly in her freshly ironed cotton dress looking at the countryside through the side window, mostly oblivious to Will's proclamations.

Wesley squirmed around in the back seat of the '48 Mercury, looking out all windows for any distraction that would make the time pass more quickly.

Each Saturday the trip was as predictable as the last. When they reached a place on the road referred to as "Dead Man's Curve," Will never failed to mention how a lot of people had been killed there.

This time, in anticipation of Will's comment about the curve, Wesley imitated his grandfather, which earned him a stern look from his usually tolerant grandmother. She reminded him that his grandfather was good to him, and that no one appreciated a smart aleck. Wesley felt ashamed because he knew that both statements were true—and because his actions did not match his true feelings about his grandfather.

Wesley sat in silence for the rest of the ride. When they arrived in town, Will found his usual parking spot near Garland's Funeral Home and brought the car to a halt. He looked back at Wesley. "I'm going to be at the sale barn at noon. Why don't you meet me over there?"

"OK, Grandpa."

Beulah said, "Wesley, do you still have the half-dollar your mother gave you?"

"Yes, Grandma."

"Well, then, don't spend it all in one place, and watch the time so you can meet your grandpa."

Wesley was like a dog off a leash once he got out of the car. The sidewalks were crowded with rambling men and women who seemed in no hurry to get anywhere, but Wesley weaved in and out of the shoppers, trotting when he could. He was looking for his new friend Ernie, and he knew the best place to find him—the pool hall.

Neither boy was old enough go in the pool hall, but it was fascinating to look through the front window. Men whom they usually saw at feed stores or driving pickups were inside at the snooker and pool tables. Even Mr. Hansen, one of the Tremont schoolteachers, was often there playing pinochle with other veterans.

The boys would watch intently to see if a man's stroke with a cue would pocket the ball; then they would vicariously join in the celebration of success or cringe after a miss.

As Wesley approached the pool hall, he saw Ernie already at the window watching intently. Ernie was a wiry, farm kid with black wavy hair who was a few inches shorter than Wesley.

Wesley joined Ernie at the window and asked, "What have I missed?"

"Not much, it's been kind of slow," Ernie said. "I've been here awhile. Let's do something else."

The boys stopped by the Ben Franklin five and dime and left with a couple of peashooters and a bag of peas. They headed for the sale barn where Wesley was supposed to meet his grandfather but detoured by an adjacent stock shed to look for targets.

"Look, up by the rafters," Ernie said, as he pointed at a gray paper-like nest covered with fierce looking reddish-orange wasps.

"That sucker's huge," Wesley said. "Let's see if we can hit it."

At first the boys fired single, long-range shots without much success. Feeling a little braver, they moved to within about ten feet of the nest and employed a more advanced technique in pea shooting. They each filled their mouths with a dozen or so peas and commenced a salvo that must have connected, because the wasps were sorely aggravated.

Ernie spun around. "Let's get out of here!"

"Ouch! Something burned my head," Wesley cried.

"Keep running!"

"I'm right behind you!"

What started as a gallant assault ended in a wounded retreat. They made it out of the shed and beyond the range of the wasps, then leaned up against a dusty slippery elm tree to catch their breaths. Wesley began gently touching the spot on the back of his head where he had been stung.

"Ernie," he said, "I didn't know a sting burned like this. It's like somebody stuck a soldering iron on my head. It's worse than a bee sting."

"You just ought to be glad it wasn't a hornet. A hornet sting will lay that one in the shade any day. They'll knock you down."

Ernie was seldom impressed by what he felt was his friend's tendency to exaggerate, and he took every opportunity to properly adjust Wesley's observations. Ernie thought because Wesley came from a city up north that he needed to be educated; he didn't even know the difference between a cultivator and a two-bottom plow.

"If you put some spit on it, it'll help the pain," Ernie said.

Instead, the boys opted for pops at the concession stand outside the sale barn with their remaining change. Ernie bought a root beer, and Wesley got an ice-cold bottle of Whistle orange. He sat down on a pop case, held the cold bottle against the burning welt on his head, and thought he had never felt anything so good. When the sodas were finished, Ernie left to meet his parents and Wesley went inside.

The Pine Grove sale barn was a large Quonset hut at the south end of town where local farmers brought livestock to be auctioned. Pigs. Calves. Cows. If it walked, squawked, quacked, or mooed, some farmer was trying to sell it—and maybe acquire something else at a bargain price. Wesley found his grandfather inside and sat down beside him. Will nodded and smiled, acknowledging the boy's arrival.

The ambience of the sale barn and the smell of the animals, hay, and sawdust were exotic to Wesley. It was almost a rite of passage—all the men went there on Saturday. He was fascinated by the auctioneer's call. He tried to mimic it by drumming his fingers over his lips and saying "sold to American" like the cigarette commercials he remembered from television in Iowa.

He could never tell how much something was being sold for, or for that matter, who bought it. To him, each transaction was a series of yelps, grunts, and nods that always ended with the auctioneer indicating an item had been sold to a man in a straw hat, a blue shirt, or sitting in the back row.

The next item on the auction block was a solitary Plymouth Rock hen, caged in a wooden and wire coup.

"All right, now," the auctioneer cried, "what am I bid for this ol' dominecker? I don't know if she lays or not, but she'll surely make a fine Sunday dinner."

"You want to buy her?" Will whispered to the boy.

"Sure," Wesley said, bewildered that he could actually participate.

59

"Bid twenty-five cents," his grandpa said. Wesley looked unsure of himself. "Just raise your hand and say, 'two bits.'"

Wesley raised his hand to initiate the bidding process, but it was more in the nature of a fourth grader trying to get the attention of his teacher. It seemed to him as if a long period of time had passed and nothing had happened. He knew he had done something wrong. His grandpa nudged him, and then he remembered. "Two bits," he yelled in a high-pitched voice.

"I've got two bits, who'll give me four?" the auctioneer called.

"Yeah!" a farmer responded.

"Do I hear six?" the auctioneer continued. "The cage goes with her—that ought to be worth seventy-five cents."

"Bid six bits, boy," Will said.

"I bid six bits," Wesley shouted to the auctioneer.

"Do I have a dollar?" the auctioneer cried. Time once again slowed. Wesley looked at his grandfather for support; Will whispered for him to be still.

"Going once . . . twice . . . sold! To the young man in the red ball cap. Come on down here, son, and get your chicken. What are you going to do with her?"

"I'm not going to eat her!" Wesley said as he went down to pick up the chicken. There was spontaneous laughter in the audience, and Wesley laughed, too. He felt as if he had done something well. It was the same feeling he got when he answered a question correctly in school. He had forgotten all about the wasp sting.

Chapter Six
Code of the Hills

Big John's reputation as a gambler was legendary in Henderson County. The stories people told about him were often exaggerated as they were repeated. Big John did not mind, and because he liked being thought of as a high roller, he often embellished the events himself.

The poker game that had been arranged with the deer hunters from St. Louis quickly became the subject of local gossip. Some of the Collier clan got wind of it and passed the information to Elvin.

Elvin had not been around town in years. Part of this time was at the courtesy of the federal government: two years in the army and time at the federal penitentiary in Leavenworth, Kansas. Uncle Sam had not taken kindly to his theft of an M-1 rifle. The incident never made the wire services, and nobody around Birch View, other than his parents, knew that he had done time.

After prison Elvin had drifted between women, oil field jobs, and bars for a couple years in Texas and Oklahoma. These days he was staying at his parents' ramshackle house in a wooded, remote section of the county.

With the news of the big poker game, Elvin's plan for revenge on Sam Rockford changed. His original plan had been to break in Club 60 at night, steal whatever cash he could find, and fill his trunk with beer. With luck, he had hoped to get the pistol back that Sam had taken from him. If he couldn't find the pistol, he would have left some other calling card—a private one that would not incriminate him but would let Sam know that he had been there.

Now, Elvin had an altogether better plan: robbing the poker game. But he would need some help, so he drove over to see his brother Ethan to tell him about his new plan.

Ethan had never married and lived alone in a run-down farmhouse south of Birch View that he was buying over time on a contract for deed from a Pine Grove banker.

At twenty-eight, Ethan was the youngest of three Collier brothers. He never finished high school and had been rejected for the Korean War by the draft board because of his scoliosis. He seldom shaved, and he cut his own hair—unevenly and on an irregular basis. Most people simply thought he was a hermit and a bit slow-minded because he seldom spoke when he came to town.

There was no economy or grace in Ethan's movement. When he walked, it seemed that his joints were loose or somehow not properly hinged. He gave the appearance that although moving forward, his body was attempting to go in two different directions because his feet pointed outward.

One March morning after a storm had dumped several inches of heavy wet snow on Birch View, Burns Grady, the local banker, saw Ethan leaning against a telephone pole in front of the bank. "Hey, Ethan," he said, "I'll give you a dollar if you'll shovel the snow in front of the bank."

Ethan stared back in response. "I already got a dollar," and shuffled toward his truck without another word.

Now, at Ethan's place, Elvin was manic over his plan. "Ethan, I've got a plan and I need your help. John Crawford and that Rockford who owns the tavern have some rich, dumb city slickers coming to a poker game. There might be as much as five thousand dollars in the pot."

"What do you want from me?" Ethan asked.

"You and I are going to show up and take the money. It's perfect. And this time it will be *me* sticking a gun in Rockford's face—and making some quick cash, too."

"Oh, I don't know," Ethan said.

"Ethan, it's like this. The Lord helps those who help themselves. Isn't that what the Good Book says, brother? Got anything to drink around here?"

Ethan pointed to a crock jug, and Elvin said, "I mean store-bought hooch . . . or some beer."

Ethan pulled two cans of Falstaff from an old-fashioned icebox and handed one to his brother. "I ain't got any ice so it ain't cold." He remained standing.

Elvin took a long draw from the can and wiped foam from his mouth with his shirtsleeve. He brushed a tomcat off a pickup truck seat, which served as a chair, and sat down. Elated with the prospect of revenge, his eyes had a glassy shine as he continued to talk.

"They'll be playing in the back room, so we'll bust in through the back door. It'll probably be unlocked because they'll be drinking and need to go out back to the toilets—it wouldn't make any sense to go out the front just to get around to the back. Even if it's locked, it won't be a padlock. We crash in and show a gun, and they'll piss their pants. We'll get the kitty and any money they have on them, and I'd like to get that fancy watch Crawford wears, too."

Ethan was fidgety as Elvin talked. He kept looking around the room and shifting his weight from one foot to the other, causing a loose floor board to squeak. "I don't know. I ain't looking to get in any trouble."

"Will you stand still? That squeaking is driving me crazy! Look, there's no way we can get in trouble. Nobody's gonna complain about robbing an illegal poker game. It would be like that Robin Hood. We would be robbing from the rich to give to the poor—ourselves. Now, can I count on you as my backup man?"

Ethan stared at the floor, and without looking up, said, "I reckon."

Big John put down the broom he'd been using to sweep the dance floor when he heard the telephone ring. He made it to the phone behind the bar on the third ring. "Big John's Roadhouse . . . Hey, Sam. Nine a.m., that's pretty early for you to be calling." John's natural smile settled into a frown as he listened to Sam's voice through the receiver.

"Why isn't J. Bob going to play in the poker game?" John reached for a cigarette as Sam explained.

"Well, that's a piss poor excuse," John grunted. "If he'd quit charging ten dollar legal fees, he would have plenty of money."

John snuggled the phone between his neck and shoulder and lit the cigarette. His frown deepened. "What do you mean you're not going to play either? Look, Cuz, I already have the boys from St. Louis lined up, and I assumed you were on board."

John held the receiver a couple inches from his ear, but Sam's complaints came through loud and clear: that one time was enough with the St. Louis boys; that he never said that he would play; and that John couldn't just assume that he would.

When Sam paused, John said, "Sam, J. Bob is no great loss, but losing you is a big disappointment and puts me in a real bind." But he knew from Sam's tone it was useless to continue the conversation.

As he hung up the phone, he also knew there was only one solution: "Memphis Mickey." And he knew Mickey would come, too.

It was Mickey who had sold him the rigged pool table that he intended to use in the upcoming gambling rendezvous. And the fewer people that knew about the table, the better. Another reason to call Mickey.

John chuckled to himself remembering how his acquaintance with Mickey began. It was V.J. Day, 1945, in the bar at the Peabody Hotel in Memphis. Drinks were free for anyone in uniform and for any woman who was with somebody in uniform—and there were plenty of both.

John was nursing a beer when he noticed another sailor sitting alone among the throng of celebrants at the bar, a few barstools down. The sailor was staring at the half-empty beer bottle in front of him, methodically peeling thin strips of the label off with his thumbnail.

The sailor's reflection in the mirror behind the bar was clear. His thin lips did not cover his teeth and gave the impression that he was continually smiling. It wasn't an unpleasant smile, but with his black ink-spot eyes and pointed nose, he resembled a rodent.

John moved next to the sailor. "My name's John Crawford," and extended his hand.

"Malcolm Waters. Pleased to meet you," the sailor said, as the two shook hands.

"Are you going home now that the war is about over?" John asked.

"You ain't just whistling Dixie, I'm headed to Magee, Mississippi, tomorrow or the next day. But there's too much action in Memphis to leave right away. Free drinks . . . broads . . . and cards if you're the sporting type."

John's face, which beamed with the mention of drinks and broads, became more serious when he heard *cards*. "Are you a gambler, Malcolm?"

"Friends call me Mickey. Memphis Mickey. I don't gamble, I play percentages. I win a little, and I try to lose a little less."

Two GIs, a sergeant and a corporal, entered the room and paused at the door way as if they were looking for someone. The corporal nudged the sergeant, nodded in Mickey and John's direction, and then the pair strode toward them.

The sergeant tapped Mickey on the shoulder. "Pal, my buddy and I would like to have a word with you in private." In a swift move, they lifted Mickey from his stool by his arms and started walking him toward an alcove partially hidden by a potted palm.

John didn't like the looks of this situation: two GIs and one sailor. But, he told himself, it wasn't his fight. Then the sergeant, the bigger of the two, doubled Mickey over with a punch to the stomach, while the corporal held him.

Enough was enough. John was off his stool and into the melee. With a cupped hand, he blindsided the corporal with a blow that landed flat against his ear, sending him to the floor screaming. Before the sergeant could react, John gripped his size 12 hand around the GI's throat, slammed him against the wall, and started squeezing.

John smiled as he held the sergeant pinned. "Do you always gang up on smaller people?"

Gasping, the sergeant said, "He cheated us."

From the floor, Mickey coughed and said, "You two dumb bastards were so stupid, I didn't have to cheat."

#

The St. Louis men arrived the following Sunday night and began hunting on Monday. They were a rowdy group by the time they arrived at Big John's for supper. At the doorway, Mack yelled, "Hey, Big John," I hope your food's better than the deer hunting. We didn't see a single deer."

"Would you city boys know a deer if you saw one?" John answered. "I'll bet before you all get back to St. Louis, some farmer will be missing a cow or two."

Everyone in the group started laughing. Mack said above the laughter, "We need beers," and as a group they headed toward the bar chanting, "Beer! Beer! Beer!"

John filled their beer orders and told them their supper was ready when they were. Then he said, "Fellows, I want to introduce you to another cousin of mine, Malcolm Waters." He motioned toward Mickey, who was sitting at the other end of the bar. "Sam, who you all met last time, can't join us, so I invited Malcolm.

Mickey got up from his stool and walked over to them, and in a southern drawl said, "My friends call me Mickey, and so can y'all." He shook hands with each one.

Mack squinted his eyes and looked over at John. "Big John, you haven't brought in a ringer on us, have you?"

Big John looked as indignant as a strumpet whose virtue had been sullied. "Hell, the card player in the family is Sam, and you held your own against him. Mickey is just a cotton farmer from the boot heel."

"His hands didn't feel like a farmer's."

Mickey laughed. "Well, that's because I'm no farm hand; I keep the books and do the taxes. Cotton farming is a lot more than plowing fields—it's a business."

Mack seemed to relax and smiled at Mickey. "Ah, I was just giving Big John a hard time. The look on his face was priceless. Hey, I'm hungry. Let's eat."

Mickey sat at the bar across the room as the men ate the ham, beans, and cornbread Big John had made.

After they had started eating, Marge arrived to take over bartending duties for the night. As before, the men gawked at Marge when she came in. Mack called over a greeting to her, but she just smiled back. John motioned for her to come behind the bar.

As Mickey sat at the bar, he passed pleasantries with Marge and sipped on a beer. He seldom finished a beer, particularly when he was working. It was more of a stage prop than a libation for him. He peeled the label off the bottle with his thumbnail and tried not to be obvious as he sized-up the competition.

The only one that concerned Mickey was the big Irish-looking guy they called Mack. He was the biggest, and the obvious leader, but it wasn't his size that worried Mickey. The palm-sized pistol Mickey had strapped to his leg would equalize that if things got rough.

But Mack seemed sharp. He had picked up on Mickey's hands right away. Mickey had perfect hands for a card player, with fingers that were long and delicate like a concert pianist's. When he was alone, he kept them nimble by rolling a quarter from one knuckle to the next on each hand.

Mickey, still in his thirties, was short, slightly built, and looked more like a shopkeeper than a Memphis gambler. This weak appearance was a deception and disguised the fact that he could do arithmetic quicker in his head than most folks could with an adding machine.

When the St. Louis men finished eating, John asked, "Are you boys sure you aren't too tired to play tonight?"

"Hell no, we can play," Mack said. "Maybe we'll be luckier than we were at hunting."

The five men moved to the back room and took seats around a table, which was already set up for poker, including a quart bottle of Jim Beam whiskey and glasses in the center.

Big John sat at the three o'clock position of the round table with his back to the wall. Mack was to his right, Mickey was to his left, and Eddie and Joe sat across from him.

Big John always made it a point to sit with his back to a wall. From this spot, he faced the back door located diagonally across the room and could also see the door to the dance floor behind Mack.

After an hour, the play was too slow for Big John, so he poured some whiskey in a glass for himself and invited the others to help themselves.

"John, you're not trying to get us drunk, are you?" Eddie asked.

"No, sir, I'm just trying to be hospitable. Don't drink anything you don't want. You're as suspicious as Mack."

Cigarette smoke clouded the room, causing Mickey to crack open the back door, even though the outdoor temperature was in the forties.

Big John took a sip of whiskey and looked up from his cards at the other players. He caught a movement at the back door from the corner of his eye. "What the hell—"

The back door flew open. Elvin burst in, pointing a pistol at the men. Ethan was right behind, wild-eyed, toting an ax handle. The card players were shocked into silence.

"Hands on the table where I can see them," Elvin shouted. "Don't anyone make any quick movements, or you'll be sorry."

John's heart was racing, but he willed any expression out of his face, and his voice was even as he said, "Pal, you're making a mistake."

"Shut up, Crawford," Elvin said. "The rest of you, one by one, stand up real easy-like, and turn your pockets inside out. Put any valuables you got in the middle of the table, starting with this mousey-looking guy," he said, pointing at Mickey.

Mickey's eyes glanced toward Big John. "Do what he says, Mickey," John said. Mickey did as he was told and stood up and emptied his pockets, keeping his eyes on the intruders.

When it was Big John's turn, Elvin moved closer to him and said, "Crawford, don't forget that fancy watch of yours."

"Well, I'll be go to hell," John said, as he began unbuckling the leather wristband of his Longines.

"You think you're such a big shot," Elvin said, "walking around with your fancy clothes and such. Where's the rest of your crowd? I heard you were going to have a dozen players. And that son of a bitch cousin of yours from Club 60, why ain't he here?"

"This is all there is. I can't believe you're going to take my watch. Hell, you might just as well take my pen, too. It's worth as much as the watch. It's an Esterbrook. Here, look at it."

John took the pen from his pocket, removed the cap, and pointed it at Elvin. The pen exploded, spraying tear gas in his face. Elvin screamed, dropped the gun, and jerked his hands to his face.

"My eyes! You blinded me!"

Ethan froze in astonishment, and Mickey said, "Drop that ax handle, asshole!" Mickey's pistol pointed directly at Ethan. The ax handle hit the floor.

Mack sprang from his chair and caught Elvin with a roundhouse punch that knocked him to the floor. Elvin curled up in a fetal position, rubbing his eyes and moaning.

Big John picked up the pistol from the floor and stood over Elvin. "You're the same son of a bitch that Sam had to corral. You know, you're becoming quite a nuisance. What do you think I ought to do to someone that breaks in my place and tries to rob me and my guests at gunpoint?"

Elvin kept moaning and did not reply.

"Shoot them," Mack said. "They were robbing us. It'd be self-defense."

"No, the Code of the Hills says you don't shoot fish in a barrel," John answered, then paused in obvious thought. "Mickey, keep these dumb shits covered. I'm going to make a phone call."

John left the room, went directly to the telephone, and gave the central operator Sam's number. Sam answered, and John told him what had happened.

At the other end, Sam said. "No, John, it's too late to shoot them . . . yeah, J. Bob is here. I'll get him."

Sam put the receiver down and called J. Bob to the phone. When J. Bob got there, Sam explained in whispered tones what was going on.

At once, J. Bob seemed to go through a metamorphosis. He suddenly looked alert—not like a man

70

who had three beers in him. "Let me talk to him," he said, taking the receiver from Sam. "John, this is J. Bob. Look, you need to call Speedo and have them arrested."

In his excitement, Big John spouted, "Counselor, you seem to forget that I had a poker game going on. If that bastard Chester Martin gets involved in this, he'll shut me down."

"That's not going to happen, John."

"What do you mean?"

"As a prosecutor he needs your cooperation as a witness. He'll be much more interested in prosecuting an armed robbery than worrying about your poker game. It'll look a lot better in the headlines than shutting down a popular watering hole."

"You really think so?" John asked.

"Absolutely. Plus, he'll jump at the chance to get a second crack at Elvin Collier; Chester's still ticked off that he got off on that DWI."

"I like the way you think, counselor."

"Look, John, I'll call Speedo and tell him that you had a friendly game of cards going on and these men crashed in brandishing weapons, crazy and drunk. They tried to rob you, but you were able to subdue them."

Big John went back into the card room, where Mickey had his pistol pointed at Elvin and Ethan. The brothers were cowered in a corner, not saying anything, waiting for their nemesis to announce their fate. Elvin's face was flushed and his eyes were bloodshot, but he was no longer rubbing them.

Speaking in an unctuous tone, John said, "I called my old cousin, Sam." At the mention of Sam, Elvin stiffened. "He's a pretty smart guy. He told me it was too late to shoot you two sorry bastards, and that we should let bygones be bygones."

Mickey looked perplexed and squinted his eyes as if he had not heard John correctly. Elvin looked baffled. Ethan continued to stare blankly at the floor.

"That's right, Mickey, bygones be bygones."

John picked up the bottle of Jim Beam and focused on the label. "Fine Kentucky bourbon, made in Frankfort." He poured liberal shots into a couple of glasses.

Mickey, unsure, but sensing John was up to something, chimed in to follow suit. "Why, I believe that's the capital of Kentucky, John."

"Why, I believe it is, Mickey."

Looking at Ethan, John said, "I know who you are, and I was just thinking . . . does that place of yours out there in the sticks have any fire insurance on it?"

Ethan looked up. "What do you mean?" His face was pale and drawn with fear.

"Oh, nothing, friend. It's just that you can't be too careful. It would sure be a shame if a fine place like that was to burn down."

Elvin glared at John through his bloodshot eyes but didn't say anything.

John said with mock concern, "You two boys look like you could use a drink." With an extended arm, John handed Ethan one of the glasses; he had the pistol in his other hand. Ethan took the glass and looked at his brother for direction but said nothing.

Smiling, Big John extended a glass to Elvin.

"I don't want any of your damned whiskey," Elvin said, but the fear and confusion in his voice rendered the statement empty of conviction.

John's smile faded. "Friend, I don't think you're in a position to refuse my hospitality."

"Big John, it seems damned ungrateful to me," Mickey added.

Elvin took the glass and drank the contents in one swallow. He nodded at his brother, and Ethan finished his glass, too.

Outside, in the distance a siren wailed. A few minutes later Speedo and a deputy entered the back room. The deputy had his sidearm drawn.

Speedo surveyed the scene. "John, you and your friend give your guns to Deputy Woods." He motioned for the deputy to carry out his order. "Now, what's been going on here?"

After John provided details that were consistent with J. Bob's counsel, Speedo looked at the Collier brothers and asked, "Do you two have anything you want to say?"

"We're not saying anything until we talk to a lawyer," Elvin said.

"Have it your way. I'm placing you both under arrest for armed robbery."

He removed the handcuffs from his officer's belt and handed them to the deputy. "Give me your gun. I'll cover you while you cuff them."

After the brothers were handcuffed, Speedo said, "Take the prisoners to the jail and call for another officer to pick me up. Meanwhile, I'll get statements from the witnesses."

After the Collier brothers were locked up in separate cells, Ethan became virtually catatonic. Later, at the arraignment, he only mumbled when asked to enter a plea. Under the circumstances, the judge appointed J. Bob to represent him.

Elvin had remained surly and uncooperative in jail, and at his arraignment said he would represent himself and refused to enter a plea. The Court made an entry for the record and set the matter for hearing.

Within a few months the matter was concluded. J. Bob argued to Chester Martin that a jury would never convict

73

Ethan, and that if it did come to a trial, J. Bob would bring in a University of Missouri psychiatrist to testify, forcing the county to tax its already tight budget.

Ethan pleaded guilty, but in the bargain received a suspended imposition of sentence with five years' probation. Elvin pleaded guilty and received five years' hard time at the state penitentiary.

Chapter Seven

Showdown at the Brush Arbor

In the early summer of 1956, William O'Dell was not impressed with news of the revival coming to Tremont. "That's just like those deacons to bring in some outsider to stir up folks," Will said as he sat at the kitchen table drinking coffee, waiting for Beulah to cook breakfast.

Wesley sat at the other end eating oatmeal, on which he had ladled a dose of freshly skimmed cream, listening as his grandparents talked.

At the cook stove Beulah was laying strips of hog jowl on a paper towel that she had just fried. While the cured pork strips drained, she began cracking eggs on the edge of a cast iron skillet and placing them in the simmering fat that covered the bottom.

Will continued to pontificate. "The idea of having a revival in Tremont, in the first place, started after the caretaker found empty beer cans scattered in the cemetery."

"I hadn't heard that," Beulah said over her shoulder.

"And you know that caretaker," Will said, "right away, he told the Methodist minister, who wasted no time walking from the parsonage to Morgan's Store to tell Vivian Morgan, who told that Pentecostal preacher . . . what's his name?"

"Brother Folger," Wesley said.

"That's right. Thanks, Wesley. But I'll tell you, those beer cans have started a regular ecumenical movement."

"What's an *ecumenical* movement, Grandpa?"

"Ah, it's a bunch of different churches getting together. That revival committee has Methodists, Pentecostals, and probably the foot-washing Baptists."

Wesley laughed.

"If you ask me," Will said, "the beer cans were just an excuse. Those psalm-singers figured church attendance was down, and according to their reckoning, sin was up, so they used it as a reason for a revival."

Beulah turned toward Will. "That may be, but one good thing is the committee decided to ask Herb and Myrtle Gibson's son to lead the revival." To accentuate her point, she added, "You know, he's an evangelist in Indiana."

Beulah moved the skillet to a cooler part of the stove. "All right, you two, come over and get your breakfast."

On Beulah's orders, Wesley and Will brought their plates to the stove, and Beulah served up their eggs. After putting an over-easy on her own plate, she joined them at the table.

Will cocked his head toward the ceiling. "I hear Rita coming downstairs; she's finally gotten up." Between bites he said, "The last time there was a revival around here, I heard Hank Blackwell jumped over a pew . . . flatfooted right over it, according to Vivian Morgan."

Beulah, mostly in her own thoughts, said, "Well, I don't think Wendell Gibson is really an outsider. I think his return is wonderful."

At that moment Rita strolled into the kitchen wearing a bathrobe and gold chenille slippers. Will stared at her as she entered. "It's about time you got up," he said. It's seven o'clock. We've already milked the cows and done chores."

"Well, I was up later than you were," she said. Will's eyes narrowed and his lips tightened. Rita moved to the stove and poured herself a cup of coffee from the aluminum percolator on the stove. "What were you all saying about Wendell Gibson?"

"He's come back to lead the revival," Beulah said.

"That's what I heard," Rita said. "I'm surprised that chubby little boy grew up to be a preacher. In grade school, we used to sneak in the cloak room and kiss."

Wesley's eyes got wide, as if he had just overheard a snippet of ribald debauchery.

Beulah pursed her lips in disapproval, but said, "Well, I knew you two were sweet on one another. His mother always hoped he would make a preacher. Just think, we might have had a preacher in the family." She looked over at Wesley. "Maybe this young man will be a preacher someday."

Wesley's face puckered as if he had eaten something sour.

Staring into her coffee cup, Rita said with a sultry edge to her voice, "Maybe I'll take off work tonight and go sit on the front row and make eyes at him."

Will frowned and shook his head slowly without speaking. Beulah looked mortified. Wesley froze.

Rita took a sip of coffee and then looked up at the rest of the family. "Why is it suddenly so quiet at the kitchen table?" After a few more seconds of silence, she said, "Wesley, have you tried on those new jeans I brought home for you last night?"

"Yes, Mom, and they're this much too long." He held his hands six inches apart to demonstrate the length. "And I wanted to wear them to the revival tonight."

"Just roll up the cuffs; they're wearing them like that now. There'll be boys there with cow manure on their jeans," Rita said, as if that were the standard by which jeans were judged.

"Aw, Mom."

"Don't whine, Wesley," Beulah said. "They can be fixed."

"That's right, they can be fixed," Rita said. "I know you want to look nice for that little what's-her-name girl."

Wesley's face turned crimson and he said, "No, I don't."

Late that afternoon there was a traffic jam at the washstand in the corner of the kitchen. Both Rita and Wesley were primping for the evening.

Rita leaned over the top of Wesley's head to apply the finishing touches to her makeup. She rubbed her lips together to even her lipstick and looked over at Beulah. "I won't be in until late this evening."

Beulah said, "I figured as much."

Wesley knew this meant his mother was going to work at the honky-tonk and not going to the revival, and he felt relieved. It seemed to him that her lipstick was too red; none of the women at church wore lipstick.

He struggled with a rooster tail that had not been tamed by a liberal application of Wild Root Cream Oil. Rita took the comb from his hand and smoothed the reluctant strands into place. She sniffed his hair and smiled at him in the mirror. "Son, you smell *purty*—like you've just been to the barbershop."

Wesley grinned back at her.

She put her hands on his shoulders and said, "Why don't I drop you off at the revival on the way to work."

Wesley stiffened. "Uh, I was going to ride with Grandma and Grandpa."

"Don't you want to go a little earlier so you can see your buddies?" Wesley did not respond. "You're not ashamed of your mama, are you?" She looked at her son's face in the mirror—her question had hit home. Wesley looked away. "It's OK, son. You can ride with them, if that's what you want."

Not long after Rita left, Wesley and his grandparents headed eastward in their Mercury to the revival. With the windows down, the scent of recently mown hayfield breezed through the car. "What a sweet-smelling evening," Will said. "It almost makes going to a revival tolerable."

78

"Will, you shouldn't talk like that on the way to church," Beulah said.

Will fought back a smile and kept driving.

About a mile from Tremont, at the edge of a hayfield, the revival tabernacle came into view. The structure had been built for the revival just that week by the Gideons, the Methodist men's group.

They had gone into the logwoods and cut down trees to make twelve-foot poles. The poles were set upright in deep postholes, forming parallel colonnades about forty feet long. Log girders were connected to notches at the top of the poles, and cross rafters spanned thirty feet between the rows of the vertical poles. It looked like the framework for a flat-roofed pole barn.

On top of the horizontal pieces, layers of smaller limbs and leaves formed a three-foot thatched roof that could withstand all but a heavy thunderstorm, or some other serious act of God. Underneath, pews borrowed from churches in the area sat on a blanket of fresh sawdust.

It was a rough-hewn pergola that everyone called the brush arbor.

When the O'Dells and Wesley arrived a half-hour before the services were to begin, a sizeable crowd had already gathered. Many folks arrived early just to visit with one another.

Wesley was out of the car first, wearing his new jeans, which were now shorter and hemmed. He saw his friend Ernie with a group of boys and girls, including Cindy Wilson. They were milling around, whispering and giggling in awkward juvenile flirtations. He jogged over to join them.

He stopped next to Ernie, greeted him, and then looked at Cindy. "Hi, Cindy," he said. She was a year older than Wesley, and he thought she was the prettiest girl in school.

Cindy responded with an unenthusiastic "Oh, hi," and then her blond ponytail swished and her nose elevated slightly as she turned to watch James Folger, the fourteen-year-old Pentecostal preacher's son. He was walking toward the group with another boy about his age.

James had been named after an apostle, but this James sported ducktails that he slicked back on both sides of his head. Wesley had once overheard Cindy tell one of her girlfriends that James Folger was "dreamy cool" and that she could "melt for him."

James was wearing black Ivy League pants that hung low on his narrow hips. These were his Sunday-go-to-meeting best, barely held up by a thin white belt with two buckles in front. As he and the other boy sidled toward the group, they were talking to each other with their hands next to their mouths to hide what they were saying.

Wesley asked who the other boy was, and Ernie told him that he was the evangelist's son, David Gibson.

David was a pursy boy with a soft belly that lopped over the waistline of his pleated slacks. His fair, slightly flushed face suggested he did not spend much time in the sunlight.

The two older boys stopped in front of the group. With a crooked smile on his face, James said, "David, here, says he'll wrestle any of you little punk boys." David had a smirk on his face. He was at least two years older than any of the boys in the group.

Cindy giggled. Willie Wagner and his cousin, two boys in Cindy's class, responded by heading for the brush arbor. Ernie and Wesley, who were both looking away, were the only boys remaining.

"Hey, Wesley, I'll tell you what," James said, "I'll give you a quarter if you'll wrestle David."

Wesley looked back and said, "Nah, I don't want to . . . I'd get my clothes all dirty, and church is going to start pretty soon."

"Sounds to me like you're chicken," James said.

Ernie, who was shorter than Wesley, leaned up to Wesley's ear and whispered, "Wes, don't do it—they're up to something."

"Ah, it'd just be for fun," James said. "I told David you were one of the best wrestlers around for your age. You'd only be wrestling on grass so you wouldn't get dirty."

It may be that the devil rarely appears patently evil. More likely, he comes silver-tongued, reasonable, and appealing to the vain natures of the unsuspecting. Nonetheless, Wesley could not pass up the opportunity to show off.

The four boys walked to the edge of the field, fifty yards from the brush arbor. David and Wesley squared off, circled, and wrapped their arms around each other's necks maneuvering for an advantage. Wesley tried to put his leg behind David's to trip him, but the older boy's weight was too much, and David pushed him backward to the ground.

"Come on, Wesley, you can do better than that," James said.

"Here, I'll help you up," David said as he grabbed both of Wesley's arms at the elbows and lifted Wesley toward him as he was getting up. Then, quick as a snake, he drove his knee hard into Wesley's crotch. Wesley screamed, doubled over, and collapsed to the ground. He curled up and made the high-pitched moaning of an injured rabbit.

David looked at James and said, "Let's get out of here."

As they trotted off, James laughed and said, "Boy, you got him good."

Ernie bent over his hurt friend. "Wes, just stay here, and I'll go get someone."

"No! Don't get anyone," Wesley said between sobs. He raised up to his hands and knees, and with Ernie's assistance he stood up, wobbly.

Services were about to start, and Will was looking around for Wesley, when he saw James and David approaching. *A couple of preacher's kids probably up to no good,* he thought. Then he saw Wesley leaning on Ernie, and instinctively he dashed to the boys. "What happened?"

Wesley whimpered and stuttered a sketchy response, but Ernie provided the play-by-play details.

Will put both hands on Wesley's shoulders and squeezed them gently. "Son, you're going to be all right; you're still young enough that I don't expect there's any permanent damage. Just try to breathe deeply, and when you feel better, we'll go back to the service."

"He's a dirty fighter and I'll get him back!" Wesley said, clenching his fists.

"Take it easy," Will said in a gentle voice. "I know you're hurt and mad . . . and I guess you're entitled to a good lick on him—he certainly deserves one—but right now you need to settle down."

Will turned to Ernie. "You go on back to the services. I want to talk to Wesley." In the background, the congregation was singing "Standing on the Promises."

Fifteen minutes later, Wesley indicated he was ready, and they trudged to the back row of the brush arbor and sat next to Ernie.

From the pulpit, Wendell Gibson said, "Now, I want to call on my son David to come forward to sing a special hymn that I know will bless your hearts."

David strolled to the front of the congregation with the ease and confidence of a veteran performer. He stood at the side of the podium, smiled at his audience, and began to sing, "The Lord is my shepherd and I shall not want . . . ."

David had the sweet tenor voice of a seraph and sang in a pious tone, with his eyes glancing toward heaven at appropriate times. He finished the song, and as he walked to his seat, he glanced to the back row and gave Wesley a gloating look of smug satisfaction.

Wesley glared back and silently mouthed the words, "I'll get you."

Business at Club 60 was fairly slow for a Saturday night. Only a dozen customers were present, including J. Bob, who sat at his usual spot at the end of the bar talking to Sam. Rita had arrived a few minutes earlier.

Sam remarked that business had been slow on Saturday nights ever since the Wisdom Drive-In started triple-feature dollar nights.

"Well, Sam," J. Bob said, "it might also have something to do with the fact that it stays light longer in the summer and some folks don't want to park their cars in front of a tavern until it gets dark."

"You might be right," Sam said.

J. Bob nodded his head toward Rita, who was filling a napkin holder at the other end of the bar. In a low tone, he said, "What's wrong with Rita? She's awfully quiet tonight."

"I'm not sure," Sam said. "I asked her the same thing earlier, but she wouldn't say. My guess is it has to do with Wesley. She thinks she's a bad mother because she works here most nights. Plus, she thinks that *her* mother is coming between them."

"Well, Sam, why don't you go over and put your arm around her and say something nice for a change."

Sam's face changed in an instant from indignant and irritated to a frown that looked more like a smile. "You know, pal, if you weren't such a good customer, and business weren't slow, I'd eighty-six your ass out of here."

J. Bob smiled. "I know that's a hell of a position to be in, Sam, but seriously, go give her a hug."

"All right, you win." Sam turned and walked to Rita. He put his hand on her shoulder and said, "What the hell is wrong with you tonight?" J. Bob heard the comment and shook his head in disbelief.

Rita jerked her head toward Sam and glared at him. "I'll tell you *what the hell is wrong* since you were so kind to ask. My nine-year-old son thinks his mother is a floozy and was ashamed to have me drop him off at a church service tonight." She turned from him and started to walk away.

"Hold on." Sam clutched her arm and pulled her into a one-armed hug. "He said *floozy*?" Sam asked, with his voice inflected and a smile on his face as he struggled to keep from laughing.

"No, he didn't have to," Rita said, not finding humor in the situation.

With a sympathetic voice, Sam said, "Maybe you're overreacting." He hesitated, as if looking for a solution, and then said, "Why don't you take off early tonight and give him a ride home."

Caught off guard, Rita said "Really?"

"Yeah," Sam said. "Take some Cokes and a few bags of peanuts and potato chips with you—he'll come around. Or, instead of going home, take him to the triple-feature at the drive-in. You could make it for the last two movies."

"You really wouldn't mind my leaving early?" Before Sam could respond, she kissed him quickly on the lips and said, "Thanks, Sam, maybe you're not such a tough old bird after all."

"Well, don't tell anybody."

"Don't worry, nobody would believe it. I feel bad about leaving you shorthanded, but I just have this feeling that I need to go."

"Get out of here before I change my mind. I'll make J. Bob tend bar if I need help."

With his well-worn bible in hand, Wendell Gibson moved to the front of the congregation. In his early thirties, he was a fleshy man with dark Irish eyes and a thick head of black wavy hair that glistened with hair oil.

One look and you knew he was a man not given to manual labor, but by reputation he was a physical force behind the pulpit. His penetrating stare and fiery tone could make some even doubt their salvation from previous conversion experiences.

Wendell gazed at the crowd of about sixty that had gathered on this sultry summer evening. Women in cotton dresses fanned themselves with paddle-like fans that had the picture of Christ and a lamb on one side and an advertisement for Dugan's Funeral Home on the other. Men in khaki work trousers and bib overalls held their hats in their laps, revealing white foreheads that contrasted with the deeply tanned skin on the lower part of their faces.

Wendell gripped the podium with both hands and leaned forward as if to get closer to his audience. "Brothers and sisters," his voice a clarion call, "I believe there is one among us tonight who is going to hell." A woman gasped, but otherwise the congregation was silent. The only sounds came from cicadas in the nearby woods and from insects buzzing around the light bulbs that hung from the rafters of the brush arbor. Every eye was on Wendell Gibson.

Then with soft compassion he said, "Is that someone you?" The congregants reacted by looking around at their neighbors for telltale signs of sin.

It was a powerful sermon. Midway, he cried out, "I call on the Power in heaven to root out sin, thrash the devil, and bind him in the bottomless pit." He pounded the podium with his fist and blasted away about the fires of hell. The redeemed were going to a heavenly reward, and sinners would be cast on a lake of fire and brimstone and tormented forever. There would be no place to hide for those that strayed from the straight and narrow path.

Throughout the sermon Wesley kept staring at David and James, seated several rows ahead. Something looked strange about James. His face was pale and he kept swallowing as if something were stuck in his throat, but his attention never wavered from Wendell.

It was over an hour later when Wendell began to wind down. Finally, his face wet with perspiration and his voice nearly gone, he pleaded: "Friends, it may be later than you think. The sand in your hourglass may be running out. Have you strayed from the path of righteousness?"

He paused, and with a soft tone of urgency, said, "Don't be that one who is going to hell."

He looked at Hank Blackwell, who had been appointed song leader, and said, "Brother Blackwell, please lead us in 'Just as I Am'."

Hank led the congregation in the altar-call hymn, and over the soft singing, Wendell urged folks to come forward and make a decision.

In the parking area by the brush arbor, Rita pulled to a stop next to a couple of pickups. She had a good view of the brush arbor and had no problem hearing the singing, but Wendell's now-raspy voice was barely audible.

The congregation was on the third verse of "Just as I Am" when James Folger bolted up from his seat and charged down the sawdust aisle toward the front. His gait became more of a trot, and he ran into the open arms of Wendell. "I feel that I have been called to preach," James shouted.

"Amen!" said Wendell. A scattering of "Amen's" rippled through the congregation.

The singing continued, and Cindy Wilson, with tears streaming down her face, also went forward and stood next to James. James's eyes were on the heavens, and Cindy's eyes were on James.

After a short while Wendell ended his pleading, acknowledged those who had come forward, and closed with a prayer of thanksgiving.

At the end of the prayer, David was a broken-field runner getting to the front. He grabbed James by the arm and pulled him outside, beyond the light cast from the brush arbor. They stopped in front of the cars parked on the side. Cindy tagged behind like a puppy.

"Hey, man," David said, "what were you thinking? We were going to have some fun this week."

The three were silhouetted against the lights of the brush arbor, ten yards in front of Rita as she sat in her car.

She saw Wesley striding toward them. The trio stopped talking as Wesley approached. David stepped toward Wesley. "You looking for some trouble, punk?"

Rita grabbed the door handle, ready to get out, but hesitated.

"No, I—I just wanted to ask you about my shoe," Wesley said.

"What about it?"

"Well, look at it," Wesley said, pointing at his left shoe. David looked down. Wesley caught him with a right hook to the nose. The sucker punch drew blood. David let out a yell and covered his nose with both hands. Cindy's eyes got wide, and she covered her mouth with her hands.

"Damn you—you bloodied my nose," David whined.

"Nice talk for a preacher's son," Wesley said.

"You shut up!" David yelled.

"What's going on over there?" Wendell had heard David's yell and hustled over to investigate.

Rita turned on the headlights, causing Wendell to shade his eyes with his hand and the kids to turn their backs to the glare.

"He hit me in the nose," David said, pointing at Wesley.

Wendell pointed his finger at Wesley, and with the condemning voice of an Old Testament prophet, said, "Young man, you should be ashamed of yourself—fighting at a revival of the Lord." Wesley cringed and looked at the ground, a sinner caught in blasphemy.

Rita sprang out of the car. "Now wait just a minute, Windy," Rita said. Wendell's head snapped toward the voice. Nobody referred to him by his childhood nickname anymore. Rita moved in front of the headlight beam.

"And just who might you be?" Wendell asked, obviously insulted.

"Let's just say I'm an old friend, and this boy's mother." Wesley ran to his mother and leaned against her. "And how dare you use your position as *a man of the cloth* to shame a little boy."

"Well, madam, someone obviously needs to teach him right from wrong."

"Is that right, Windy. It seems to me that you weren't much older than he is when you were kissing girls younger than you in the cloakroom." Rita motioned for Wesley to come over to her, but continued to stare at Wendell.

A crowd was gathering around the scene. "David, come with me," Wendell said. "Madam, I will pray for you." With his son in tow, Wendell parted the crowd on his way back to the brush arbor.

Rita called out to him, "Maybe you better pray for yourself while you're at it."

Will and Beulah were at the back of the crowd. Will had held Beulah's arm to keep her from intervening in the argument. Now, as they walked toward her, their eyes met Rita's.

"Wesley is going with me," Rita said. "We may be out late, but don't worry." She put her arm around Wesley's shoulders and said, "Come on, son, let's go."

"Yes, Mama."

As Wesley passed in front of Cindy, she gave him a hateful look and said, "Wesley Sanders, I could never like a boy who fights."

"Unless he fights dirty," Wesley said, looking back at her but not slowing his pace.

Inside the car, Rita said, "How would you like to go to the triple-feature at the drive-in?"

"Really?" Wesley asked.

"Yep, and I've got sodas, potato chips, and peanuts."

"Oh boy!"

"Wesley, that was quite a haymaker you put on that Gibson boy. He was a lot bigger than you, too. Why don't you tell me about it."

"OK, Mama."

Chapter Eight
Killer

*R*ita, still half asleep, rolled on her side and scrunched up the feather pillow underneath her head. Like the attic rafters above, her mind was dusted with cobwebs of gauzy thoughts. Sunlight coming through the window made her eyes squint, and muffled conversation from the kitchen below caused her to blink awake.

She rubbed her eyes with her knuckles, getting her focus, and without sitting up, she reached for her watch on the nightstand next to the bed. It was nearly nine o'clock.

She propped herself up on one elbow and leaned sideways to see around the chifforobe that partitioned the attic in the center. The spaghetti strap on her nightie fell off her shoulder as she leaned.

A glance at the fallen strap reassured her that her breast was not exposed, and she looked back to the other side of the attic. Wesley's bed was empty. Everyone would be leaving for church before long.

It had been a late night, even though Wesley had fallen asleep and they had left before the third feature started. But it had been special: hot dogs from the concession stand; peanuts and Cokes; and the antics of Dean Martin and Jerry Lewis. She and Wesley had both giggled like kids.

With Wesley asleep in the front seat, she had turned the lights off and eased the car to a crawl when they got to the farm just before midnight. In spite of her caution, Beulah had met them at the door in her ankle-length cotton nightgown.

Without her hairnet, Beulah's gray-streaked hair, brushed out and parted on one side, had given her a more witch-like appearance than her usual tightly-wrapped look.

91

The glower on her face had been that of a mother waiting up for a miscreant teenager out past curfew.

"I told you that we'd be in late, Mother," Rita had said, with a tone harder than she had intended and instantly regretted.

Beulah's response had been quick and well played. "I was just worried, that's all. It's dangerous on that winding road late at night—a woman and a little boy alone."

Now, fully awake, Rita's uneasy feeling from the night before returned. Her morning-after reflections were interrupted by the sound of Will's car. The engine revved and the throw-out bearing screeched as Will rode the clutch out of the driveway. She sat upright on the edge of the bed and put her bare feet on the rough plank floor.

Standing, she pulled her nightie over her head, tossed it on the bed, and treaded lightly and nakedly to the burled oak chifforobe.

She slipped on a house coat from the large center compartment and grabbed a shirt she had ironed and hung the day before. From a side drawer she pulled out clean panties and a brassiere.

Holding the underwear under one arm and the black striped shirt under the other, she padded downstairs.

In the kitchen the galvanized metal bath tub sat on the floor between the table and the cook stove. On the stove a three-gallon bucket of water was warming. Beulah had also draped a clean towel and a wash cloth over the back of a chair. *Was this a peace offering or a religious message that I'm unclean?* Rita wondered.

She poured a cup of coffee and made a sandwich with a biscuit and bacon leftover from breakfast. She bit into the tender biscuit; even cold it flaked in her mouth. The hint of baking powder against the sweet saltiness of the sugar-cured bacon made Rita smack her lips.

She chased the bite with a swallow of coffee and sauntered across the kitchen to the window that faced the woods to the north. That old woman can bake biscuits, she thought, as she took another bite.

Rita had seen Beulah do it hundreds of times. Rolling the dough; cutting out the round discs; spreading a few tablespoons of bacon grease on the baking pan; and then swabbing both sides of each raw biscuit in the grease as if she were painting a board. Yet Rita could never duplicate the result.

The coffee raised her spirits but only masked another anxiety she felt. The feeling had started after Wesley's fight the night before and had subsided during the movie, but it now returned as if it had been some bird of prey perched above the bed just waiting until she was completely awake before attacking.

Wesley was growing up without a father. Will was the best man she had ever known, but he was a grandfather, not a father. Wesley needed a younger man to teach him things that a boy needed to know, like how to defend himself. He might not be so lucky next time.

She stepped to the stove and poured the bucket of water into the tub.

Sam watched as Rita got out of her car in front of Club 60 and unlocked the door. She was wearing blue jeans with cuffs rolled to mid-calf and a man's shirt with the tail out. He opened the door and let her in. "Nice shirt you're wearing; I think I recognize it."

"You should, it's yours, but you never wear it."

"It's too loud for me. I think shirts should be seen and not heard." He kissed her briefly on the lips. "You want a cup of coffee?" Rita replied that she did.

On the other side of the bar, Sam poured Rita a cup, topped off his, and returned the glass carafe to the coffeemaker. The photograph of R.C. Jefferson, Heavyweight Champion of the Navy, sat next to it.

Rita slid onto a bar stool. "Sam, tell me about that fighter in the picture that you trained."

Sam turned around and sat Rita's cup on the bar. His face was a mixture of curiosity and suspicion; the space between his eyebrows narrowed to a V-shaped crevice. "Why do you suddenly want to know about him?"

"Oh, I don't know. He has kindly, sort of sad eyes, but such a big chest and arms. I'll bet he could hit you pretty hard."

Sam's passion overrode his suspicion. "R. C. Jefferson. Man, could he punch. Six feet tall, 210 pounds, and the quickest hands I ever saw. His jab was like a machine gun." Sam's hands went up in a boxer's pose, and he began jabbing an imaginary opponent with his left. In a staccato outburst, he blared, "Rat, tat, tat, tat, and then the combination," as his right hand hooked upward into the pretend-foe's chin.

Breathing heavier, he looked at Rita. "You should have seen the championship bout when he KO'd that big Swede from Minnesota."

"Sam, you looked pretty good yourself."

"Nah, I'm just a ham-an-egger . . . but I know boxing. Jefferson was after me to train him for six months before I finally agreed."

Rita's mind was shadow boxing, too. Should she continue with the fancy footwork or move in with the big leveler? She opted for the latter. "Sam, would you do a big favor for me?"

The crevice in Sam's brow returned. "What kind of favor?"

"Teach Wesley to box."

"So, that's the reason for your sudden interest in boxing. What brought this about?"

Rita told him the story about Wesley's fight.

94

"Sounds to me like he did all right," Sam said.

"Well, actually, I think it may have been a lucky punch."

"Even better," Sam said, and then laughed. "Now he's got a reputation, and the kids will leave him alone." He emphasized *reputation* as if he were talking about an old west gunslinger.

"Sam, that's not the point. I want him to learn the right way. He needs to know, and you would be perfect to teach him."

Sam sighed and reached for his Chesterfields. "I suppose I could show him a few things."

"You're the best, Sam."

"Bring him by here after school later in the week. I've got a couple pair of boxing gloves packed in an old sea bag that I'll dig out."

After hearing that Sam had real boxing gloves and had trained a heavyweight champion, Wesley's imagination soared. Now he would know what to do if a bully tried to pick on him. It would be better than Charles Atlas and his *dynamic tension* advertised in the comic books.

Wednesday after school Rita drove him to Birch View for his lesson. On the way Wesley had been full of questions about Sam and boxing, but when they arrived at Club 60, the excitement had left his face and was replaced with a look of apprehension.

"Well, are you ready, son?" Rita asked.

"I . . . guess so." Along with the unmistakable hesitancy in his voice, both his hands clutched the edge of the seat.

"Oh, come on, now. Why the long face? You're going to have fun."

Inside, Sam was behind the bar talking to three sawmill workers who sat on barstools across from him. J. Bob sat at the return end of the bar, keeping company with a bottle of

95

Budweiser and a law book that he was reading. The three men broke into laughter at something Sam had said.

"Excuse me, gents, but I have to say hello to Rita and her boy," Sam said, gesturing toward the door.

The three men turned toward Rita, and one said, "Hey there, Rita. Who's that stranger you got with you?"

"Aw, he's just some hitchhiker I picked up on the road." The men, fueled by beer, burst into hearty laughter as they had at Sam's story. Wesley smiled but looked down at the floor. The men's laughter subsided, and they turned back around.

As Sam approached Rita and Wesley, Wesley was still looking at the floor. Sam winked at Rita and grinned. "Rita, is this the fellow that punched that palooka in the snot-locker?"

A spontaneous giggle escaped from Wesley; he glanced up at Sam and then back at the floor.

"Wesley, look up, I want you to meet Sam," Rita said.

Wesley looked up, but did not speak.

Sam squatted down until he was eye-level with Wesley. "Wesley, my name is Sam. This is my place, and I want you to know that you are welcome. Now, let me see your hands."

Wesley extended both hands, which Sam took in his, and examined them as if he were a physician looking for a fracture. "Rita, he has a great set of hands. He's going to grow up to be at least a light heavyweight."

Wesley radiated a smile at Sam and then looked over at Rita, with pride showing on his face.

"Tell you what, Rita, watch the bar and I'll finish setting things up in the storage room. Get Killer, here, a soda; it won't take me long."

Rita nodded and Sam started toward the rear. As he passed the bar, he called over to the three men, "If you fellows need anything, Rita will get it for you."

"No, thanks, Sam," the talkative one said. "Our wives will be waiting supper, so we need to go."

Rita guided Wesley behind the bar, got him a 7-UP, and continued to the end of the bar where J. Bob sat.

J. Bob stood up as they approached. "Good afternoon, Rita." He leaned forward and extended his hand over the bar to Wesley. "Hello, Wesley. I'm J. Bob Dalton, at your service." Wesley smiled and shook J. Bob's hand.

"Wesley, let's go around the end, here," Rita said, gesturing to the space between the end of the bar and the back wall, "and sit next to J. Bob." She put her hand on his shoulders and nudged him through the opening.

"What are you studying?" Rita asked. Then, looking at Wesley, she added, "J. Bob is a lawyer."

Wesley's head nodded in acknowledgement, but his face registered that he had no idea what that meant.

"Rita," J. Bob said, tilting the book upward, "this is a volume of the Revised Statutes of Missouri. I brought it in to show Sam how you could possibly circumvent the law that prohibits establishing a tavern within 100 feet of a church."

Rita narrowed her eyes, nonplused. "Why would he need to know that?"

J. Bob exhaled a long sigh. "Well, on Sunday I was having dinner at my mother's and that old Methodist preacher was there pontificating about the evils of alcohol, so I made up a yarn to annoy him."

"You lied to the preacher?"

J. Bob's mouth formed a lopsided grin. "Well . . . "

"What did you tell him?"

Wesley locked on the conversation, and his eyes went back and forth between his mother and J. Bob as if he were watching a ping-pong match.

J. Bob wet his lips with a sip from his beer. "I told him that Sam was going to move Club 60 to that vacant lot across the street from the Methodist Church."

"You didn't," Rita said in disbelief.

"I most certainly did."

"What did he say?

"He didn't say anything . . . he couldn't. He was choking on his mashed potatoes."

Wesley and Rita both laughed. Then Rita said, "Is he all right?

"Yeah, mother and I slapped him on the back a few times and he was fine. But my mother, that's another case. She gave me the most contemptible look you can imagine. What's worse, she bailed out the old windbag."

Wesley's mouth dropped open and his eyes got wide when heard the preacher being called a *windbag*.

"How did she bail him out?" Rita asked.

"Mother pointed out that this statute prevented it," J. Bob said, tapping on the relevant section of the page. "And then the preacher gloated as if he had known it all along."

"J. Bob, how did your mother know about the law? Had you told her about it?"

"I may have, but she probably knew it anyway. She's read all the Missouri statutes. That's what she does when she sits in my office answering the phone for me—she reads law books. She's read the King James Bible several times, so it's no trick for her to absorb the nitwitery of state legislators."

Sam came in from the back room to the opposite side of the bar. "What are you all talking about?"

"Sam, I'm about to explain my theory on how you could put a tavern on that vacant lot by the Methodist Church."

"Why would I need to know that?"

"Just listen, Sam."

"Well, hurry up, counselor, Killer and I have some boxing lessons we want to get to."

"This will just take a minute. The statute says you can't have a tavern within 100 feet of a church, but it doesn't specify how to measure."

98

He pulled a fountain pen from his shirt pocket, yanked a paper napkin from the metal dispenser on the bar, and began sketching. All eyes were on the napkin.

J. Bob drew an X on the napkin. "For example, let's say you have a church here," he said, pointing his pen at the X, "and you wanted a tavern here, 95 feet away." He made another X a couple inches away and marked a straight line between them. "You could build a four-story building and put the tavern on the top floor." He sketched a rectangle to represent the building.

"But it's still within a hundred feet," Rita said.

"Yeah, but he's going to measure from the top of his four-story building," Sam said.

"That's right, Sam," J. Bob said, as he drew a line from the top of the rectangle to the first X, which formed a triangle between the church and the tavern. "Now, if you measure the hypotenuse of this right triangle," he said, pointing to the longest side, "according to the Pythagorean theorem, it would be more than 100 feet."

Eyebrows raised, noses wrinkled, and heads shook, but no one asked what *hypotenuse* or the *Pythagorean* theorem meant. With the visual-aid napkin, everyone could see the point he was making.

Sam stared down his nose at J. Bob's sketch through the smoke of a cigarette dangling from his lips. "J. Bob, what if the church put up a really tall steeple?"

J. Bob frowned, obviously annoyed at this possibility, and looked up at Sam. "That would be about what I would expect from Methodists."

As Rita and Sam chuckled, J. Bob's frown turned into a smile. "Well, don't spread it around or old Reverend Windbag will bring up building a taller steeple at the next deacon's meeting." He paused. "On second thought, maybe we should spread the rumor that a tall steeple will prevent a tavern from being built across the street."

"J. Bob, you get great pleasure from tormenting that parson," Rita said.

J. Bob smiled, but said nothing more.

Looking at Wesley, Sam said, "Are you ready to get started?"

"Yes, Mr. Rockford."

"Now, let's get something straight. Just call me Sam. Got that?"

"Yes, sir."

"And, don't call me *sir*—I work for a living."

"OK, Sam."

"That's more like it, now, let's go. J. Bob, I need you, too. Rita, you can stand in the doorway in case customers come in."

In the center of the storage room, a canvas sea bag with S. H. Rockford stenciled on the side, hung by a rope from an exposed rafter. Two sets of boxing gloves, tied together by their laces, were entwined around the rope.

"Sam," J. Bob said, "what do you have in the bag?"

"Just a few blankets; it makes a perfect heavy bag."

J. Bob sidled toward the bag, gave it a head fake, and started bouncing on his feet, bobbing and punching. He stepped back and looked at Wesley. "I just gave it the old one-two."

Sam said, "My money is on the bag."

"Thanks a lot, Sam." J. Bob gave the bag another punch and said with a tone of triumph, "The *coup de grace*."

Sam looked at Wesley and shook his head in an unsubtle communication that J. Bob was not a fine example of a pugilist.

Sam untied the gloves from the rope and separated them, tossing one pair to J. Bob. "You'll need these later, counselor." He looked back at Wesley as he knelt to one knee. "Come over here, Killer."

Wesley proceeded over with his hands stuck in the front pockets of his jeans and his eyes fixed on the boxing gloves. They seemed huge, brownish red with sweat-stained Everlast labels sewn in the wristbands.

"These gloves are not toys," Sam said. "Real boxers have used them, and they have battle scars from colliding with flesh and leather and canvas. Stick out your hands."

Wesley extended his hands and made two fists.

"Unclench them."

Wesley obliged and Sam put the gloves on Wesley's hands and tied the laces, wrapping the extra length around the wristband of the gloves.

"These are 14-ounce gloves. They look big, but weigh less than a pound. You ought to be able to handle them. You can lift a pound can't you?"

Wesley nodded that he could, standing with his gloved hands hanging at his side, barely a foot from the floor.

"Go over to the bag and start punching it. Let me see what you got. J. Bob, hold the bag; I don't want it punching back."

Rita watched from the doorway, where she could also see the bar.

Wesley stepped to the bag, drew back his right hand, and unfurled a roundhouse. As the punch connected, J. Bob pulled back on the bag. "Wow, Sam, this young man packs a wallop."

Wesley punched the bag two more times. Each time, J. Bob jerked the bag backwards giving the appearance that the force of Wesley's blow had moved it.

Sam said, "Killer, use your left hand, too."

Wesley hit the bag three times with his left hand, and Sam said, "OK, that's good. Now that you've knocked your opponent down, come over here to a neutral corner."

Wesley let the boxing gloves hang to his knees and went over to Sam. Between deep breaths, he said, "That was fun."

Sam squatted to eye level with Wesley. "I need to show you a few things. You need to jab with your left. Don't lead with your right."

Wesley's eyes reflected that he did not understand.

"Here's what I mean." Sam demonstrated with a series of short, quick punches with his left hand that stopped short of Wesley's nose. Wesley blinked and jerked his head back as Sam verbally augmented his punches. "Bam! Bam! Bam!"

"Now, about your right hand," Sam continued, "what I mean by *not leading* is you don't punch with it first. You don't throw it until you've set up your opponent with jabs like I showed you."

Sam extended his arms, wrists bent upward at ninety degrees, with his palms facing Wesley. "Hit my palm" he said, waving his right hand, "with three left jabs and then hit my other with your right—that's called a right cross. The right cross is your power punch. Put your body into it and punch straight to your opponent."

After Wesley's first punch, Sam said, "Stop. You need to be in fighter's stance. First, get your feet apart about the width of your shoulders. Bend your knees a little and don't stand flatfooted; weave and bob and move in and out. Like this." Sam began moving forward and backwards like a baggy pants vaudevillian fox-trotting without a partner. "Now, you try. Let me see some footwork."

Wesley mostly slid his feet from side to side and hopped as he tried to imitate Sam.

"That's good," Sam said. "Get your gloves up to protect your face . . . not that close to your face, someone could hit your gloves and knock them right back into your puss."

Wesley moved his gloves outward, and he stopped hopping.

102

"Get your left hand a bit higher, and drop your right a little so you can throw it with power. That's good. You look like a young Rocky Marciano. Now, give me three jabs and a right cross." Sam extended his palms and Wesley threw the punches.

"How was that?" Wesley asked.

"That was outstanding."

"Counselor, put on the other set of gloves and let Killer poke at a moving target."

J. Bob slipped on the gloves and tucked the laces inside the wristband. He got on his knees, positioned the gloves in front of his face, and rubbed his nose a couple times with the overstuffed thumb. "OK, I'm ready."

"Remember what I told you, Killer," Sam said, "start with the jab."

Wesley jabbed twice with his left and the punches slid off J. Bob's gloves. A right cross did the same.

"Show me some footwork," Sam said.

Wesley scooted his feet back and forth, more like he was sanding the floor than dancing. More jabs bounced off J. Bob's gloves, but a right glanced off a glove and connected with J. Bob's forehead. J. Bob had anticipated the punch and keeled sideways to the floor.

"Way to go there, Killer," Sam said.

J. Bob stood up rubbing his forehead. "Sam, he's got a pretty good punch, I'll tell you."

A wide-open smile showed all Wesley's front teeth. "I've never used real boxing gloves before."

Sam put his hand on Wesley's shoulder. "I think you've had a pretty good first session. I want you to have these boxing gloves so you can practice."

"Really?" Wesley said, astonished.

"Yeah. Both pairs. A contender like you will need to find a sparring partner."

103

"I'll get Ernie." Wesley looked over at his mother in the doorway with an expression that sought permission to accept such a big gift.

Rita nodded that it was all right.

Sam said, "Now, Killer, I want you to remember a couple things."

Wesley's eyes met Sam's.

With the tone of a venerable coach, Sam said, "A good boxer is not a bully and doesn't go picking fights and bragging how tough he is. That's what a punk does. Because a good boxer has trained hard, he is confident and can protect himself when necessary. And, because he is confident, he can walk away from a fight and not be ashamed. That doesn't mean you have to take lip from some jerk, but use your head before your fists." Sam's face softened. "If you don't use your head, you might just as well have an ass on both ends."

A laugh erupted from Wesley.

Rita stepped a few feet into the room. "He's right, Wesley, so pay attention."

Wesley averted his eyes toward his mother, and then back to Sam, whose eyes had never left Wesley.

On the way back to the farm, Wesley sat on the passenger's side with the boxing gloves in his lap. He stroked and patted them like he had a lap full of kittens. "Mom, these gloves are soft like a horse's nose."

Rita reached over and touched one. "Yes, they are." She put her hand back on the steering wheel and looked straight ahead. "Wesley, what did you think about Sam?"

"He's pretty nice. He calls me *Killer*."

"What about J. Bob?"

Wesley puffed up his chest as he tried to make his voice sound deeper. "Wesley Sanders, at your service," he said. "He's funny."

104

"You see, Wesley, Club 60 is not such a bad place, now, is it."

"No, Mama."

Chapter Nine

Lye Soap and Creek Water

As Rita drove toward Birch View, she reflected that it was nearing the end of her second summer back, and she still wasn't divorced. Ray had come through a couple times early on, and he had sent money for Wesley for a few months, but now she hadn't heard from him in over six months. Nonetheless, his last words were that he didn't want a divorce, and she kept putting off taking any action.

A mile outside Birch View, Rita looked at her hair in the rearview mirror for the umpteenth time since she had gotten into the car. *Nothing grows slower than a bad haircut,* she thought. She tugged at a layer on the right side that should have covered her ear, as if she could stretch it or encourage it to grow faster.

On the advice of her mother, she had tried a new hairdresser in Pine Grove, and the result was simply awful. In her mind she continued to chide herself. What had she been thinking, and would she ever stop trying to please her mother? She had known from the hairdresser's first whack that it would be bad.

Now, she had to swallow her pride and go back to her regular beautician, Eva, and see if she could fix the botched hairdo. She had been dreading today and hoped Eva would not be too feisty when she realized one of her favorite customers had gone to another beautician.

Up ahead, a man stood next to a produce stand by the side of the road. It was a makeshift setup with a six-foot sheet of plywood that extended from the tailgate of an old Dodge pickup to a wooden sawhorse. On the top, cardboard boxes and paper sacks were filled with tomatoes, squash, and corn.

A hand-lettered sign leaning against the rear tire advertised: EGGS 25¢ Doz.

Sam had told her to pick up eggs for him to pickle while she was out. She stopped the car on the shoulder and got out.

Up north the man beside the stand would have been called a bum or a hobo. But this unkempt fellow, in need of a scrubbing, a shave, and a haircut was pure-d hillbilly. He wore bib overalls caked with dirt and ragged at the cuffs, which tumbled over his Brogans and dragged on the ground as he advanced toward Rita.

He stared at her with his deep-set eyes and smiled the goofy smile of a nut but did not speak.

Rita remained by the car door and left it open. "How much are your eggs?" she called over to him. Several dozen sat on an upside-down cardboard box next to a peck of roasting ears.

He stopped walking and pointed to his sign.

"I'll take three dozen," Rita said. "That's a quarter a dozen cheaper than at the store."

"Twenty-four cents," the man said. His voice had no inflection, but it was slightly high-pitched, and he did not make eye contact as he spoke. It was as if he were talking to something on her shoulder.

"What do you mean?" Rita asked.

"The store charges 49 cents a dozen," the man said.

"Oh, OK," Rita said, agreeing, without actually doing the arithmetic. She pulled a dollar bill from her skirt pocket and gave it to him.

He turned around and in his odd stride shambled to the pickup bed where he kept his money in a cigar box.

A Club 60 customer drove by and Rita waived. The man turned around and glanced at the car after it had passed by, then muttered, "487-421," as he handed her a quarter in change. He looked down the road at another car, still a hundred yards, and said, "352-203."

"What are those numbers?" Rita asked.

"License plates."

"You couldn't have seen that number. Do you know who was driving it?"

"Nope, I just know the numbers."

"What's the number of that big green Buick that comes through almost every morning."

"A877-203."

He knows Sam's car, Rita thought.

On the way to the beauty shop Rita kept thinking about the odd little man. He was pretty rough-looking. Still, cleaned up he might be made presentable. She smiled.

A few minutes later, Rita parked in front of the Cut & Curl. The shop was in the space formerly occupied by Sadie's Café. The faded painting of a giant coffee cup could still be seen above the windows on the brick storefront. People, including Eva, had taken to calling it the "Cup & Curl." Eva agreed that enough coffee was drunk in the shop to make the nickname fitting.

"Well, look what the cat's drug in," Eva said, as Rita entered. "It's been over six weeks since you've been in to see me. I'd ask what you've been up to, but from the looks of your hair, I can guess."

Embarrassed, Rita said, "I'm sorry that—"

"No need to be sorry, I'm just glad to see you." Eva was putting the last few rollers in a gray-haired lady. "Let me put Mrs. Davis, here, under the dryer, and I'll take a look at your hair."

Rita sat down on a bentwood soda fountain chair, left over from the restaurant, next to a white metal cart littered with beauty trade publications and old issues of *True Story* and *True Romance* magazines.

The shop had a stringent smell common to beauty parlors: a sulfurous mixture of permanent wave solution, burned hair, and Spray Net.

Eva assisted Mrs. Davis from the styling chair and escorted her to the dryer chair. Eva had gone to beauty school in Cape Girardeau the summer after she graduated from Birch View High School. She was one of the few in the class of 1951 that had gone on to "higher learning."

Barely five-foot-three with natural honey-blond hair, Eva still had the looks and figure that had gotten her chosen as a cheerleader and homecoming queen.

The Cut & Curl had become Eva's life. Her high school steady, whom she had planned to marry, was killed in a car wreck, and she never developed another serious relationship afterwards.

"OK, Rita, get in the chair and let's see what we can do." Rita moved to the chair. Eva began with her usual bromide, "Looks like it's nothing that a little lye soap and creek water can't fix."

As she combed through Rita's hair, her focus narrowed, checking the length, and whispering to herself. "Hmmm, I see what she's done . . . can't use thinning sheers on your fine hair . . . now, what was she thinking with all this layering?"

"Can you fix it, Eva?"

"Well, it's not as bad as some I've seen. Folks come in here with over-processed perms and nicks and gouges they want me to fix, so I think I can handle this little mess. We may have to go a little shorter, but I think what I have in mind will be cute."

"I brought you a dozen eggs," Rita said. "I picked them up from this man at a roadside stand west of town. He was a grubby little fellow, but he seemed like he might be pretty smart. You know, he knew the license plate numbers of every car that passed."

110

"Oh, that was Ethan Collier; he sets up every year about this time. But I don't know how smart he is. Last spring I went to his place to get some eggs and noticed these pretty little flowers growing and asked him what they were. He said, 'Them's the April Whites.' And, I thought, well, he may be smarter than he looks, until the next month, when he pointed out the May Yellows."

Rita and Eva both laughed, looking at each other in the large mirror in front of the chair. "Well, Eva, he might not be too bad, cleaned up. He might be a hot potato." Rita glanced over at Mrs. Davis, "Oh, I'm sorry, Eva."

"Don't worry, she's as deaf as a post, and anyway, she couldn't hear anything sitting under that dryer."

"Well," Rita continued, "slicked up, he might be somebody to go out with and—"

"Not with anybody I know," Eva said, gesturing to Rita in the mirror with her scissors.

"Oh, are you dating J. Bob?"

"No, we're just friends."

"Well, if I could get Ethan in here, would you cut his hair?"

Eva rolled her eyes. "Rita, I see what you're up to; you're trying to fix me up. You just won't give up, will you? OK, it's your turn. What's the deal with you and Sam Rockford? Rumor has it you're still married."

"All right, Eva, I'll drop the subject," and then, under her breath she said, "—for now."

"I heard that, Rita."

Rita strutted through the door at Club 60. When she saw Sam looking, she shook her head from side to side, waving her hair. "Well, how do you like it?"

"Like what?" Sam asked.

"My hair!" Rita said with exasperation in her voice.

111

"Oh, I forgot, you went to the beauty parlor. It looks great."

"You didn't even notice. Here's your eggs." Rita sat them on the bar."

"I wanted three dozen."

"I know, but I gave a dozen to Eva as a tip." Sam frowned and narrowed his eyebrows. "It's no problem, I can get some more. That man at the roadside stand—Ethan—had more."

"Ethan Collier! Why in the hell are you buying eggs from that half-wit?" Sam asked. "That's the dumb son of a bitch that helped his brother Elvin hold up Big John's poker game."

"Oh my, I never made that connection."

Sam grabbed his Chesterfields from the counter and flipped his wrist, expelling a single cigarette. He pulled it directly from the pack with his mouth, and with the cigarette dangling from his lips and bouncing up and down as he spoke, said, "The only reason he's not in jail, too, is because of J. Bob."

"Oh, Sam, I think he's harmless. And did you know he's memorized all these license plate numbers?"

Sam struck a match and lit his cigarette, then took a quick drag and exhaled. "All I know is that if I weren't pickling these eggs, I wouldn't eat them, as dirty as he is."

"And just where do you think an egg *comes* from?" Rita paused, and Sam gave her an annoyed look. "Anyway, Sam, I don't think he would look so bad if he were cleaned up. I'm going to try to get Eva to cut his hair."

Sam looked stunned. "Now, I've heard it all. While you're at it, why don't you just get a pig out of some barnyard and take it to Sunday dinner."

Rita turned around without speaking and marched toward the door.

"Where are you going?"

Without looking back, Rita said, "To find a pig to take to Sunday dinner. Bye."

Rita had already stopped twice that week to buy produce from Ethan. After her initial visit, she had gone back the same day to pick up the other dozen eggs for Sam, and the following day she bought some ears of corn. Each time he was a little more talkative. Whenever she drove by, she would always wave, and Ethan would wave back.

Today, he watched when she got out of the car, and when their eyes met, he looked down at the ground and grinned, embarrassed, like a little boy who had accidentally caught a glimpse of some girl's underpants.

"Hi, Ethan. Got any eggs today?"

"Yes, Miss Rita. I saved some brown eggs for you. They're the best-tasting. They come from those Rhode Island Red chickens. The white ones come from Leghorns."

Something was different about Ethan. He had combed his hair—or attempted to. This is not heading in the right direction, Rita thought.

"Ethan, I was wondering if you could do a favor for me and my girlfriend, Eva. You know Eva; she runs the Cut & Curl beauty shop in town." Ethan nodded his head indicating that he did.

"What kind of favor?" he asked.

"Well, Eva wants to start cutting men's hair. She thought if she gave you a haircut, and then folks saw how good you looked, they would want theirs cut, too."

"I wouldn't want to go to no beauty parlor."

"Oh, you wouldn't have to. We'd come out to your place. How about it? What do you have to lose? I see you combed your hair a special way today; it looks nice, but it would really look good with just the right haircut. And I'd sure appreciate the favor for Eva."

113

Ethan, in his usual slouched stance, looking intermittently at the ground and the sky, shifted from one foot to the other. "Well, I reckon it would be OK. You all wouldn't tell anyone would you?"

"Of course not, Ethan, it will be our secret."

Rita headed straight for the Cut & Curl. Eva was walking out the front door when Rita pulled up.

"Hey, Eva. I'm glad I caught you. Where are you going?"

"I was going to get a hamburger at the Owl. Why don't you join me?"

"I can't. I've got some errands to run, but I need to tell you my plan."

"Well, I haven't known you all that long, Rita, but one thing I have noticed is that you always have some kind of *plan*."

As soon as Rita finished telling her the details, Eva said, "You've concocted all this because you think I need a boyfriend? I wouldn't go out with that heathen if he were the only man left after the Rapture."

"Oh, Eva-"

"Don't *oh Eva me!*"

"Eva, I was just going to say that I didn't really think you would be going out with him, but when I told Sam you were going to cut Ethan's hair—"

"You told Sam before you talked to me?"

"Eva, you should have seen his face. If a cow had walked in Club 60, sat down on a barstool, and ordered a beer, Sam's face couldn't have looked more bewildered. But he said that you'd probably be too afraid to do it."

Eva looked indignant. "Well, that settles it. I'd like to see that big blowhard do what I do every day. When are we supposed to do this?"

"Tomorrow afternoon after work?"

114

"All right, but we've got some shopping to do," Eva said, "so let's get to it."

"What do we need to get?" Rita asked.

"Soap, for one thing. I'm not touching him unless he's clean. And sheep dip or some coal oil, in case he's infested."

"Infested with what?" Rita asked.

"With head lice."

The next day Rita drove and Eva directed as they motored on the back roads toward Ethan's place. "Turn at this next gravel road on the right," Eva said. "You'll see a run-down barn. Then we'll go about a half mile. You'll know Ethan's place when you see it."

Rita did know it when she saw the single-story farmhouse with a rusted tin roof. The exterior was covered with tan asphalt sheet siding, patterned to resemble bricks. In several places, sections of siding were missing, exposing weathered gray boards with half-inch spaces between them. Rags and cardboard had been inserted to keep out the wind and rain.

As they approached, two dogs, a shepherd-mix and a black and tan coonhound crawled from underneath the front porch, which had collapsed on one end. The dogs trotted toward the car barking.

"Well, Eva, how do you like your future home?" Rita asked, grinning. Eva's stare made Rita immediately regret the smart-aleck comment. "Sorry, I was just teasing. I hope he took a bath like I told him."

"Well, he either had to go to the creek or fill up a tub with water from the cistern," Eva said. "There's no way this place has indoor plumbing. I hope you went to the bathroom before you left town. You'd be better off going in the woods than setting foot in his outhouse. You're liable to get bit on the butt by a spider."

Rita's face contorted. "No way I'm going in it."

Ethan appeared at the doorway, and Rita said, "Well, look at that. He's got on brand-spanking-new overalls . . . and he shaved, too. I hear wedding bells."

"You're going to see stars if you don't knock it off, Rita."

"All right, I promise," Rita said.

Ethan ambled toward their car in his offbeat stride. The dogs continued to bark and howl. Ethan kicked at the shepherd. "You dogs get gone now, hear?" Both dogs padded back to the porch.

The two women got out of the car with their supplies. "Ethan, don't you look nice," Rita said. "You know Eva, here, she's going to give you a haircut."

"Hi, Miss Rita and Miss Eva."

"Ethan, go in the house and bring out a kitchen chair. Rita, take the bucket to the cistern and fill it with water while I get set up here."

Ethan returned, carrying a ladder-back chair with a torn cane bottom. "That'll do fine, Ethan. We'll be ready to start in a moment."

"Yes, ma'am."

"Ethan, I'm not a *ma'am*. My name's Eva. That's what I want you to call me."

Ethan looked down and scuffed the toe of his shoe in the dirt. Then, still facing downward, he looked up with his eyes, which had the shine of someone who had been given a special privilege, and said, "All right . . . Eva."

Rita screamed from over at the cistern. Eva and Ethan pivoted toward the sound. "There was a snake in the bucket!" Rita yelled. She had dropped the bucket and was now ten feet or more from the cistern.

"Oh, it's just a ring-neck snake," Ethan said. "It won't hurt you."

"Ethan, do you drink water from that cistern?" Eva asked.

"Yes, ma'am, I mean, Eva . . . the snakes don't hurt it none."

After the snake slithered away, Rita returned to the cistern, lowered the bucket, and this time retrieved it full of water, without a snake, and joined Eva and Ethan.

Eva leaned the chair against the car, put a towel around Ethan's neck, and told him to sit down and lean back. He obeyed, and Rita braced against the chair to keep it steady.

Eva dipped a glass in the pan sitting on the fender and poured water on Ethan's head. He gripped the chair seat with both hands. His now blanched face, with the fresh shaving cuts, gave him the look of someone who had just been in a car wreck and was about to be treated for shock.

"Now, Ethan, don't be nervous. I just need to shampoo your hair before I cut it. Just shut your eyes and relax. I don't want to get shampoo in them."

Eva's expert hands began massaging the shampoo onto Ethan's scalp. "Now, doesn't this feel good, Ethan?" She looked at Rita. "He really has nice thick hair; Mrs. Davis would die for a head of hair like this."

Eva and Rita continued to chatter quietly, but Ethan was not listening—he had dozed off. When Eva poured the rinse water over his head, he jerked and woke up but did not say anything. She swaddled his head with a towel and began rubbing his hair dry. To get rid of the tangles, she made a rinse solution by adding a few drops of Suave hair dressing to a glass of water.

"Ethan, I'm going to start cutting your hair."

"OK, Eva."

Eva, in action, became a combination of Michelangelo and Clara Barton, the field-efficient Civil War nurse. She was General Patton at the forward edge of the battle area. She was a sheep shearer. She was Delilah.

Hair fell in clumps around Ethan's shoulders. She cut on one side and then the other. No wild hair escaped her attention. There was no conversation. It was all quiet on the western front.

After thirty minutes of labor, she stepped back to gain perspective, and said, "I think that does it." The look on her face was that of a proud mother on graduation day. "Rita, what do you think?"

"I can't believe it." Rita's voice was filled with awe. "He's been transfigured."

"Oh, no," Ethan whimpered, his face fearful.

"He misunderstood you, Rita. Ethan, you poor thing, she means you've changed. You look beautiful." Then, with no appearance of obvious thought involved, she bent over and kissed him on top of his head. Immediately, she looked over at Rita, whose mouth had dropped open, "Now, don't you say a word."

The moment had arrived. She gave Ethan a hand mirror. He looked, at first, as if he were seeing someone other than himself. Maybe someone better than himself. With his free hand he patted his hair, his styled hair that had lift and body. His clean-cut hair that was tapered tightly around his neck and ears. His Clark Gable hair.

He smiled a big smile and his eyes moistened. "Much obliged, Eva."

Chapter Ten

Ethan and the Marquess of Queensberry

𝐵urns Grady, the president of the First State Bank of Birch View, watched Ethan through the front window of the bank. Ethan stood on the sidewalk, leaning against the street-side telephone pole between the bank and Eva's beauty shop.

This was the second day in a row. The day before, Ethan had been there for over an hour before Eva came out, took a paper sack of tomatoes from him, and shooed him away.

At fifty, Burns Grady was not an impressive-looking man. He stood only five feet six inches, with skinny legs and a potbelly. He looked a bit like a potato supported by two matchsticks. His pate was a round bare spot that he hid with the town's only toupee, which Eva had described as a dead tarantula.

He continued staring out the window, where Ethan was now holding vigil over a peck basket chock-full of green zucchini and yellow summer squash. "Why does he have to stand outside the bank? It's bad for business," Burns mumbled.

"Shirley," Burns called to his secretary, "go out there and tell Ethan not to loiter in front of the bank or I'll call the constable."

Shirley, a petite recent high school graduate, looked at her boss and tried to manage a compliant smile. "Mr. Grady, I hate to get near him. I think he's scary."

"Nonsense, he's just shiftless and lazy. I'll do it myself," Grady said and marched out the doorway.

With arms akimbo, two feet from Ethan, Grady said, "Why are you standing here in front of the bank? You're

119

loitering, and your old truck is taking up space that a bank customer could use."

"I can stand here if I want to."

"Look, if you have a gift for the object of your affection, why don't you just go inside the beauty shop and give it to her, and quit standing in front of my bank."

Ethan looked at the ground with his face grimaced. "I ain't got an *affection* . . . and I can stand here if I want."

Jesse Weaver was striding up the sidewalk toward them. He had dropped his wife at the beauty shop and was headed toward the bank.

"Hey, Jesse, wait a second," Grady said. "Did you know that old Ethan, here, has got himself a girlfriend?"

"Who'd go with *him*?"

"Why, Eva," Grady said, "the beauty operator." Then, looking at Ethan, he said, "Think you're man enough for her, stud? I reckon you wouldn't be that little filly's first."

Ethan's head snapped up and he looked straight at the banker. "You shut up about Eva."

"Now, look out boy, you better watch your mouth—and I'll say whatever I damned well please."

Ethan clenched both fists and struck a boxer's stance. The pose resembled that of a nineteenth-century prizefighter using the Marquess of Queensberry rules. His left arm was curled and extended with the palm of his fist toward his own face. His right fist was held *en garde* at the waist.

The banker's face reddened in a mixture of surprise and outrage. "What do you think you're doing?"

"I'm fixing to hit you with a chin hook."

The banker guffawed and turned to Jesse. "Did you hear that? He threatened me because I said something about that hairdresser next door."

As he turned back toward Ethan, Ethan's fist popped him smack on the nose. The banker's head jerked back.

"Ouch! By God, Jess, that son of bitch just hit me."

It had been the punch of an amateur and inflicted more insult than serious injury. Grady felt his nose with his hand; it was trickling blood. He pulled a handkerchief from his vest pocket and dabbed at his nose. As he looked at the crimson spot on the fresh linen, his lip curled exposing an incisor. He looked up at Ethan. "You've done it now, you half-wit, I'm going to kick your ass."

Panic showed on Ethan's face as Grady lunged at him. Ethan sidestepped the banker's charge and grabbed a foot-long zucchini from his basket. From his crouched position, he hurled it at Grady. Grady ducked, and the squash grazed the top of his head, sending the tarantula flying.

Grady's hands moved to his bald spot faster than a woman covering a windblown skirt. In the background of the unfolding scene, Jesse's laughter was punctuated by his leg slapping. Ethan was not laughing. His face was bleak and wide-eyed, as if he had scalped his opponent.

Grady pounced on the hairpiece, and with no pretense of dignity, attempted to reapply it. The spider was, now, more on the side than the summit of the banker's head.

"Jesse, get that fat-ass constable over here. I want this heathen arrested." Grady shifted his glaring eyes to Ethan. "Don't you even think about leaving, or you'll be charged with leaving the scene of a crime, too."

#

Orin "Stubby" Davis pulled to the curb in a '54 Ford station wagon that served as the town's police car and ambulance. Stubby barely had half of his two hundred and forty pounds out of the car when the banker yelled, "Get up here and arrest this criminal. He just assaulted me, and Jesse, here, saw it all."

"That so, Jesse?" Stubby asked.

"That's right, Stubby. He just hauled off and hit Mr. Grady . . . when he wasn't looking, too."

Stubby hitched up his trousers and waddled over to his suspect, pulling his handcuffs from the leather Sam Brown belt that he wore with his khaki shirt and trousers. "Ethan, what in the name of God do you have to say for yourself?"

Ethan backed against the telephone pole and crooked an arm around it as if he might otherwise fall. His face was pale and his breathing was shallow and quick like a captured bird. His head drooped and he stared at the sidewalk.

"Turn around, Ethan," Stubby said. As he was putting the handcuffs on Ethan, Eva opened the door of her shop. Instinctively, she charged to the scene.

"Hey, what's going on? Why are you arresting Ethan?"

"He assaulted Mr. Grady," Stubby said, nodding at Ethan.

"I can't believe that."

"Jesse here saw it," Stubby said.

"Ethan," Eva said, "did you hit Mr. Grady? No, don't answer that. I'm going to get J. Bob."

"I brought you some squashes, Eva."

J. Bob had been at the courthouse in Hamilton for Law Day, a special time set aside by the court to hear motions and matters requiring a hearing. It made for a long day, and on the way home, J. Bob stopped for a beer at Club 60.

When he walked through the door, Sam pulled a Budweiser from the cooler, poked a couple holes in the can with a church key, and set it opposite J. Bob's usual stool.

Several regular customers were at the other end drinking cold ones and listening to a logger's story about a bear he had seen near the Eleven Point River.

"Did Eva Thomas ever get hold of you?" Sam asked. "She called here looking for you."

J. Bob sat down. "Yeah, she called the court clerk—I was over in Hamilton—and he gave me the message." J. Bob took a drink from his beer.

"What'd Eva want? That is, if you can tell me."

"Well, it seems that old Stubby locked up Ethan Collier."

"What did that dumb son of a bitch do?"

"Now, Sam, you're just still sore because he was an accessory to the holdup at your cousin's place. Hell, that was a case of undue influence on a simple mind."

"He's simple-minded, all right," Sam said.

"Well, Sam, I'll tell you one thing, he may be simple, but he's not stupid. My mother taught him at a one-room school, and she says he could do arithmetic from a high school book in the fourth grade.

Sam lit a cigarette, took a drag, and exhaled. "When I was training recruits in the Navy, we had a guy like that. He scored real high on tests, but he couldn't tell his left from his right."

J. Bob raised his eyebrows and nodded. "That's about like Ethan. But he is so timid that I can't believe he took a poke at Burns Grady. I never have liked that old fussbudget. I ought to defend Ethan *pro bono*.

"You'll probably have to do it for free—or get paid with eggs."

"Actually, the last time I represented him, he paid me five hundred dollars in cash. He's probably got enough green stashed away to burn a wet elephant. But I'll tell you, this case is a serious problem; Ethan is still on probation. If he gets convicted, even of common assault, he'll join his brother at the state penitentiary in Jeff City."

J. Bob took a long draw on his beer. "He wouldn't survive a week in the pen." The vision J. Bob imagined gave the beer a coppery taste, and he passed on Sam's offer of a second one.

Chester Martin, the county prosecuting attorney, and J. Bob stood up as the Magistrate Gerald Elliot entered the courtroom. Chester would not agree to let Ethan out of jail without posting a bond.

"Mr. Martin," Judge Elliot said, "you have amended the charge from common assault to aggravated assault, plus destruction of public property. What public property was destroyed?"

"Well, Your Honor, the defendant relieved himself in the Birch View city vehicle."

"I object," J. Bob said. "I've not heard anything about this."

"Well, he did, Your Honor," Martin shot back.

Judge Elliot leaned forward over the bench and under his breath said, "Was this urination or defecation?"

"I object—"

"Counselor, your objections are falling on the deaf ears of the court until I find out what happened."

"Judge, I know justice is blind—I didn't know it was deaf, too."

"Mr. Dalton, another comment like that, and I'll hold you in contempt."

"I apologize, Your Honor."

Chester cleared his throat. "It was urination, Your Honor. The defendant peed his pants in the police vehicle and got the rear seat wet. I can get Stubby over here to testify to that if necessary."

"Your Honor, it's obvious that my client was scared to death. I fear it will do irreparable harm to him if he is forced to stay in jail. He's not a threat to society."

"On the contrary, Your Honor," Martin said, "the Court will recall that the defendant is currently on probation for attempted robbery."

"The Court's recollection does not need to be refreshed, Mr. Martin. Why has the present case been elevated to *aggravated* assault?"

"The assault was perpetrated with a weapon," the prosecutor said.

"What kind of weapon?"

"A zucchini, Your Honor."

J. Bob made a painful face. "Judge, now I have heard it all. Doesn't our esteemed prosecutor have anything better to do than charge a citizen with aggravated assault for defending himself with a vegetable?"

Martin glared at J. Bob and then directed his attention to the bench. "Judge, the State's evidence will also show that the defendant struck Mr. Grady." "Counselors, save your extended arguments for the preliminary hearing. What's the state's position on bail?"

"Your Honor, for a felony of this degree, and given the fact that the defendant has no visible means of support and is likely to flee the Court's jurisdiction, the State submits that bond should be posted in the amount of five thousand dollars."

"Judge, that's pure nonsense," J. Bob said. "According to the prosecution's reasoning, half the people in this county have *no visible means of support.* It'd take a hundred acres, free and clear, to post a five-thousand-dollar bond. His old truck would be lucky to make it out of the county, let alone the Court's jurisdiction. He has ties to the community—family and such—and I'll bet he's never been out of the county in his entire life."

"Bond is set at five hundred dollars," the Judge said and accented his order by banging his gavel.

J. Bob sat at his office desk preparing the paperwork for Ethan's release. He leaned back in his swivel chair and gazed at the books and furnishings that surrounded him. His office was a sanctuary from ignorance. Sometimes when he was there on Sunday mornings, as he often was, it felt almost spiritual.

The turn-of-the century roll-top desk had been in old Doc Davis's office. As a child he had been fascinated by the many pigeon holes stuffed with bills and receipts. The desk didn't look much different now. Two of the drawers were locked. In one he kept at least five hundred dollars in cash for weekend bail money when the banks weren't open; in the other he kept a bottle of Jack Daniels.

J. Bob's secretary came to the doorway. "Mr. Dalton, Eva Thomas is here to see you."

"Send her in."

J. Bob stood up when Eva entered the room and motioned her to a chair. "Have a seat, Eva. I wondered how long it would take for you to show up. I guess I know why you're here."

Sitting on the front edge of the chair, Eva said, "I just want to know what's going to happen to Ethan. Do you know what exactly happened?"

"You raised two questions. As to the first, I'm not sure what's going to happen, but I do know what provoked an otherwise timid soul to poking the banker."

"Well, what caused it?"

"Now, Eva, conversations between an attorney and his client are privileged."

"Oh, horse feathers, J. Bob. You know it won't go any further."

"In a beauty shop?"

"You know I can keep a secret. I've never told anyone about that night you and Shirley Barnes went—"

"All right. Hold on, Eva. That was an evening involving John Barleycorn. But let's get back to the case at hand. Why are you so interested in this matter? It seems to me that you are taking this rather personally. Have you become fond of our little scofflaw?"

"No, it's just that he doesn't have anyone to watch out for him. That's all . . . and, well, it's partly my fault. If he

126

hadn't been bringing me the vegetables, none of this would have happened. I mean, you should have seen him, when he said, 'Eva, I brought you some squashes.' It just breaks my heart . . . the poor thing. And that nasty banker . . . I just wish there was something I could do."

J. Bob held his gaze on her. "Maybe there is."

Eva's eyes widened. "What can I do?"

"In the interest of helping my client, I am going to confide in you. Ethan hit Burns Grady because Grady made an untoward remark about you. He, in effect, accused you of being a woman of easy virtue."

"That old scoundrel, I'll give him a piece of my mind the next time I see him," Eva said.

"You can do better than that. You can threaten to sue his ass and help Ethan out at the same time. Grady has slandered you, and not just garden-variety slander, either. He has impugned the chastity of an unmarried woman. That's slander *per se*. You don't even have to show damages—they're presumed."

"Oh, I don't want to get involved in a lawsuit."

"I said *threaten* to sue. If you were to retain me to represent you, Grady might be persuaded to drop his complaint against Ethan. We'll have to be careful. Chester Martin will be raising hell, saying that I'm interfering with his prosecution by trying to intimidate the complaining witness."

Three days later J. Bob received a telephone call from the prosecutor. "Well, hello, Chester. To what do I owe the pleasure of this call? . . . Oh, I guess Burns Grady got my letter."

J. Bob's mouth tightened as Chester's voice got louder. When Chester paused, J. Bob said, "Hell, yes, she's going to sue him. Miss Thomas came to me concerned that her reputation in the community has been ruined."

J. Bob held the receiver a couple inches from his ear and could still hear Chester rant.

When he thought he could get a word in, J. Bob, with his voice raised, said, "Let me tell you something. By the time I finish cross-examining Grady, he will have established my client's defamation case—under oath. He's a big, fat puffed-up deacon in the Baptist Church, and I'm going to let some air out of him . . . What? . . . I double-dog dare you to report me to the Bar Commission. I'll report *you*! You're using your prosecution to deny my client's day in court."

The receiver slammed on the other end of the line. A smile came to J. Bob's face, and he calmly placed the receiver on the phone hook. Then he leaned forward and unlocked one of the desk drawers.

Chapter Eleven
Autumn Winds

*T*he colorful foliage of the Ozark autumn was beginning to fall. Rita watched from behind the bar as leaves swirled across the highway in front of Club 60. Winter weather wouldn't be far behind.

Two customers had just left and were about to get in a pickup, but they hesitated as J. Bob turned off the highway onto the parking lot. J. Bob got out of his car and began chatting with them.

Rita disposed of the empty beer cans left by the two customers and wiped the counter. It had been over a week since the excitement of Ethan Collier and Burns Grady, and Rita perked up with the thought of quizzing J. Bob about the case. Eva had been tight-lipped about the matter, as if she were trying to distance herself from the incident.

Rita sat a can of Budweiser on the bar as J. Bob entered, and he sat on a stool in front of it. "What's new in the lawyering business?"

"A few things. Where's Sam?"

"He left after the lunch crowd thinned out and went to see Big John, but he should be back before too long."

"I didn't need to talk to him anyway. In fact, I'm glad I caught you here alone." He paused. "Rita, your maiden name was O'Dell wasn't it?"

Rita looked suspicious. "Yes. Why?"

"My secretary said an older woman named O'Dell stopped by my office and wanted to talk to me about obtaining legal guardianship of her grandson. She left her address, and when I got the message, I felt certain it was about your boy, Wesley."

"That just can't be right." Rita crossed her arms in front of her chest and audibly sucked in her breath. "What do you think is going on, J. Bob?"

"It sounds like she's trying to steal your son."

"Over my dead body. I'll—"

"Hold on. Nothing's happened yet. And don't worry, I wouldn't take the case, but I thought you should know. Why don't you have a beer, too."

Rita got a beer for herself. "She couldn't do that, could she?"

"Well, in a nutshell, if a grandparent can technically show that a child has been abandoned—"

"I haven't abandoned Wesley."

"I know, but let me finish. The actual facts aren't what's most important; it's what you can make a judge *believe*. How old is Wesley?"

"He's ten."

"That's good. At least between you and your husband, you would have an advantage. In the eyes of the law, young children are presumed to be better off with their mother. Where is your husband, anyway?"

"God only knows. He ran off with a truck stop waitress, and I haven't seen him in months. He supposedly drove by to see Wesley and my parents a few months ago. He was passing through on a trip and drove his big truck out to the farm. I expect he's back in Iowa now."

"You're living with Eva now?"

"Most of the time," Rita said.

"What about the rest of the time?"

Embarrassed, Rita said, "Well, sometimes I stay at Sam's house in Ridgeview, but sometimes I stay at my parents' place."

"Wesley, I assume, lives with his grandparents."

"Yes, he goes to the little school near there."

"How long have you lived . . . at Eva's?"

130

"About six weeks." Rita took a hurried swig of her beer. "Hey, whose side are you on, J. Bob?"

J. Bob raised his hand up like a cop stopping traffic. "Hold on, now. As I said, between you and your estranged husband, you would have the upper hand. It could be a little more complicated as far as your mother is concerned."

"How's that?"

"Well, my friend, you work in a honky-tonk; your boyfriend runs the honky-tonk; and you live part-time in a house with said boyfriend and not with your son. This isn't the big city. It could be argued that you abandoned him or are an unfit mother."

Appalled, and raising her voice, Rita said, "I most certainly have not abandoned my son."

"When was the last time you saw him?"

"I don't remember, exactly, it was—"

J. Bob cut her off. "A month?"

"Not that long. I think, maybe, three weeks. But one weekend he went to a lake in Arkansas with his friend Ernie and his parents. Then Sam's friend from the navy and his wife came through, and we entertained them.

"Do you ever see him during the week?"

"Yes, but there isn't much time between when he gets out of school and when I start work. I've been meaning to go more, but every time I go out there my mother gives me these looks. I get so mad. I miss him more than you can imagine."

"I understand, Rita, but you need to understand that if you don't take some action, you're going to have a lot of problems. First, you need to get divorced and get a custody order."

"It sounds like I'd have a better chance going against Ray than my mother."

"Maybe so, but the divorce isn't a cakewalk either, if your husband decides to contest it."

"Why? He's the one that ran off with the other woman. I've got grounds, don't I?"

"You're right, adultery is grounds for divorce, but there is a little stumbling block in the Missouri divorce law. You have to be the *innocent and injured party*."

"Well, I am."

"Not exactly. What that means is that even though you have grounds against him, if he can show grounds against *you*, you're not the innocent and injured party. If he has a photograph of you and Sam coming out of a motel, for example, he can keep you from getting a divorce."

Rita's eyes filled with tears, which she swabbed with a bar rag, and then wiped her nose with it. Her face suddenly morphed into a clinched fist. "J. Bob, Ray has cooked up this dirty scheme with my mother."

J. Bob nodded. "It does seem that someone has cooked up something."

Chapter Twelve

Eva's Story

*A*s Eva stood at the sink washing dishes left from breakfast, she peered out her kitchen window at the hickory tree in the back yard. The late afternoon sun filtered through the branches, casting a spider web silhouette on the lawn. The leaves were a bright dead yellow, which she took as an autumn sign that it was time to return to the cemetery. The thought didn't seem as bad this year. *Was it just a ritual now after five years?*

The kitchen was spic-and-span in the house she had lived in all her life. It looked the same as it did when she was a child: two wooden wall cabinets painted a buttermilk enamel on either side of the window above the sink; a red tin bread box and blue glass canisters for flour and sugar; and the round oak table that had been her grandmother's.

She felt a sinking feeling remembering the first year after Sonny was killed—it had been the worst. It was six months before she could speak his name without her voice breaking. Some memories she still avoided altogether. She had not returned to the high school since the day before graduation, the day he was killed in the car wreck.

Now, of all things, she was going back to the basketball homecoming game. At the half-time coronation, the school would be honoring past queens. "Why, you simply have to be there," Mrs. Wendling, the venerable English teacher and homecoming sponsor, had told her. "You are the only one I can recall that was voted in twice."

Eva had explained to Mrs. Wendling that she had previous plans. She had assumed that was the end of the matter, until J. Bob showed up at the Cut & Curl the next week on Tuesday morning.

Eva was alone in the beauty shop sweeping the floor when J. Bob walked in. "Eva, what's this I hear about you not going to homecoming?"

"Well, good morning to you, too, J. Bob." Her eyes moved up and down, looking at him from his hair, which needed a comb, to his black bluchers, which needed a shine. "It looks like you must have come in for a haircut."

"No, I didn't come for a haircut. I was over at the Owl having coffee and Rita told me."

Eva rolled her eyes. "That little heifer . . . and just why is it any of your business whether I go to a stupid basketball game?"

"Because I'm your friend . . . and I care about you."

"Well, I appreciate that, but I'm afraid it would just make me sad and I'd be up all night crying. Anyway, I'd feel foolish. Half the people in town treat me like I'm the sad young widow."

"No, you act like a sad young widow, and you and Sonny weren't even engaged. You're preoccupied with death—first Sonny, then your mom and dad six months apart. When are you going to start living?"

Eva looked stunned. Tears came to her eyes. Her lower lip trembled as she closed her eyes and clutched the broom for support.

J. Bob rushed over and put both arms around her and hugged her tightly. In her ear he whispered, "I'm so sorry, Eva."

Eva let the broom fall. Their bodies meshed together. Her sobs reverberated against his stomach, and the softness of her breasts molded against his chest as she clung to him.

They held each other without speaking until her crying subsided. She began the controlled breathing of one struggling for emotional stability, and after a long sigh, she

134

turned the side of her face against his shoulder and said, "I just . . . didn't want to go there . . . alone."

J. Bob took her shoulders in his hands and stepped back until he could look into her eyes. "I'll take you . . . if you'd like."

She pulled him closer, hugged him, and with her cheek against his chest, said, "Thank you, J. Bob. I'll think it over."

Rita entered the kitchen as Eva dried the last dish. "Eva, what time is J. Bob coming over to pick you up?"

Eva put the dish in the cabinet, turned toward Rita and said, "He should be here by seven o'clock," and then proceeded to the hallway mirror at the kitchen entrance. "Do you think this blouse looks OK?" She patted her hair with her hand and puckered her lips, inspecting her lipstick.

Rita watched her with the interest of a big sister. "You'll be the prettiest girl there."

Looking at Rita, Eva said, "I don't know about that. I'll be there with all those cute little girls sashaying around. I feel as nervous as a high school freshman."

"Well, you haven't been on a date in a while."

"Oh, this isn't really a date. J. Bob just said he would take me to be kind."

With a devilish grin, Rita said, "I don't know. That perfume you're wearing smells like a night-across-the-tracks."

"Oh, do you think it's too much?"

"Not for a girl going on a date with her feller."

"He's not my fellow."

"I have a feeling about this—"

"Oh, Rita, you've been trying to get me fixed up with a man ever since I've known you. You would have married me off to Ethan Collier."

#

J. Bob parked his car in front of Eva's, and before he was on the front porch, she opened the door and stepped outside.

"Hi, J. Bob."

J. Bob watched as she pulled the door closed behind her. She was wearing a pleated skirt, hemmed at mid-calf, and a white blouse under a red button-up sweater. Her honey-colored hair shone in the glow of the porch light. She wore it shoulder length, parted on the side and held in place with a single white barrette. She looked as if she might only be seventeen. J. Bob suddenly felt very old at thirty-one, and he found himself at a rare loss for words.

"Well, J. Bob, aren't you going to say anything?"

"You look lovely, my dear." *Jesus, I'm not her father*, he thought.

"Why, thank you, Mr. Dalton."

J. Bob thought she had emphasized *mister*, and he wondered whether she was trying to tell him that this was an arms-length transaction or the opposite—that he shouldn't be so stuffy.

"Well, Eva, I was just thinking that it's so nice out, we ought to walk to the school."

"Sounds good to me," Eva said with a lilt in her voice.

As they walked from the porch, Rita peeked from behind the curtain in the living room and smiled. "Yes, I've got a feeling."

Eva and J. Bob strolled side by side in the middle of the unlit street by the light of an orange harvest moon.

"J. Bob, this is certainly nice weather tonight."

"Yes, it is, Eva. I expect there will be some kids out stealing pumpkins."

"I wouldn't be surprised."

They continued their stroll without speaking, and after a short while, Eva said, "You know, when we walk in the

136

school together, it's going to give the town gossips something to talk about."

"Well, I'm not too worried about that."

"That's easy for you to say, you come from an old, respected name in this town."

"There's nothing wrong with your name, and I guarantee you they talk about me already. My own mother even talks about me."

"J. Bob, about the only thing I've ever heard anyone say negative about you is that you spend too much time at Club 60."

"Maybe so, but those same folks will be the first ones to come running for help as soon as they have a problem."

Eva nodded. "That's about right."

"And another thing, Eva, every time someone sees my car at Club 60, it doesn't mean I'm in there drinking. Some days I have lunch there, and I enjoy talking to Sam."

"Sam! Why do you like talking to him? I've heard he's mean. I don't know what Rita sees in him. Oops! Rita just works there."

J. Bob laughed. "I suppose 'Rita and Sam' is the town's worst kept secret, but Sam is all right. He's a very smart man, and he's been all over the world—India, China, all kinds of places. His stories are fascinating. Hell, I want to go to China."

"Then, why don't you go there, I mean, sometime on a vacation."

"Well, I wouldn't really want to go alone."

As they rounded the curve at the top of the hill, the two-story school building came into view. It loomed like a castle at the edge of a hamlet, all lit up for games and a coronation, with townsfolk gathered to pay tribute to the athletes and the new queen. Eva uttered a quiet moan.

Tentatively, J. Bob reached for her hand, and when their fingers touched, she clasped on and said, "Thanks."

Once among the throng of villagers at the front steps, J. Bob released her hand.

The smell of hot popcorn permeated the air as they passed over the wooden hallway that creaked under the game-night traffic. FFA boys dressed in their blue corduroy jackets barked snacks and sodas, urging support for the Future Farmers of America. From the gymnasium further down the hall, cheerleaders yelled "Go Tigers!" The B-team game was in progress.

Familiar faces passed pleasantries: "Nice to see you at homecoming, Eva" and "Hey, J. Bob." Eva forced smiles for each and simply said, "Hi" or "Thanks." J. Bob extended his hand to each, never missing a first name, but never lingering to chat.

They sat on the third row of bleacher seats on the hometown end across from the stage, which was decorated with blue and gold. Crepe paper streamers crested to form a canopy above muslin-draped chairs for the queen and her court to be seated.

Memories began coursing through Eva's mind: her own coronations and homecoming kisses, first from *a senior* when she was a junior—my, how jealous Sonny had been—and then as senior when Sonny was the captain.

A boy on the opposing team caught her attention with his forelock of black hair that reminded her of Sonny; again, she felt that too-familiar sinking feeling. Unconsciously, she grabbed J. Bob's forearm.

J. Bob leaned to her ear. "Are you OK?" She indicated she was fine, but her voice was shaky. "I'll go get us a couple Cokes. Do you want any popcorn?"

"No, a Coke would be fine."

J. Bob headed to the concession stand and had only been gone for a few minutes when, from behind Eva, a voice said, "I hope homecoming doesn't bring up bad memories for you."

Eva knew the voice. It was Loretta Smith. *Nosy old Mrs. Smith—she's worked at the community library since before I was born. What on earth is she doing here?"*

Eva turned around and saw that Mrs. Smith had moved to sit in a spot behind her that had been vacant. "Hello, Mrs. Smith. No, I'm fine. You look nice this evening." *I wish J. Bob would get back here.*

Mrs. Smith smiled thinly but didn't return the compliment or thank Eva. "I see you are here with J. Bob Dalton. I'm surprised."

"Oh really?" *What's taking J. Bob so long?* Eva looked past her to the aisle for J. Bob.

Mrs. Smith continued, "What I was wondering is—"

"Oh look, there's J. Bob, now," Eva said, noticing that Mrs. Smith's smile had waned.

J. Bob held a paper cup in each hand, with a bag of popcorn squeezed between. "Here, Eva, take one of these Cokes." As J. Bob sat down, he glanced at the newly occupied seat behind them and said, "Hello, Mrs. Smith. Eva, did you know that Mrs. Smith was homecoming queen a few years back?"

"I didn't know that," Eva said.

J. Bob turned in his seat so he could see both Eva and Mrs. Smith. "It looks like this game is about over and the ceremonies can start."

Mrs. Smith's lips were twitching from side to side as if a question were fighting its way out to be heard. Finally, the question overpowered her weak lips. "J. Bob, can I ask a stupid question?"

J. Bob's mouth tightened into a wry smile, and his eyes twinkled. "Why, Mrs. Smith, I'm sure you can."

J. Bob's timing was perfect. The horn sounded, ending the first game. The principal, already center stage, announced through a scratchy microphone, "Will the queen candidates come up to the stage, and former queens move under the goal to my left."

Of the former queens, Eva received the most applause by far. When she was announced, she gave a shy smile, but with the crescendo of the crowd, she beamed into a wide full smile and waved at the hometown fans. Her eyes were moist, but nothing about her looked sad.

The old royalty returned to their seats, the lights dimmed, and the coronation ceremony began. Eva and J. Bob watched as a rangy, and somewhat embarrassed-looking team captain, crowned and kissed the junior queen candidate and escorted her to the throne.

J. Bob whispered to Eva, "You seemed to survive just fine, and you got a lot more cheers than Mrs. Smith."

Eva grinned. "Now that you mention it, yes, I did. Maybe I should go ask her if this brought back bad memories for her."

"I've got a better idea. The mission here is accomplished, so before the next game starts, let's mosey out of here."

"That's fine with me; it's a little stuffy in here."

Outside, the crisp fall air was scented with tobacco smoke as they passed through scattered groups of men replaying the game and reliving past glories. "Truman Lehman was the best I ever saw," one man said. "He scored twenty points in the second half against Pine Grove."

J. Bob smiled as he overheard the discussions; he loved stories of how great things used to be and wondered if he were an anachronism. Maybe he would have fit better in an earlier time.

J. Bob barely noticed as he and Eva crossed the edge of the light cast from the schoolyard and into the darkness of the street, until Eva clasped his hand. It was unexpected and exciting, and almost by reflex he squeezed back. He felt euphoric, and at the same time, oddly guilty—but of what, he was not sure.

"J. Bob, thank you. I couldn't have done this without you."

"No need to thank me for escorting you to your coming-out party."

"Coming-out party?"

"In wealthy families young women are presented to society at debutante balls sometimes referred to as coming-out parties. These soirées have dinners and dancing and are quite posh affairs."

Eva laughed. "J. Bob, you certainly use some two-dollar words. All I can say is if this was my debutante ball, it wasn't an official one . . . you know the school board won't allow dancing at the high school."

"Too many Methodists and Baptists on the board," J. Bob said, "but there are alternatives." Their hands were still entwined, and for J. Bob, her hand had become an unconscious extension of his body.

"What kind of alternative?" Eva asked.

"Rita told me to bring you by Club 60 for a post-game celebration. She said Big John was making a special trip just to meet the girl J. Bob was taking to homecoming."

"I've heard of him, but I don't know. I don't drink, and if my little old ladies found out that I was at the den of iniquity—that's what they call it—I'd lose half my customers."

"Eva, I doubt if any of them will be there. Besides, there are enough closet drinkers in Birch View that if they all gathered together on Saturday nights, they'd put Club 60 out of business."

"J. Bob, I swear, you don't take anything at face value." Her voice had a playful quality that reflected the glow of the homecoming ceremony. "But I guess I can go wherever I please, and if this is my *coming-out* party, I should go where there is dancing, even if it's a honky-tonk."

#

As they pulled in the parking lot at Club 60, J. Bob announced, "Saturday night at Club 60, where you'll find the 'Who's Who' of local sinners, most of my friends, and a great source of clients."

Eva leaned toward the dashboard and stared through the windshield straining to see if she could see anyone she knew through the front windows. She saw Rita behind the bar waiting on customers. "OK, take me to the ball."

They stepped through the front door into cigarette smoke and the sound of jukebox music and laughter. From behind the bar only Rita seemed to pay any attention as they entered, and she motioned them over.

But from the far end of the bar a voice boomed over the din, "Hey, Counselor, get your scrawny ass over here." Big John had already arrived.

They maneuvered around three men hovering over the pinball machine toward the end of the bar where Big John was holding court. Eva gripped J. Bob's upper arm with both hands.

Big John glanced at two men on either side of him and said, "You fellows will have to excuse me." He rose from the barstool to his full height, flashed his best killer smile, and said, "Counselor, introduce me to the vision of loveliness on your arm."

Rita, who had moved parallel with J. Bob and Eva, intervened. "Big John, don't scare that kid; she's not used to someone with all your charm."

Big John grinned. Bending forward like one stooping to the level of a child, he extended his ham-sized hand to Eva and said, "Darling, I'm John Crawford. Everyone calls me Big John—I don't know why."

"John," J. Bob said, "may I present Miss Eva Pruett."

Eva extended her arm for a handshake, but Big John raised it to his lips and kissed it.

"Don't get smoochy, Big John," Rita said. Directing her attention to Eva and J. Bob, she said, "J. Bob, I'll get you a beer. Eva, do you want a Coke?"

Eva nodded that she did and took a step toward the bar. Leaning over she whispered, "Rita, I need to use the ladies' room."

"Hold on a minute," Rita said. She left and returned with a Coke and a Budweiser.

"If you gentlemen will excuse us, we're going to the ladies' room. Eva, meet me at the other end of the bar."

As they walked to the rear, Eva said, "Rita, you could have just told me where it is; you didn't have to come with me."

"It's outside, Eva. Why do you think I have the flashlight?"

The beam of the flashlight revealed a wooden outhouse with peeling paint that could accommodate no more than a single person who wasn't too tall. It listed to one side, and with its pitched roof and quarter-moon ventilation opening, it resembled humorous postcards that tourists sent from the Ozarks. Over the door, which wasn't square with the frame, a hand-painted sign on a board read "Ladies Room."

"Rita, this doesn't look much better than Ethan's, and you wouldn't go in his."

"Well, it's cleaner because I *have* to use it, and it's still early in the evening . . . some of these old bags get a little careless, if you know what I mean. You can wash your hands in the kitchen."

When Eva came out, Rita said, "Tell me what went on this evening with you and J. Bob. Anything good to report?"

"I actually had a good time. As much as I dreaded it, I'm glad I went."

"What about J. Bob?"

"Well, he's J. Bob, but tonight it seemed different somehow . . . almost romantic."

"In what way?"

"I don't know. We walked in the moonlight, and talked. And we held hands there and back."

"Really?" Rita said. "This is too good."

"He said tonight was my coming-out party and that I needed to go where there was dancing. Do you think he'll ask me to dance?"

"I'll take care of that. When you hear 'Tennessee Waltz,' get ready. You do know how to dance, don't you?"

"Yes, a little. My mother gave me some lessons in case I ever moved away."

"Don't worry; just relax and let him lead."

Back inside, when they left the kitchen, Rita proceeded to the jukebox, and Eva returned to the end of the bar where Sam had joined J. Bob and Big John. J. Bob introduced Eva to Sam.

"Eva," Sam said, "Rita and I were hoping you would come by tonight. She said you were attractive, but you look gorgeous this evening. I can't say as much for your escort."

"Well, Sam," said Eva, "my mother told me that pretty women should go with smart men. Do you think that's true?"

Sam hesitated before answering. "I think that smart women should go with smart men."

Rita nudged in between Sam and the corner of the bar. "What are you all talking about?"

"Sam was passing on the wisdom of his age," J. Bob said.

Big John said, "That'll be the day when Sam passes on any wisdom."

From the jukebox, Patti Page began singing and couples glided to the dance floor hand in hand, and a few single men sauntered about in search of partners.

"Well, J. Bob, aren't you going to ask Eva to dance?" Rita asked. Eva looked at her and smiled.

144

L. D. Whitaker

J. Bob looked at his feet like a shy schoolboy. "I haven't danced since I took social dance for a physical education credit at the university and—"

"Then you know how, so get with it," Rita said.

"All right, Rita." J. Bob bowed slightly to Eva and said, "May I have the honor of this dance?"

"Of course you may," Eva said.

After Eva and J. Bob had moved to the dance floor, Rita narrowed her eyes at Big John and said, "Don't even think about cutting in."

"But Rita," John said, "I'm so light on my feet. Eva should have the opportunity to experience my grace."

"Now, that takes the cake, John. I've seen you dance. You hop around like an old hen with an egg broke in her behind. It looks like the barnyard Charleston."

"You crush me, Rita."

J. Bob ushered Eva to the edge of the dance floor with his hand on her shoulders until they faced each other. Eva grasped his extended hand and placed her other hand on his shoulder. He stepped toward her, and with his hand on the small of her back, pulled her closer.

"Two things I remember from social dance class are that the man starts by stepping forward with his left foot, and he guides his partner by applying gentle pressure with his hand on her back."

"That's nice to know. I'll just follow you and listen to the music."

They were hardly a matched pair, structured and cautious, and moving by the numbers, but gradually their movements became more synchronized and their steps shortened. Eva placed the side of her face on his chest and closed her eyes.

J Bob's face nestled in her hair, with his lips next to her ear. Her hair was fresh and smelled of lilacs. Her ear seemed

145

sensual to him. He felt awkward and turned so his cheek was next to her head.

From the jukebox, Patti Page's old friend completed the theft of her sweetheart and the song ended. "In dance class," J. Bob said, "we were told to applaud the band at the end of the song. I guess we skip that part when there's a jukebox."

"I can't believe the song went by so quickly; I was just getting the hang of it," Eva said.

"What do mean? You're a wonderful dance partner. In class, I had to dance with some big old corn-fed farm girls that were like dancing with sacks of feed."

"J. Bob you're awful; I'm sure they were very nice."

"They were, and I forgot to add, they made their own dresses."

Laughing, Eva said, "Oh, J. Bob, that's terrible."

From the jukebox, Nat King Cole was now singing "Mona Lisa, Mona Lisa men have named you . . . ."

"J. Bob, I just love that song. Let's stay for one more dance." She assumed a starting pose with both arms extended. J. Bob reciprocated and they began slowly moving with the music. By the end of the song, they simply scooted their feet and held each other, and Eva quietly sang along with the record.

After leaving the dance floor, they did not stay long at Club 60. When they got back to the bar, Rita got them another Coke and a beer. Neither had finished their first, nor did they finish the re-fills before making excuses to leave, despite protests from Big John.

As they drove back to Birch View, Eva gazed at the moon, which was still bright, though it had turned a pale yellow. "J. Bob, from now on when I see a full moon, I'll think of this night. It's so lovely."

J. Bob leaned over the steering wheel for a better view. "You're right about that." Then glancing over at Eva, he said, "But it pales in comparison to the way you look tonight."

146

"What a nice thing to say, J. Bob."

The front windows of J. Bob's Ford were slightly open and the fresh air contrasted with the smoky smell of their clothes.

"One thing that I hate about going to Club 60 on the weekends," J. Bob said, as he sniffed at his shirtsleeve, "is that you smell like you've spent all day in a pool hall shooting snooker."

"I know what you mean. When smokers come into the shop, the smell really settles in their hair."

At the city limits, J. Bob said, "Look how deserted this town is. We could get a cup of coffee or something to eat, but we'd have to drive to Pine Grove."

"Oh, J. Bob, I think I better get home."

"You're probably right"

They drove on in silence. J. Bob kept trying to get a clear station on the radio, but by the time he got KMOX, a broadcast out of St. Louis, they were in front of Eva's house. He pulled to a stop and turned off the engine.

"J. Bob, this evening turned out so much better than I ever imagined, and I want to thank you. It seems I keep thanking you."

"I'm glad you had a good time, but there is no need to thank me. The pleasure was all mine."

"J. Bob, I don't mean to be personal, but you know all this stuff about me, and I hardly know anything about you. I mean, I don't even know who you dated in high school."

"Well, I wasn't very *dateable* in high school. I wasn't an athlete and I made good grades—I was the valedictorian— but most of the girls that I might have been interested in weren't interested in me."

"So, you never dated anybody?"

"I'll put it like this—I never had a serious girlfriend. Everybody tried to push Roberta Thompson and me together, but we mostly competed for grades; she was the salutatorian.

I suspect if I hadn't been so naïve, she might have been more romantically inclined."

"What about in college?"

"College was a different matter. I joined a fraternity and they had all these social mixers and dances, so there were always a lot of sorority girls to date. Hey, am I on the witness stand?"

"No, of course not. I'm just interested. Did you have anyone serious?

"I suppose I did. I got pinned to a Tri-Delta, and they say that is being engaged-to-be-engaged."

"What happened?"

"She wasn't at all interested in my future plans to come back to Birch View after law school. She was from Kansas City and couldn't imagine living in the sticks."

"You didn't date anybody in law school?"

"No, I really didn't. There was only one girl in the entire law school. About all I did was study. I wanted to make law review." The look on Eva's face told him that she didn't understand. "If you're grades are good enough, you can be selected to a group of students who write articles for the quarterly law publication."

"Did you make it?"

"Yes."

"Why *did* you come back?"

"It never occurred to me not to, not really, but I suppose I did what I thought was expected of me. Maybe that's why I rebel at some things now."

"Like what?"

"Seldom go to church . . . to my mother's consternation. Try to vex the prosecuting attorney any chance I get, and I hang out with sinners and winebibbers at Club 60."

"J. Bob, this evening has been nice for another reason. Getting to know you a little bit—it makes me feel special."

"Well, I suppose I should walk you to the door."

148

"Wait a minute." Eva slid over to J. Bob's side. She lifted a hand to his cheek and leaned forward and kissed him on the lips.

At first she was tentative; her eyes were open and her lips barely touched his. J. Bob put his hand on her shoulder, as if they were dancing again, and pulled her closer. Eva's lips parted more and she relaxed in his arms.

It wasn't a long kiss, and afterwards they sat silently, staring ahead at the windshield, holding hands, and J. Bob thought she had the softest lips he had ever felt. Still looking ahead, he said, "You make me feel like a fraternity boy again."

"I knew I wanted to kiss you, and I kept thinking about the rhyme my mother used to say: 'Kiss in the car and not by the gate, love is blind, but the neighbors ain't.' I can think about the oddest things sometimes."

"That's a new one on me, but I agree. Now the question is, should we do this again?"

"Do you mean *kiss*?"

"Well, actually, I meant *go out*."

"Kiss me again, and I'll think about it."

Chapter Thirteen

Jack of Diamonds

*B*eulah rolled over to the edge of the bed. The dream had been so vivid that it took a few moments to realize that it was not real. In the dream she was seven years old, and a bugler was playing Taps. *They always played Taps when one of the children died.*

The sadness of the dream soaked her like the perspiration she felt on her neck and forehead. She threw back the quilt in spite of the chill in the bedroom. Her husband Will lay next to her snoring.

It was not yet daylight, but she was awake, and the dream was still lucid and penetrating.

"How could you do that, Mama?" she whispered to herself. What kind of woman would allow her daughter to be put in an orphanage for most of four years, and then take her back when she was old enough to work on her new husband's farm?

The hurt and bitterness she felt turned into silent sobbing. Almost audibly, she said, "I swore that none of my children would be abandoned, and by God, neither will Wesley." A peace, born of purpose, came over her and she allowed her mind to drift back many years.

By the time Beulah was a teenager, her mother, Ella, had run off every boy that had ever paid any attention to Beulah. Ella's reputation, that she had once killed a man with a pitchfork, was sufficient to scare off potential suitors— except Will.

Ella particularly did not like Will, and when she used his name, her voice had a hissing, mocking tone. And because he worked on the railroad section gang, she referred to him as *that gandy dancer*.

In spite of Ella, Beulah and Will would sneak around and see each other. Once, for some unknown reason, Ella deigned to allow Beulah to go to a pie supper with Will at the old community center in Tremont. Beulah had baked a fresh apple pie that Will was to buy at the pie auction for the privilege of eating it with her.

Will had arrived to pick her up in his horse-drawn buggy, and as he was getting down from the buggy, Beulah bolted out the front door and said, "Something has set Mama off. Let's hurry and go."

Will had helped Beulah up and was about to snap the reins, when Ella hurried toward the buggy. She grabbed the horse's bridle and said, "Just where do you think you two are going?"

"Mrs. Reynolds, we're going to the pie supper. You know that," Will said.

Ella was a stocky woman with a round pock-marked face and thin lips that seldom formed a smile. She scowled at Will and said, "William O'Dell, you'll not take my daughter anywhere."

"But Mama, you said—"

"You keep your mouth shut, girl," Ella snapped, cutting Beulah off in mid-sentence.

Will had three older sisters and had been raised to treat women with deference and respect, but he had never seen this type of behavior in a woman. Anger added to his confusion, but he met Ella's stare and began rolling up his shirtsleeves in the manner of a father preparing to discipline a child. He got down from the buggy not taking his eyes off Ella.

"Mrs. Reynolds, you put yourself in the place of a man. You'll take what a man takes."

Ella's mouth opened, speechless, and she took a step backward. If she was shocked, she recovered her composure quickly. "Well, maybe you'll amount to something after all," she said and turned and retreated to the house.

Beulah's attention came back to the present as Will rolled on his side. "You awake, Beulah?"

"Yes, I'm just lying here thinking."

"About Ray coming?"

"That, and about that pie supper we went to years ago. I was only sixteen," she said, turning on her back.

"I remember—you were the prettiest girl there."

"Well, I don't know about that," Beulah said, "but it was barely a year later that we got married—two weeks after I turned seventeen.

"November 17, 1918, thirty-eight years ago," Will said. He reached over and gently squeezed her hand. "What time do you suppose he'll get here?" Will asked.

"I hope before Wesley gets back—he's going to Ernie's today. We need to talk to Ray alone."

By late afternoon, Beulah had finished two tub loads of laundry and had it hanging on the clothesline that stretched between two trees behind the house. Where the line sagged in the center, it was supported by a forked sassafras pole.

As Beulah took wash from the clothesline, a gust of wind billowed the sheets like sails and dislodged the pole from the ground. The line drooped and the sheets flapped against the ground. With synchronized precision, she put the clothespin she was holding into her mouth and grabbed the pole with both hands looking like a pole-vaulter about to launch upward.

"Will!" she yelled. It came out muffled. She spit out the clothespin and kicked at it. "Will, come out here and help me before all the wash is in the dirt."

Another gust wrapped a sheet around her waist. "Will!"

"Hold your horses, I'm coming." Will pulled up the water bucket by its chain and hung it, empty, on the cistern housing and marched toward Beulah. He stopped a few feet from her. "Listen," he said. "I hear a truck."

Beulah heard it, too, and turned loose of the pole and strode past Will toward the house. She looked back at Will. "Well, don't just stand there, set the pole back."

Will gave his head a confounded shake and then secured the pole, raising the abandoned wash off the ground before following Beulah to the house.

Beulah and Will waited on the concrete slab patio that extended from the two-step kitchen stoop. The strain of a diesel engine could be heard as a truck was downshifted to make it up the hill at the railroad crossing a half-mile away.

"Well, I expect that'll be Ray," Will said.

Beulah's eyes watered, and through the thick glasses she wore, it looked as if her eyes were quivering. "He was just like a son to me . . . the son I could never have."

"Now, Beulah, don't go thinking about little Will. It's been over thirty years."

"How can I not think about him? Every time we pass the cemetery, I think of my Sweet William buried in there. He wasn't even a week old." She took off her glasses and wiped her eyes with her apron. "And Doc Davis said we couldn't have any more children. Rita was the only one . . . and the best thing she ever did was marry Ray."

"Now, Beulah," that's not true. You thought she should have married that pantywaist boy who became a preacher."

"Well, that was different. I thought he might have been a settling influence—she had that willful streak. But then Ray came along, a real man, and I knew he was the one. He started calling me 'Mom' even before they got married."

A cloud of dust followed the orange semi-trailer rig as it pulled off the gravel road and onto the driveway of the farm. The engine sputtered and then belched as it was turned off.

Through the windshield they could see the big smile. *Smiling Ray*, that's what the truckers called him.

Ray opened the door of the cab and stepped to the ground. He hitched his green khaki trousers and attempted to tuck in his matching uniform shirt, which had "Midwest & Southern Van Lines" embroidered in orange above the left pocket.

His shirt gapped open below the last button and exposed his belly where it extended over his belt. He weighed 230 pounds and was a shade under six feet tall.

Ray pulled a small comb from his pants pocket and ran it through his curly, sandy-colored hair, combing it over a spot on the crown that was beginning to thin.

Beulah met him before he was halfway to the house. Will lingered behind.

"Hello, Mom," Ray said, his voice was tentative and his smile, now, more of a lop-sided nervous grin.

"Hello, son," Beulah said. "How have you been?" She extended her arms and they embraced.

After they separated, Ray said, "Oh, can't complain, I suppose. Where's Wesley?"

"School's out for a teacher's meeting, and he's visiting a friend today. I thought it best that we talk first without him here."

Ray looked confused, as if uncertain whether he was going to receive sympathy or a scolding.

Will, who had made no effort to move forward, stood with his hands in his overall pockets and said, "You two come on in the house. Let's sit down and have a cup of coffee. Ray looks as if he could use one."

Will and Ray sat at the kitchen table and waited for Beulah to serve the coffee. The blue Depression glass cups and saucers, usually reserved for holidays, were striking against the red-checkered tablecloth.

After she poured the coffee, Beulah sat down at the table and wasted no time getting to the point. "Ray, have you thought about what's going to happen to Wesley when you and Rita are divorced?"

"Well, I supposed that he would live with his mother, since I'm on the road all the time."

"Ray, do you really think that is a good idea? You know, after she started working at that honky-tonk in Birch View, she moved in with a girlfriend. And I hear she spends a lot of her free time at that honky-tonk, too. If she sees Wesley more than once every two weeks, I'd be surprised." Beulah's face was stern as she watched Ray and waited for a response.

Ray broke eye contact and stared into his coffee as he stirred it with a spoon. He sat the spoon on a paper napkin and looked up. "Mom, I'm so sorry," and the big man's voice erupted in to a sob as he started to cry.

Beulah popped out of her chair and put her hand on his shoulder, patting it, and said, "It'll be OK. I have a plan."

When Ray settled down, Beulah said, "Will and I think that we should get custody of Wesley and become his legal guardians."

"Now, Beulah," Will interrupted, "I said we should talk to Rita about this, too."

Beulah glared at Will and resumed talking to Ray. "It would really be best for Wesley. Like you said, you're on the road all the time and are in no position to take care of a little boy. And you surely don't want him left by himself, while she's at the bar. She'd probably end up leaving him here most of the time, anyway. Of course, you'd still be his father."

Ray took a sip of coffee and lit a cigarette. He inhaled deeply and seemed to reflect on what Beulah had said. His face appeared more relaxed as he exhaled. Part of the familiar smile returned—the part that said, "Yes, Mom."

"You know, Mom," Ray said, "I could continue to send money directly to you and not child-support payments to Rita, and that way, I'd be sure the money would be used for Wesley."

"You're absolutely right, Ray. I hadn't thought of that," Beulah said. "And another thing, we would be able to get assistance from the state if we were his legal guardians. Every little bit helps. Will's likely to be laid off at the mill before long, and we don't know when he'll get called back."

Will stood up abruptly, bumping the table in his haste. "I'm going to the barn. I've got chores to do." He left without saying more.

"Ray, let me fix you some supper."

"That would be great, Mom."

As Beulah was building a fire in the cook stove to prepare super, she said, "Ray, I'm fixing your favorites: chicken-fried steak, mashed potatoes, and gravy."

"Mom, that surely sounds good. Nobody makes sopping gravy like you do. You can't get home-cooking in a truck stop, that's for sure."

Will opened the screen door and walked back in.

Beulah looked at Will. "I thought you had chores to do."

"It looks like it's going to rain," Will said. "I better go and pick up Wesley. It's three miles, and I don't want him caught on his bike in a gully washer."

"Well, get going, then. Ray and I can visit while you're gone, and I'm fixing supper."

After Will picked up Wesley, the sprinkling turned into driving rain that forced Will to pull to the roadside because he could not see well enough to drive. He turned off the engine and looked at Wesley. "No use in wasting gas—this may go on for a while. It's raining like a cow pissing on a flat rock."

Wesley giggled at Will's language, which made Will smile for a moment. When Wesley got his mirth under control, he asked, "What's the surprise grandma said she had for me?"

Will's smile faded. He started to mention that Ray was at the farm but changed his mind and said, "You'll have to ask your grandma."

Sensing that Will was through with the subject, Wesley said, "All right, grandpa."

They sat silently peering through the side windows at waves of rain falling from ominous, gray clouds. After ten minutes the rain let up, and Will got back on the road.

Will pulled to a stop in the driveway of the farm. Ray's rig was gone, but as they got out of the car, Ray appeared at the doorway. "Daddy!" Wesley squealed and ran to his father.

Ray stepped off the stoop and met Wesley halfway across the patio. "Hello, Sport." He squatted down and rustled Wesley's hair with his hand. "Boy, you're growing like a weed."

Wesley threw his arms around his father's neck and hugged him. He released his hold and said, "I'm almost as tall as Grandma. You're my surprise, aren't you?"

"I suppose I am. Your grandma has dinner ready, and I'm starved."

"Me, too, and something smells good."

Will, standing a few feet behind Wesley and observing the reunion, said, "Ray, where's your truck?"

"Mom told me to pull it behind the barn. No need to advertise that I'm here."

Later that evening, as they sat at the kitchen table finishing supper, the storm came in full force. Lightning flared and illuminated the room like a flashbulb. A thunderclap followed that shook the windows in the old house.

"That one was close," Will said. Wesley covered his ears with his hands. "Wesley, those rumbles are just the old man in the sky and his potato wagon." Beulah and Ray laughed at Will's tall tale, and Wesley joined in.

Another flash and boom shook the house, this time knocking out the electricity. "Will, grab the flashlight and get out the coal oil lamps," Beulah said.

Will followed orders, and once lit, the two glass-globed lamps cast an eerie glow across the room. In the flickering light, Wesley thought the grown-ups at the table looked like they were holding candles in front of their faces getting ready to tell ghost stories.

"Gee, what are we going to do now? We can't even listen to the radio," Wesley said.

"Well, we could play a game of pitch if I can find the cards," Beulah said. She went into the pantry and returned with a deck of Bicycle brand playing cards.

"Wesley, do you know how to count the points?" Ray asked.

"Sure. High, low, jick, jack, and game."

"I can tell your grandma taught you," Ray said. "I learned it as ace, deuce, off-jack, jack, and the ten."

From the barnyard, Bessie the milk cow was bellowing. Will said, "I better go see what's wrong with her."

Beulah said, "I want to get this table cleared off. Ray, you and Wesley take one of the lamps and the cards into the living room."

Wesley and Ray went into the adjacent room. Ray set the lamp on the coffee table in front of the davenport, which Wesley flopped on. Ray pulled an oak spindle-back chair closer to the table, opposite Wesley.

The turned stiles of the chair extended above its back crest rail like two blunt spears and cast a shadow on the wall like a giant inverted tooth.

Wesley watched as his dad shuffled and back-shuffled the cards. "I didn't know you were such a good card shuffler."

"There are a lot of things you don't know about me."

159

"Like what?"

"I invented the Yo-Yo."

Wesley laughed. "You did not."

"Yes, I did. And I played football for the Green Gooses."

"No, you didn't," Wesley said, laughing again.

"Did, too," Ray said with a theatrical, solemn face that was betrayed by twinkling eyes. "Hey, do you want to see a card trick?"

"Sure."

Wesley squinted in the dim light of the kerosene lamp as he watched Ray give the cards another shuffle and push the deck toward him.

In the voice of a carnival barker, Ray said, "Pick a card. . . any card."

Wesley lifted the top half of the deck and set it aside. Then he chose the top card from the remaining stack.

"Don't show it to me."

Wesley pulled the card close to his chest and examined it. It was the jack of diamonds.

"OK, put your card back in the deck."

Wesley slipped his card back on one of the stacks. Ray reassembled the cards, shuffled them, and brought the deck to his forehead. He paused dramatically, then inhaled deeply as if he were experiencing the scent of a freshly cut flower.

Ray assumed an aura of deep concentration and appeared to be in a trance. He tightened his closed eyes for a moment, and then the tension in his face relaxed into a slight, knowing smile. He opened his eyes, returned the deck to the table, and spread the cards faceup in the shape of a fan.

He pushed the ten of clubs toward Wesley, and with elongated vowels and the Eastern-European accent of a Gypsy fortune-teller, he said, "Dees ees not jour card, no?"

Wesley shook his head, indicating that it was not. Ray then pushed the jack of diamonds across the table, and the Gypsy said, "Ah, I tink dees is jour card, no?"

"How did you do that?" Surprise radiated from Wesley's face.

"It's magic," Ray said.

"Show me how to do it."

"I don't know. It takes a lot of practice, and you have to understand magic.

"Please," Wesley said in a childish whine.

Sighing, Ray said in the pedantic tone of a long-suffering teacher, "All right, Wesley, I'll show you," and in a hushed voice explained the secret of the card trick.

As Wesley practiced the trick, Ray went back into the kitchen, barely able to contain the deep belly laugh growing inside him.

The next morning after an early breakfast, Ray said goodbye to everyone and promised to be back before Christmas in a few weeks. He pulled away from the farm minutes before the bus came to pick up Wesley for school.

Wesley hopped on board the school bus for the short ride, with the deck of cards concealed in his jacket pocket.

The Tremont schoolhouse, a white clapboard, two-room structure built in the 1920's, served all eight grades for the rural community. The structure was crowned with a louvered cupola centered on a pitched roof of green shingles that housed the bell. Outdoor privies and a cistern provided the plumbing amenities.

Inside, two classrooms were separated by a heavy, floor-to-ceiling sliding partition. On the north side, Wesley's room, Mrs. Hansen taught the first four grades; on the other side, Mr. Hansen, her husband, taught grades five through eight. The rooms were referred to as the *big room* and the *little room*.

Feeling impressive, Wesley wasted no time telling Ernie and Cindy how he could pick cards from a deck by magic, and that he would show them at recess, away from the watchful eyes of the teachers.

About ten o'clock, Mr. Hansen sent a student to get permission for Wesley to come to the big room for a moment. Wesley hoped Mr. Hansen was going to ask him to play on the big room's softball team.

When they entered the big room, the other student took his seat and then Mr. Hansen motioned for Wesley to come over to his desk.

"Wesley, Cindy tells me you can do a magic card trick. Is that right?" Mr. Hansen asked.

Wesley looked at Cindy sitting smugly at the front of the fifth grade row. A low-grade alarm went off in Wesley's mind—like the feeling he got when his grandma wanted him to sing for their neighbor. "I guess so," Wesley said.

"Where'd you learn it?" Mr. Hansen asked.

"My dad showed me."

"Well, son, would you like to show us?" As the teacher spoke, he gestured toward the rest of the students.

"I don't have any cards," he said quietly, wishing he were back in the little room.

"Well, then, just tell us how you do it? We'd all like to know," Mr. Hansen asked.

Wesley shoved both hands in his jeans pockets and shrugged. "You pick a card, and then I tell you which one you picked."

"I understand that, but how do you do it?"

"Well . . . you smell the cards." Some of the students started laughing.

"Really?" Mr. Hansen asked. "You're not pulling my leg, are you?"

"No, really," Wesley said. "The ace of spades smells like gravy and the jack of diamonds smells like oranges."

162

Laughter erupted in the big room. It was more than laughter—it was spontaneous howling. Freckle-faced Willie Waggoner, kept slapping his leg as if he were in some kind of a fit. He slid halfway out of his desk and covered his mouth with the bib of his overalls to hide his laughter. All the girls were giggling. Worst of all, Cindy was laughing, too.

For a moment Mr. Hansen joined in the levity, but when he looked back at Wesley, he stopped immediately. The features on the boy's face seemed to have fallen, as if a smile got stuck in embarrassment and was never finished.

"All right, that'll be enough," Mr. Hansen said to the class.

Collectively, the students seemed to understand the moment. In the room where there had been laughter only seconds before, now a cat could have been heard walking across the floor.

Wesley's eyes were cast downward; his ears could only hear the blood that was rushing to his now crimson face. His heart had sunk to that sick place in his stomach where fear and shame reside.

Mr. Hansen's face now registered that the situation hadn't turned out as he intended. He looked toward the back of the eighth grade row at Jack Weaver, his biggest and brightest student. "Jack, come up here and take charge." It wasn't unusual for him to put an older student in charge if he needed to leave the room.

Mr. Hansen escorted Wesley outside to the foyer and closed the door behind them. "Wesley, I'm sorry if you felt embarrassed. There's no need to—we weren't laughing at you. It was just a funny story. Do you understand?"

Wesley, still looking downward, said, "I guess so." His voice had a tremble.

"Now, go on back to your desk."

Wesley stepped toward the door to the Little Room.

163

"Wait a minute, Wesley. We may need you to play on the big room's team when we play Hidden Glen School next week—think you can handle it?

Wesley, now facing Mr. Hansen, smiled and said, "Yes sir."

Chapter Fourteen
Revelation at the Hacienda

*T*he grayish-purple sky warned of a storm brewing over the west Texas flatlands. Shafts of sunlight filtered through the clouds, illuminating a grove of mesquite trees next to a shotgun house on the outskirts of Fort Worth.

A hairy woodpecker, not as big as a robin, flew from the grove and attached itself to the side of the house and began slamming its beak into a window header. Like a tiny jackhammer, it drilled the soft wood, searching for a carpenter bee's nest buried below. The pecking was relentless.

Inside, Ray Sanders, flat on his back, squinted to see with one eye. He was afraid to open both. It was a pathetic, almost childlike, attempt to determine where he was. His nose was throbbing with pain, and he could not breathe through it. He touched it with his finger; it was crusted over.

The bed he was on smelled of vomit. His head was splitting and his tongue felt coated. He would have sold what was left of his soul for a beer at that moment. Two feet away a portrait of Jesus on a 1956 wall calendar stared at him.

The last thing he remembered was leaving his truck at the warehouse in Fort Worth . . . no there was a Mexican cantina . . . and some woman.

The smell of a lit cigarette drew his attention to a doorway by the head of the bed. At the sight of a squatty round-faced Mexican man, Ray lurched to sit up, screamed, grabbed his chest, and fell back. It felt like a rib had punctured his right lung.

"You better stay down, hombre," the man said.

Ray hurt too much to respond. He struggled for shallow breaths to avoid the knifing pain in his chest. Breathing slowly through his mouth, Ray managed, "Who are you? And where am I?"

"My name is José, and you're at mi casa, but you can't stay. My wife and children are at Sunday mass, and you need to vamoose before they come back. You don't remember her screaming when I brought you here?"

"No, I don't remember coming here. Would you have a beer I could buy, Jose?"

"Amigo, I don't think you have any money, but I can get you a cerveza from my truck. Then I will drive you to the main road."

The beer was warm and green tasting, but Ray already wished José had brought two.

"You're one dumb pendejó," José said. "I think you're nose is broken—maybe you're ribs, too—but you are lucky to be alive."

Ray's memory was returning like the gradual recall of a dream. In his mind fuzzy images segued from one to another: being jerked by his shirt collar over a bar and punched in the face, a Mexican woman, his face smashed against a dirt floor, pointed cowboy boots kicking him, and a voice that had said, "Jesus, help me."

Ray rose up enough to take a couple more swallows of the beer. "What exactly happened to me? I must have been in a fight."

"You and a couple of your amigos were drinking in the Armadillo Cantina. They didn't want to stay. You were buying drinks for Maria Martinez so she would dance with you. Mi amigo, you went too far—she could not leave with you—she belongs to Miguel, the bartender."

"He pulled me over the bar and hit me, didn't he?"

"Yes, but it was his brother Manuel who was kicking you. It is a good thing you are fat, or you would be worse broken up. Maria jumped on him or he would have killed you, I think. She gave me five of your dollars to bring you here. Manuel took your wallet."

Ray looked at his left wrist for the time, but instinctively knew his watch had been stolen, too. "What time is it? I've got to call the dispatcher and get to my truck by noon. Do you have a phone?"

"We do not have a telephone, but it's nearly four o'clock, and the church bus will be bringing my wife and children home soon, so we must be going."

José's old Ford pickup looked like a sharecropper's truck. Ray knew trucks, and this one needed a mechanic. The floor board, littered with empty Wizard Oil cans and loose tools, shook each time José shifted gears, sending flares of pain to Ray's ribs. Like the truck, Ray was feeling his hard miles.

Ray stared through the open window at scrub trees and scattered houses until the truck slowed and pulled into a Texaco station on the edge of Fort Worth. "This is where you got to get out," José said.

Ray felt in his pants pocket and fingered some loose change. "José, can you tell me where the cantina is so I can get my wallet back?"

"Man, you better not go back there."

"Could you loan me a couple of dollars then? I'll pay you back. I'll mail it to you."

"No, I got no money to loan." José pulled a piece of paper from his shirt pocket. "But Maria from the cantina told me to give this to you."

Ray unfolded the piece of paper torn from a spiral pocket tablet and read the hand-printed information.

The Hacienda
119 Vaquero
Fort Worth, Texas
Ask for Joe

"What's this?"

"I don't know," José said. "She just told me to give it to you."

The mirror in the service station restroom told the story as Ray attempted to clean up: bloodshot and blackened eyes and a nose that was angled to the side.

Ray jerked his nose to the left. His knees buckled. Blood spurted. "Goddamn it," he screamed and fell forward on the basin, then screamed again as pain shot through his chest. Several moments of agony passed, and he ripped toilet paper from the roll on the basin and pressed a wad to his hemorrhaging nose.

The phone call to the dispatcher was more bad news. "Ray, you've already had too many second chances. I had to give your load to another driver. The regional manager told me to tell you that you were fired, and if you showed up on company property, he would have you arrested for trespassing."

Ray hung up the phone and slid down the wall of the phone booth and began to sob like a wounded soldier left behind.

A rap on the door brought Ray from his semi-conscious state. A voice followed with more rapping. "Hey buddy, come out of there." Ray looked up. The voice belonged to a law officer wearing a Stetson.

Bent over and listing, Ray opened the door and staggered from the booth staring at the lanky officer's silhouette framed by the sun sitting low in the December sky.

"What's your name?" the officer asked.

"Ray Sanders." Ray attempted a smile.

"Let me see some identification."

"Well, officer, I lost my wallet and it had my money and driver's license in it."

"That's too bad, because we don't cotton to vagrants here in Fort Worth. Unless you have somewhere to go, I am obliged to drop you outside the city limits. On second thought, a night in the drunk tank and a few days on a work detail might do you some good."

Ray fumbled in his shirt pocket and yanked out the paper José had given him. He glanced at it before handing it to the officer. "I'm trying to get to my friend Joe's place. Do you know where The Hacienda is?"

The officer's lips tightened below his neatly trimmed mustache. "Get in the car and keep your mouth shut."

Twenty minutes later they stopped in front of a single-story adobe-style house on Vaquero Street that sat between two trash-covered vacant lots. Strands of Christmas lights were draped inside the front windows, and above the front door a sign, with letters that could have been painted by a child, indicated they had arrived at The Hacienda.

"Get out," the officer said. "I'll escort you to the door to make sure you go inside."

The officer knocked on the door and a short, wiry man with a craggy, lined face wearing navy-style dungarees and a white T-shirt came to the door. The man looked to be in his fifties. "Good evening, deputy."

"Padre, I've got another broken-up wet one for you."

"Hey, what is this place?" Ray asked.

"I'm Joe. Come inside. You look like you could use a cup of coffee, that is, unless you want to go with the deputy. What's your name, son? "

"My name is Ray, and I'll take that cup of coffee."

The officer was already turning around when Joe said, "Thanks, deputy."

Inside, the place was smoky with a shabby masculine ambience: a couch with exposed stuffing, orange crates serving as coffee tables, and ashtrays on every horizontal surface. At the back of the room, three men in vest undershirts sat around a wooden table on unmatched chairs. They glanced up from their card game as Ray and the man the deputy had called *Padre* entered.

Padre ushered Ray through an archway to the kitchen. From a percolator that sat on a gray linoleum-covered counter, Padre served Ray a cup of coffee. Ray's hand shook so badly that he had to use both hands.

"Where are you from, son?" Padre asked.

"Mostly Iowa, but I'm a trucker." The smell of the cigarette Padre lit made Ray's stomach retch, but he got a sip of the coffee to stay down. "The policeman called you *Padre*. You don't look like any priest I ever saw."

"It's a nickname. I was once in the seminary, but I couldn't stay away from the communion wine and they kicked me out. At the time I was very ashamed and thought it was the worst thing that could have happened to me. As it turned out, it was a blessing."

"How could that be a blessing?"

"It allowed me to come to a turning point and to do what I do now."

"What's that?"

"Help people like you and me . . . drunks."

"I'm no drunk, and as soon as that sheriff—"

"Hold on, partner. Just think for a few seconds. How far do you think you would get? Do you have any idea where you are? Why not give God a chance to help you?"

"Hey, is this some kind of Holy Roller church?" Ray stepped back to put more distance between him and Padre.

"No, but we do talk about God helping us help ourselves, and it seems to me you can use all the help you can get."

Padre continued. "As you can see, The Hacienda is not a very church-like place. It's more of a mission, and not a very official mission at that. It's quite unofficial, actually, but a judge and a few of the officers I know send folks like you here

L. D. Whitaker

instead of to the drunk tank. If I can get them dried out, it saves the court paperwork and the cost of meals."

Ray sat the coffee cup on the counter. "Thanks, Padre, but I've got to go."

"Look, Ray, I know you are hurting. I can see it in your eyes . . . and it isn't just physical pain. Let me get you a Coca-Cola, a few crackers, and some aspirin."

"I could sure use the aspirin," Ray said.

Padre served the left-handed sacrament of Coke and crackers with three aspirin. "Ray, if you won't stay, at least get a few hours sleep; we've got an extra cot in back. It's dark out, and you don't know where you're going. If that deputy catches you again, he'll lock you up, and you'll end up facing a judge."

Ray's mind told him to go, but he felt dog-tired and said, "All right."

Ray plummeted into a fitful sleep strewn with voices and strange images. He thought he was awake. Rats with large red eyes and ears like police dogs' glared at him. He screamed at them to leave him alone, but they hissed at him, exposing their pointed teeth, and called him a gringo.

Ray was awake before sunrise, sweaty and weak. It was a full five minutes before he was sure the room did not have rats. He faltered to the door, unsure of each step, and steadied himself against the jamb before entering the main room.

Padre was sitting on the couch backlit by a floor lamp and engulfed in cigarette smoke. He closed the book he was reading. "Well, Ray, you survived your second night—that's often the worst."

"Padre, I think I saw *something* last night."

"Ray, I expect you did. I heard you talking and went in to check on you. You were standing by the bed staring at the corner—you looked terrified. You kept whispering, 'Go away, go away.' I put my hand on your shoulder and told you to be still, and you went back to bed."

"Padre, I thought you said God was going to help me."

"He will, Ray, but sometimes we get hit with His backhand first. You have all the answers inside you, but you just can't see them now. If you stick around here a few days, I believe you'll begin to see some of them."

"Thanks, Padre, but I don't have a few days. I need to make a long-distance collect call. Do you have a phone here?"

"Yeah, there's a phone here, but why don't you have some oatmeal first."

Chapter Fifteen
The Telephone Call

*W*ill headed the Mercury onto the farm-to-market road in front of the farm. Beulah sat on the passenger side. It was nearly 7:30 p.m. and late to be going to the Tremont Grocery, which seldom stayed open past dark.

But earlier that afternoon puny old Fred Morgan had showed up at the farm and announced: "Your son-in-law called on the telephone—*collect*." After pausing for effect, he had added, "The wife told me to tell you that he will call back at eight o'clock tonight."

When it came to financial matters, Fred's face often contorted to a smile that looked more like a sneer, revealing teeth yellowed from countless cups of coffee and an ever-present cigarette.

Beulah's cowed reaction to the *smile* had been trumped by the specter of a long-distance telephone call from Ray. But now, as she replayed the scene in her mind, her anxiety increased; they already owed too much money on their bill at the store.

The Tremont grocery was a mile away at Highway 60, which ran from the east through Birch View, Pine Grove, and Ridgeview. The store supplied most everyday items for surrounding farm families, from livestock feed to groceries.

They rode mostly in silence. Twice Beulah began to express her worries about Ray, and each time Will said, "We'll find out soon enough." When she shared her concern about the bill, Will remained silent, but the knuckles in his right hand expanded as he tightened his grip on the steering wheel.

The storefront lights were turned off when they arrived. The interior was dimly illuminated by a fluorescent fixture hanging behind the checkout counter in the rear of the one-room grocery area. The Morgan's living quarters on the side were well lighted. A silhouette behind the drawn shade was sitting in a front room chair. Fred, no doubt, was in his favorite spot next to the floor model radio.

Vivian Morgan, Fred's wife, who, if not the bookkeeper, was certainly the personality and good will behind the business, unlocked the front door and welcomed them.

"It was a person-to-person call," Vivian said, "so I told the operator you weren't here. I could hear your son-in-law's voice in the background saying he would call back at eight o'clock. That's when I sent Fred to tell you."

"Well, Vivian," Beulah said, "we appreciate your doing that. We brought money to pay for the call."

"That's fine, but I wasn't worried about it. I put on a pot of coffee. Let's not stay out here in the store or people driving by on the highway might think we're open."

Before any of them finished the first cup of coffee, the telephone clanked a series of three short bursts. "That's our ring," said Vivian.

The trio scurried to the phone—Fred stayed put in his chair. Vivian picked up the earpiece from its cradle on the side of the wooden telephone box on the wall. "Tremont Grocery . . . yes, she's here." Her voice conveyed a sense of urgency.

Beulah took the hand piece from Vivian and put it to her ear. Her five-foot frame required that she stand on her tiptoes to reach the black mouthpiece that protruded from the telephone box.

"Hello, son. Are you OK?" Her eyes moistened as she strained to hear his voice through a crackling connection.

Vivian and Will stared at Beulah and listened to her one-sided conversation.

"Rita's in Birch View, and Wesley is with us." Her lips grimaced as she continued to listen.

174

"Western Union in Fort Worth?" She again listened.

"Trailways . . . we'll try to send it tomorrow or the day after."

"Bye, son." Beulah hung up the receiver and turned to Will and Vivian.

Vivian, out of politeness, didn't say anything.

Will started to speak, but hesitated. His focus had changed. The shadow cast by the fluorescent light veiled one side of Beulah's face and gave the impression that she had suddenly aged. Her gray hair looked whiter, and her eyes appeared deeper set. "What is it, Mom?" he asked his wife.

Straining to remain calm, Beulah spoke slowly. "He had a wreck with his truck. He's been laid up for two weeks and needs money to get out of Texas. I'm not sure what all is going on, but he needs thirty dollars for a bus ticket here. We're supposed to wire it to him."

"Well, I'll swan," Vivian said. Her tone was sympathetic, showing an understanding that Ray's emergency had just created a new level of hardship for the O'Dells.

"Where are we going to get thirty dollars?" Will asked. "That's nearly a week's wages at the mill, and I don't get paid until Saturday and that's two days away. The sale barn in Pine Grove isn't open until Saturday; I can't even sell that hog we've been fattening until then."

Beulah looked from Will to Vivian; she didn't say anything, but her look was as pitiful as a calf in a hailstorm.

"I can let you have the thirty until Saturday," Vivian whispered, ". . . but don't say anything to Fred. Just slip it back to me when you come in on Saturday."

Ray had been at The Hacienda for three days when he made the phone call to Tremont; three days that marked the passing of one year and the start of a new one. Ray's hope of a new beginning began to fade when the money didn't arrive the next day.

It finally arrived on Saturday, and he purchased a bus ticket to Springfield, Missouri, and would leave the next day. He could make a connection there that would pass by Tremont, and with luck, the driver would let him off there on Monday.

As Ray stood in a line of people to board the Trailways bus at the Fort Worth depot, he had ten bucks and some change left over from the money Beulah had wired. He would be able to get a meal during the layover in Oklahoma City.

The line moved slowly and Ray became concerned that the trip had been oversold and that he might have to stand. He remembered the war years when the buses and trains were so crowded. Old men would offer their seats to men in uniforms, but Ray had never accepted. Now the thought of standing was worrisome.

His turn came, and he stepped up inside. He grabbed the metal pole next to the driver's seat, hesitated, and surveyed the inside for a vacant seat. With passengers still standing in the aisle, it appeared all the seats were taken. Then he saw the one remaining empty seat. *Jesus H. Christ.* It was next to a nun.

"Come on, buddy, move it," a voice at the rear of the line called. It was like marching orders from a sergeant. Ray moved numbly forward.

The nun looked up from what Ray assumed was some kind of prayer book and smiled slightly as he leaned over the aisle seat next to her.

"Hello, ma'am . . . mind if I sit down?"

"I'm not *a ma'am*," she said lightly. "I'm Sister Margaret Catherine, and of course, you may sit down."

Sister Margaret Catherine was not a big person. All swaddled in black fabric, she was like some kind of bird that appeared big, but underneath all the feathers was something very scrawny. She had a hint of peppermint and smiling eyes

176

that accented her cloistered-from-the-sun wheyface, which contrasted starkly with her habit.

Her age was a mystery to Ray. Except for telltale laugh lines by her eyes, her face was smooth and round, but did not sag, nor did she have the wattle of an older woman. Maybe she was in her forties, Ray thought.

"My name is Ray. Pleased to meet you. She did not respond; it was clear she was examining his face. "I was in a wreck. That's why my face is so bunged up."

"Oh, I'm sorry, I didn't mean to stare. It's just that your face looks so sore. I can be so rude sometimes, without intending. Please sit down."

Ray sat down. "Where are you headed, Sister Margaret?"

"I'm going to a convent in Richardson, Missouri. I'll be teaching at a girl's school there."

"You don't say. I'm going to Missouri, too. Looks like we'll be travel partners for a while."

The sister gave a faint smile and resumed reading.

Ray turned his head toward the aisle and closed his eyes. When the bus lurched forward, Ray's eyes fluttered, but in his reverie he was shifting gears in his rig somewhere in Florida.

Ray awoke, disoriented, to tapping on his arm. "Young man. We have arrived at our lunch stop. I thought you would like to get something to eat, and I would like to get out."

Ray collected himself mentally. The bus was nearly empty and parked at a familiar-looking truck stop. Sister Margaret was leaning toward him and looking somewhat impatient. Her face didn't seem so pale.

"Sure, let me get out of your way." Ray stood up and moved back a step, allowing Sister Margaret to pass.

Ray went inside the restaurant to use the restroom and smelled grilled onions and hamburgers that were sizzling in the kitchen. His stomach growled. He was famished, but he

177

did not want to spend his money on a meal yet; it was several hours until Oklahoma City. He bought a Coke and a bag of redskin peanuts and willed himself back to the bus. He finished both before he got to the bus.

Sister Margaret returned to her seat smiling and cheerful. Did you get something to eat, young man?"

"Ray," he corrected."

"Oh yes, *Ray*. I had a wonderful cheeseburger. My medicine often makes me hungry."

"Are you sick?" Ray asked.

"Sometimes I get carsick . . . motion-sickness I think they call it. So on trips I take my medicine. It has a calming effect."

"What kind of medicine is it?"

"Oh, I forget. Brother Hopfinger at the monastery fills it for me. I better take a little before we start again."

She reached in her shoulder bag and retrieved a pint-sized amber pharmacy bottle, unscrewed the cap, and took a generous swallow. "Ray, maybe you could use a little," and extended the bottle to him.

With no conscious thought, Ray put the bottle to his lips and took a gulp.

"Doesn't it have a nice refreshing smell?" Sister Margaret asked.

"Yes, it does, Sister." Ray passed the bottle back to her.

Within seconds Ray felt a tingling sensation in his arms like the prickly feeling of circulation returning to nerve endings deprived of oxygen. He felt a shiver pass over his body. *Schnapps, and it's good-quality stuff.*

"Sister Catherine, if you don't mind, I might like another small drink, I mean dose, of your medicine."

She nodded and Ray took another swig.

"Thanks, Sister," Ray said, replacing the cap and handing the bottle back as the bus lugged forward.

Ray sighed, leaned his head back, and closed his eyes, thinking. Maybe things will work out. I could live with Beulah and Will and help them during the day; maybe get a job at the mill with Will on the night shift. If I save every one of my paychecks for a year, I could buy my own truck—and pay cash for it—and then drive it right up to that warehouse and tell them to kiss my ass. He drifted off to sleep.

Still dozing, Ray twisted in his seat to get comfortable and then opened his eyes. Outside the Oklahoma landscape, flat and scrubby, still looked like Texas. *I couldn't have slept long,* he mused.

Sister Catherine's eyes were closed, her head rested against the seat back. Her purse sat on the floor between her feet and the bus wall.

Ray leaned forward, adjusted his shoe string, and glanced at the seats across the aisle. The woman in the window seat was gazing at the landscape and the man across from him was sleeping.

He reached to the sister's bag with his left hand, unsnapped the two-prong clasp at the top, and slipped the medicine bottle out. Still bent over, he brought it to his mouth and sucked down two good snorts before returning the bottle. He leaned his head back against the seat and closed his eyes again.

"Oklahoma City," the bus driver announced after the bus stopped at the Trailways depot. From the corner of his eye, Ray saw the nun looking around as if she had just awakened with great joy on a holy day. Ray nodded at her without speaking, then butted in line as the man across the aisle assisted the woman next to him.

"How much time do we have?" Ray asked the bus driver, who stood outside the bus door as passengers descended.

"An hour and forty-five minutes. You'll get a new driver, and he has a reputation for being on time, so I wouldn't be late."

"Thanks," Ray said and moved on. He tucked in his shirt and tugged at his undershorts, which were bunched and uncomfortable from sitting in the bus for so long. He rubbernecked around, gauging his surroundings, and tried to get his bearings. The schnapps had made him thirsty—the kind of thirsty that demanded a beer or something stronger. Ray started a quest in search of a drink.

A black man wearing a red depot cap and pushing a janitor's broom looked up when Ray stopped next to him. "Can I help you, sir?"

"Where can I get a quick bottle of booze?"

"Why, sir, you're in Oklahoma; we still got prohibition. All you can buy *legally* is three-two beer."

"Yeah, I know all that—I'm a trucker—but where can you get something *illegally*."

"Well, now, that depends." The black man leaned on his broom handle and stood a bit taller, but with his stooped shoulders, he was still a head shorter than Ray. His deep-set, filmy eyes, surrounded by a brown leathery face, narrowed to a squint as he began to speak. "Young sir, I might be able to help you if you'd be willing to make a deal."

"What kind of deal?"

"You see, I know where a bootlegger—"

"I'm not interested in moonshine," Ray interrupted.

"No, sir, this man has 'bout any kind of store-bought booze you could want. It's what they call a speakeasy. I've got the money, but he won't let me in, you know. He won't sell to Indians either. But if you'd get me a bottle, too, I'll tell you how to get there."

Ray made the deal and returned with a bottle of Schnapps for himself and a bottle of sneaky Pete for his associate.

Beulah and Will sat in the Mercury at the side of Morgan's store. Even though it was 8:30 a.m. and the store was open, they did not go in. Since finding out about the thirty dollars, Fred Morgan had been peevish.

Ray's bus wasn't due for thirty minutes, so Will turned the radio on to listen to the news and farm reports from the radio station in Ridgeview.

Beulah had taken time to powder her face, an act usually reserved for Saturday trips to Pine Grove or church. Will had mentioned that to her as they were leaving and received a glare in return. Their conversation during the ride to Tremont had been sparse.

Talking over the radio announcer, Beulah said, "I wonder how he will look, being in an accident and all."

With a slight sideways glance, Will confirmed that Beulah was warming up a bit. "Well, if he can ride a bus from Fort Worth to here, I reckon he's not in too bad of shape. He's a young buck and stout."

Will leaned his head to the open window. "I can hear the bus coming now." The whining sound of the diesel engine changed pitch as it slowed to make the curve and pull onto the gravel shoulder not more than ten feet from them.

"There he is," Beulah said. "He's standing up in the aisle."

The door opened and Ray stepped down from the bus. He had barely cleared the door when the bus lurched forward, headed to the next stop in Birch View.

"Oh my, he doesn't look well at all," Beulah said. Ray's eyes were bloodshot, and his wiry hair stood out in peaks like a clown who had slept on his side.

Where was his big grin? Beulah thought back to the last time she had seen her son-in-law, when he had stepped out of the big semi-trailer rig all handsome in his green khaki driver's uniform. Now, he was wearing wrinkled dungarees and a half tucked-in flowery shirt.

"What have they done to you, son?" Beulah's concern registered in her watery eyes, magnified through the thick lenses of her glasses.

"It's been pretty bad, Mom." They hugged, and Ray looked at Will standing by the car. "Hello, Will."

"Hello, Ray. Let's get on back, now."

"I'll fix you a good breakfast, son," Beulah said, clinging to Ray's arm and guiding him toward the car.

Back at the farm Beulah served bacon, eggs, and toast made in the oven from homemade bread.

"I haven't had a breakfast like that since the last time I was here. And nobody makes better coffee than you do, Mom. Isn't that right, Will?"

Will looked directly at Ray's eyes. "I agree, but we'd like to hear what happened to you."

"Now, Will, he'll tell us when he's ready."

Ray cleared his throat and looked at his mostly empty plate. He looked up and focused on Beulah. "Oh, I suppose now is as good as any. I had driven all night from Oklahoma and had reached the edge of some little town east of Fort Worth when this Mexican in an old pickup pulled out in front of me."

Ray paused to drink some coffee and continued. "Turns out, he was hopped up on tequila and some pills they call Mexican jumping beans. All I could do was cut to the right. I nearly jackknifed, but I crashed into a light pole and cracked some ribs and blacked both eyes."

Beulah appeared raptly attentive. With her mouth slightly open, she intermittently nodded her head and looked as if she wanted to speak but said nothing.

182

"Then, this cowboy sheriff comes up to the truck and says, 'We don't cotton to speeders around here, and you just wrecked my cousin's truck.' I tried to tell him what happened, but he accused me of drinking and driving, arrested me, and locked me up in their jail."

Beulah said, "I'll swan."

With his peripheral vision, Ray tried to measure Will's reaction. Will's face was that of a man pondering unanswered questions. He had positioned his bifocals lower on his nose to get a sharper view of Ray's face. Occasionally, an eyebrow would raise or he would take a sip from his coffee cup, but he said nothing.

Focusing again on Beulah, Ray said, "The next morning the sheriff says I can go. I asked for my wallet back—it had eighty dollars in it—and he tells me that the money was for the fine and damages. But if I waited for the judge, it would be three days in jail."

Beulah put her hand over her heart and sucked in a breath. "That beats all I've ever heard."

Well, Mom," Ray said, "that's not all. Spending the night in jail made me late for a delivery and a pickup, and the company fired me. And they said they were keeping my last check for the damage to the truck."

Will cleared his throat. Beulah and Ray looked at him. "Ray, when you didn't show up for your delivery, didn't the company check with the state troopers?"

Ray hesitated. "Well . . . I think they hid my truck in an alley because when I got out, that's where it was."

"That's quite a story, Ray," Will said, "but now that you're here, what are your plans?"

Ray looked blankly at Will and then over at Beulah.

"Will," Beulah said, "he needs to rest first, and he can figure that out later."

Looking relieved at Beulah's intercession, Ray said, "The first thing I have to do is write to Iowa to get my driver's and chauffeur's licenses replaced. By the way, is Wesley in school?"

"Yes, he had a spelling test or we would have brought him with us," Beulah said.

Chapter Sixteen
Little Hearts Opening to God

On Sunday, the week after Ray arrived in Tremont, Will, Beulah, and Wesley returned to the farmhouse from church shortly after noon. When they entered the kitchen, the aroma of green pepper, sage, and onion lingered from the pork roast Beulah had started in a Dutch oven that morning.

She had asked Ray to watch it on top of the stove for an hour, and then put it in the oven to simmer. A note on the table from Rita said she and Ray were going to Pine Grove, and that she had put the roast in the oven at 11:00 and closed the stove damper.

"Well, it looks like it will just be the three of us," Beulah said. "Will, make a pot of coffee, and I'll have dinner ready by one o'clock."

After the coffee finished perking, Will removed the metal basket of coffee grounds and went outside to spread them on the flower bed by the side of the house. As he sprinkled the wet grounds where the tiger lilies would bloom in the summer, he heard the creaking sound of the front porch swing.

He eased to the corner of the house and looked around. Wesley was gliding back and forth, still in his good winter coat, and with Felix, a twelve-pound tomcat, in his lap. Petting the cat, Wesley said, "Felix, we'll just tell them to quit fighting."

The calendar had unfolded a sunshiny winter day, but the weather didn't offset the sadness that now hit Will. For some reason it came to him that as he got older, the winters were longer and the summers were shorter; he supposed winters and summers still seemed endless to Wesley.

Will waited until the boy was quiet and then stepped around the corner. "Hey, you mind if an old man swings a bit?"

"No, Grandpa." Wesley drug his feet on the deck and stopped the swing. Felix jumped down and hightailed it off the porch.

Will sat down with a sigh and gazed at the dried-out front yard. "Just look at that grass. It's as yellow as straw. About the only thing that is still standing are some of those pesky buckhorn weeds. They beat all I've ever seen. In the summer, those rascally things with their tall skinny stalks and foxtail tops even seem to prosper in dry weather."

"They get caught between my toes when I'm barefoot, Grandpa."

"Well, I'll grant that they're tough. They kind of remind me of you—tall, skinny, and tough."

Wesley smiled.

They sat in silence, gently swinging back and forth, making it even cooler as they generated their own breeze. Wesley stared into the distance, not appearing to focus on anything and unconsciously picking at the cuticle on his right thumb.

"What are you worried about, son?" Will asked.

"I don't know."

"Well," Will said, "I expect it's something. If you're not worried, you ought to tell your face, because it looks worried."

Wesley smiled again.

"Are you worried about your mom and dad's problems?"

"Maybe a little," Wesley said.

"How so?" Will asked.

"I don't know what is going to happen."

After a moment of respectful silence, Will said, "I expect that's enough to get a fellow worried." He paused again. "You know, Wesley, when I sit here on the porch in the

186

spring, I like to look at your grandma's azalea bush. I see the red buds opening and imagine they're little hearts opening to God." He looked over at the boy. "How do they know to do that?"

Wesley looked up at his grandpa and said, "I don't know."

"Well, they don't know either," Will said. "Let me ask you this: Should you worry more than an azalea bud just because you don't know what's going to happen? God will take care of you the same way he does the azaleas. Anyway, why don't you let Him worry about it—he works on Sunday—you're supposed to take it easy."

"I thought God rested on the seventh day, Grandpa."

"Well, he's gotten a lot busier since he created man," Will said.

The view over the bottomland from behind the barn always helped Will sort things out. He had retreated there after dinner. This was his private sanctuary, under a splayed-limb post oak. Sometimes he talked to God here. Sometimes he just whittled. Sometimes he whittled and talked to God.

The dark green ridgeline of pines against the cloudless blue sky was punctuated by a half-dozen soaring buzzards in the distance. The sun's reflection on the glossy black feathers gave the appearance that their wings were white-tipped. Will knew that was not true, but it had allowed his mind to wander from his worries.

He reached in his trousers, pulled out his pocket knife, and stepped to a stand of sassafras trees a few yards away. He cut off a slender branch from a sapling, brought the cut end to his nose and inhaled the aroma. The scent reminded him of dill or pennyroyal. He thought it cleared his head the way camphor did, but mainly, it was his favorite whittling wood.

He sat down on a cedar stump, which had been there since the tree had been cut down to make way for the barn, braced the branch against his thigh with his stub arm, and began peeling long thin strips. He remembered making whistles out of sassafras as a kid, but he wasn't a kid anymore. Now, he was a man and needed to bring his attention to prayer.

"God, it's me, Will, again. It seems like I have been coming here a lot lately. The fact is, I don't know what to do about this mess with Beulah and Ray. I'm afraid she's put too much faith in him. What I'm really afraid of is that he might take off with Wesley to Iowa. Lord, if I do what I think is best, I'll be going against my wife . . . and that's a hard thing."

Thirty minutes later all that remained of the sassafras limb was a mess of shavings scattered on and around Will's shoes.

Chapter Seventeen
Church

Sunday mornings in Birch View before the church bells started ringing was as peaceful as any place J. Bob could imagine. He flipped his pillow to the cool side but continued lying on his back and didn't open his eyes. He liked to wait until the last possible moment before viewing the day.

His eyebrows tightened as he tried to restart a dream, but a dog started barking in the distance, and he lost all hope. He opened his eyes to the alarm clock on the night stand, the tin-colored Baby Ben with the two bells and clanger on the top. He pondered, *If the striker is the clanger, why isn't the bell the clangee.* It made perfect sense to his legal mind. It was a quarter past eight o'clock.

He propped himself on his elbow to see out the windows across from his bed. From his second-floor apartment above his office, he had a view of Main Street and First Street, which ran parallel to each other and composed Birch View's business district. The two streets were separated by a narrow public park that featured a bandstand, where old men sat and whittled, and an arched wooden bridge over the dry creek that went through town.

Old-timers said that in days gone by the creek regularly flowed with clear water and had river birches along the banks, but an earthquake in the 1800s stopped the regular flow. Now the creek only had water after a cloudburst, and the birches had been replaced with oaks.

Through the trees, over on Main Street, J. Bob could see two of Birch View's feature attractions: the Owl Café (which closed at 3 p.m. every afternoon) and David's Rexall Drugs, which was the after-school hangout for teenagers.

But on Sunday mornings the two streets were deserted.

J. Bob had just turned thirty-two and officially, at least, still lived at home with his mother on what was known locally as the *Old* Dalton Place, even though Daltons still lived there. But his unofficial—and usual—residence was the apartment above his office in the old Farmers Bank building on First Street.

The Farmers Bank had gone out of business during the Great Depression, in part because his grandfather and great uncle, the managing partners, were benevolently slow to foreclose deeds of trust the bank held on many of the farms in the county. The town's other bank down the street, not given to altruism and still in existence, actually prospered during the hard times.

With the fee from his first personal injury case, J. Bob bought the old building and began converting it to his office. Much of the refurbishing was paid for though bartering. He drafted wills and deeds or handled divorces or criminal matters in exchange for plumbing and carpenter work.

His law library was in the room-sized vault that had once housed the bank's cash and collateral instruments. The heavy steel door was always left open. The combination had been forgotten years before, and J. Bob feared losing all his books, or what he called *half his brain,* if the door were locked. He often laughed that he needed a safecracker for a client.

J. Bob sat up on the bed and put both feet on the floor. If he hustled, he could have a cup of coffee with his mother before she left for church. In bare feet and pajamas he padded over the oak tongue and groove floor to the bathroom.

His upstairs two-room apartment was appointed with a shower, which was one of his prized possessions. The Dalton place only had bathtubs that evoked memories of childhood scrubbings accompanied by cautionary statements about wasting water and his mother's favorite Methodist aphorism:

cleanliness is next to godliness. J. Bob relished his shower, and with a large-capacity water heater, he could stay in it as long as he liked and waste as much water as he wanted.

J. Bob drove between the limestone gateposts surrounded by crepe myrtle bushes and proceeded up the short driveway to his mother's place. The columned two-story antebellum house had been in the family since before the Civil War. These days, just his mother, Lodema Blaylock Dalton, lived in the main house. A married couple, who served as caretaker and cook, lived in the guest house in the rear. Mr. Dalton had passed away during J. Bob's sophomore year in college.

His mother's 1950 Chevy coupe was parked under the porte-cochere, and J. Bob came to a stop behind it. He frequently checked up on his mother, although at sixty-five, she did not need much checking-up-on. He often said, "Mother can still work all day in the garden and blister you with her tongue on matters of religion and politics. She's a Methodist and a Democrat and thinks both are revelations from the Almighty. John Wesley and FDR are saints to her."

Mrs. Dalton appeared in the side doorway. Her posture was erect as she descended the steps from the house with ease. "Good morning, Sonny Boy. I see that you are not dressed for church." J. Bob wore yesterday's slacks, which bagged at the knees, and a wool crew neck sweater over a plaid shirt.

"Well, neither are you, Mother." Mrs. Dalton was wearing a cotton dress and an older button-up sweater.

"Well, I'll be ready for services, but I had a few chores to tend and some seed catalogues to review."

When it came to growing things, Mrs. Dalton was generally acknowledged to be without a peer. In her garden, she was a meditation in motion. She would focus on one plant, then another, inspecting leaves as if they were children with dirty ears and occasionally whispering to them in a low soothing tone. "Now, you're growing to be a big boy," she'd coo to a tomato plant. But her countenance could cloud up and become bellicose in an instant at the sight of a potato bug or a cut worm.

Her hair was mostly gray and thinning, and during the week, it showed the telltale signs of the farmer's straw hat she wore in the garden. But on Sundays, every hair was in place when she anchored the front row of the choir at First Methodist. She had a standing appointment at Eva's beauty shop on Saturday afternoon, and on Saturday nights she slept in a silk head scarf to avoid mussing her style.

They walked arm in arm through the side door and past the butler's pantry to the large kitchen that accommodated a rectangular cherry table with six chairs.

"Let's have a cup of coffee, son."

"Mother, its after nine; you'll be late for Sunday School."

"Oh, I'm boycotting Sunday School until that simple-minded Trellis Powell's tenure as teacher is up next month. I swear she would be more suited with the Pentecostals." She filled two cups with coffee, added milk to J. Bob's, and then sat down.

"What's wrong with old Trellis?" J. Bob asked.

"Don't get me started on her. Are you coming for dinner today?"

"Did you invite the preacher?" J. Bob loved Sunday dinner with his mother, which was usually fried chicken served promptly at two o'clock. Except when she invited the minister and his wife.

"What difference does that make?"

"It's always the same. He'll make his usual comment that he hasn't seen me at church in a month of Sundays; you'll add a nodding approbation; and then I'll say something smart and end up feeling like an outcast."

"He's just concerned about your welfare."

"No, he's an officious intermeddler."

"Well, it wouldn't hurt you to show up at church more often. It would be good for you."

"Mother, I probably know more bible verses than that bible-college parson. Anyway, I *do* go to church on Sundays when I'm not at First Methodist."

"Where do you go to church?" Her voice was excited and carried a tone of disbelief. "You're not sneaking off with those beer drinkers at that Catholic church in Ridgeview, are you?"

"No mother, it's non-denominational and focuses more on fellowship than scripture—you wouldn't approve. But don't worry, they don't do full emersion, and I just visit."

"James Robert, sometimes you try my Christian patience."

By 10:30 J. Bob was in his car headed for his Sunday fellowship meeting. By 10:45 he was parking his car behind Club 60. He entered through the unlocked back door and followed the aroma of cooking bacon to the kitchen.

With a cup of coffee in one hand and a spatula in the other, Sam presided over a dozen sugar-cured pork strips simmering on the grill. He was vested in a white T-shirt, cloaked by a restaurant utility apron, and "toqued" in sailor's cap with the brim pulled down. A cigarette cantilevered from his lips.

Sam glanced over as J. Bob entered and sat his coffee cup on the counter to withdraw the cigarette. "Good morning, Brother J. Bob. Glad to see you could make it to church this morning."

Church at Club 60 started a few months after Sam bought the tavern. He discovered after closing up on Saturday nights that he was too tired to drive 35 miles over the winding highway to Ridgeview. He began sleeping on a cot in a backroom and driving home on Sunday.

One Sunday morning J. Bob realized he had not replenished his beer supply, and the thought of a hot summer afternoon, after dinner with the preacher, would be intolerable without beer. He charged to Club 60, hoping to talk Sam into selling him some.

He got there and found Sam and Big John Crawford sipping libations and cooking ham and eggs. Sam said he couldn't legally sell beer on Sunday, but he was welcome to join them for a cold one and some breakfast. It soon became a regular event in which Speedo Green, the county sheriff, often joined them.

"Good morning, Brother Sam. I see that Reverend Big John has not arrived yet."

"No, but I'm sure *The Reverend* John will be here shortly, unless he is shacked up someplace. He loves knocking down a few snorts and imitating a colored preacher." At the sound of a car outside, Sam stepped to the window. "Here he is now."

Big John presented himself at the door. "Good morning, brethren! Reverend John has arrived; give me an 'Amen!'"

"Ah, knock it off, John, it's too early," Sam said. "Sounds like you've already had an eye-opener."

John looked as if his feelings had been wounded, but then he grinned. "Well, I may have had a road toddy."

"Where's Rita?" J. Bob asked.

Sam's face went solemn. "She's at her parents' place this morning—her husband is back. Apparently, he lost his truck driving job and is out there trying to mooch a grubstake."

"When did he show up?" J. Bob asked.

"Monday morning. Rita wasn't in at all yesterday. By the way, where were you?"

J. Bob brought his thumb and index finger to his chin and looked out the window. In a quiet, thoughtful tone he said, "Interesting. Now, maybe I can get service of process on him for Rita's divorce." He looked over at Sam. "As you know, every time he's in the area he hides out in Winn County to avoid being served."

"Hiding in the shadow of wings. Say, yes, brothers!"

"Dammit, John, knock it off," Sam said.

John held up both arms in surrender.

"Is Speedo coming today?" J. Bob asked.

"No, he was coon hunting last night."

"That's no reason to skip church," J. Bob said. "Anyway, where's Rita's old man going to get any money? Not from her parents. I hear they can barely make ends meet."

"Hell, I don't know," Sam said. "All I know is that Rita will be a lot happier—and so will I—when she can get rid of that jerk."

J. Bob pulled a can of beer from the portable ice chest on the floor. "Where's the church key?"

"Over there, counselor," Big John said, gesturing to the window ledge.

J. Bob grabbed the beer opener, punched two triangular holes in the top of the Falstaff can, and took a long draw. He wiped foam from his upper lip. "How much money do you suppose he needs?"

Sam inhaled smoke from his Chesterfield and raised both eyebrows. As he blew smoke out his nose, he said, "Maybe a couple hundred."

"Why don't you loan it to him, Sam."

A spontaneous laugh erupted from Sam. "Well, counselor, you little traitor."

"You want to get rid of him?" J. Bob asked.

Sam crushed out his cigarette butt in an ash tray by the grill. "You're thinking that he's such a deadbeat that if he owes me money, he'll never come around, again."

"Something like that, Sam."

"Hey, you never told me where you were yesterday."

\#

By Tuesday of that week, Rita was racked with jumbled emotions. She had gone to her parents' farm and picked up the man she hoped would soon be her ex-husband, and now she was driving him to her boyfriend's tavern to obtain a loan. And Ray, weepy and maudlin, kept encroaching from the passenger's side and whining about starting over together—if only for Wesley's sake.

"Rita, we could get a little place—"

"Ray, don't start this again. It's too late."

"What's the matter? I hear this Sam is your boyfriend now. Don't forget, I'm still your husband."

"Our marriage never stood in *your* way."

At Club 60 the Tuesday night crowd was meager. When they arrived, the after-work crowd had left, and the honky-tonkers wouldn't be around until the weekend. Sam was behind the bar, and J. Bob was talking with two men at the end of the bar.

Rita and Ray sat on stools at the middle of the bar in front of Sam. J. Bob excused himself from his audience and moved toward them.

"Sam, this is Ray," Rita said.

Sam looked from Rita to Ray, his face showing the same level of emotion as when he was dealing cards. He reached to the cooler below and pulled out a bottle of Rita's usual brand. He casually removed the cap and sat the bottle, a glass, and a paper napkin in front of her. He looked at Ray again and said, "What can I get you, pal?"

"Just give me a Bud." Ray's smile, which he usually relied on to charm people, was absent.

Not waiting for an introduction, J. Bob said, "Hello, Rita." Then, extending his hand to Ray, he said, "I'm James Dalton—folks call me J. Bob. You must be Ray."

"You're the lawyer."

"Guilty as charged," J. Bob said.

As they shook hands, Ray said, "Well, Rita may not need your services, J. Bob. You see, we've been talking things over."

From behind Ray's back, Rita shook her head, indicating this was not the case. Her lips were tight and closed.

J. Bob smiled. "Well, Ray, a client's welfare and happiness are my only concerns."

Sam, who had been listening, interjected himself into the conversation. "Ray, I understand you've had some problems and want to transact some business with me."

"That's right. Is there some place we can talk?"

"Sure, right here. I've got a business to run. Besides, my lawyer is here and he can make sure we're legal. How much do you need to borrow?"

"I figure a couple hundred ought to do it. I just need to get to Iowa, and work some things out with the company so I can get back on the road. I make pretty good money, you know."

"I'll bet you do. Why don't we make it five hundred? If you don't need it all, you can just leave it in the bank. This isn't a regular loan—I'm not charging interest. I'm spotting you the money because Rita is a good employee, and they're hard to find around here."

The smile came back to Ray's face. "Well, it's hard to turn down an offer like that."

"How much time are you going to need?" Sam asked.

"Maybe a month."

"Write me a check for five hundred dollars and date it thirty days from now."

By nine o'clock, only J. Bob and two other customers remained, and Sam said, "Last call, fellows." The two mill workers said they had to be going and left. Sam locked the door behind them, turned off the front lights, and went back behind the bar.

"All right, J. Bob, are you ready to tell me where you were Saturday?"

J. Bob shrugged and smiled.

Sam stared at him for a moment, said "Okay," and paused again. "You want another beer?"

J. Bob, still smiling said, "How about a half?"

Sam gave him an annoyed look. "The only *half* around here is your ass." He moved back to the center of the bar and pulled a can from the cooler underneath, opened it, and slid it to J. Bob at the end of the bar without spilling any beer.

"Hell, Sam, it's no wonder you beat everyone in shuffle board; you get all this practice sliding beer cans."

Sam walked back to the end of the bar across from J. Bob and sat on a tall stool he kept behind the bar. "Counselor, you won't tell me where you were Saturday, so how about telling me this instead: tell me how I have made such a great investment with my five hundred dollars."

"Now, listen Sam, this is slick. First of all, you're never going to see the five hundred because I guarantee you when you cash that check in thirty days, it's going to bounce."

Sam nodded in agreement.

"Writing a hot check is a crime, and one as sizeable as that is a felony, which could carry a year in the state penitentiary. The statute of limitations is three years. If he shows up during that period, you can swear out a warrant and have him arrested. You have a three-year reprieve from him."

"I understand that, J. Bob, but there's still one. problem—he's married to Rita . . . unless you're planning on horse trading the bad check charge for his cooperation in the divorce."

"Hell no, Sam, a lawyer can get into trouble threatening prosecution to help a civil case. Besides, I don't need his cooperation anymore."

"How's that?"

"Well, shortly after Rita drops him off at her parents' farm this evening, one of Speedo's deputies is going to serve him with the divorce process that he has been avoiding. The only reason he chanced showing his face in this county was that he needed some quick money.

Sam nodded. "It's still a pretty damned expensive way to do business."

"But, here's the clincher. Do you remember me warning you and Rita about being too public with your relationship?"

"Yeah, what about it?"

"I will refresh your recollection. In the state of Missouri you have to have *grounds* to obtain a divorce. She's got grounds—he committed adultery. Moreover, you have to be the *innocent and injured party*, which means the other side can't have any grounds against you. Are you following this, Sam?"

"Pretty much, I think," Sam said.

"This is my point. If he were to testify that Rita has an open and notorious affair with you, she's not an innocent and injured party, and she can't get a divorce."

"It's a wonder anybody can get divorced, counselor."

"Hell, Sam, most of divorces I handle are based on collusion because the parties lie to get the divorce. And frankly, some of the testimony amounts to extortion; it's the old 'I won't give you a divorce unless you give me what I want' routine. But now, if he tries to pull that and shows up to testify at the divorce trial, he'll end up in the slammer on the bad check charge."

Sam rose to his feet and beamed.

J. Bob sat down his beer. "What?"

"Nothing." Sam went dead pan and turned to swipe at the counter with a wet rag.

"Do you have something you want to say, Sam?"

Sam smiled, with his side to J. Bob.

J. Bob leaned over the bar. "Is there a compliment brewing, Sam?"

Swiping the counter again, Sam said, "Nope. Nothing like that." Sam smiled again, looking down at his knuckles. He stopped swiping and looked over at J. Bob. "You never did tell me where you were."

Chapter Eighteen

A Day of Reckoning

*W*ednesday morning Beulah was teary-eyed and still upset about the deputy sheriff serving Ray with papers the night before. She likened it to Judas and the betrayal of Jesus. And Ray had started making threats that confirmed Will's fears and bolstered his resolve.

Will told Beulah that he was going to Birch View to get the spare tire for the car repaired. Beulah barely paid attention.

Driving down the gravel road, Will refused to second-guess his plan. As soon as guilty feelings started to crawl into his mind, he blocked them by returning, in his mind's eye, to his sanctuary behind the barn.

He had made up his mind, and it was the right thing to do—he owed that much to Rita. There used to be a special bond between them. Now, as he thought of Rita, he remembered her as a little girl, and how proud he had been when Tom Mix, the movie star, had put her on his famous horse Tony the day Will shod the horse in his blacksmith shop.

His eyes welled up as he recalled those days. When he lost his arm, she was only six and became his left arm, holding nails so he could hammer them. In his mind he could still hear her voice: "We can do it, Daddy."

He steadied the wheel with his stub arm, wiped his eyes, and then pulled out his pocket watch. Rita would be at Eva's beauty shop. She had started apprenticing under Eva. She had said, "In a year, I'll be able to take the state boards, Daddy, and get my own license." Had he been encouraging?

Had he cheered her on even once? *Well, I'll do the right thing now.*

Before reaching the highway, he turned up the lane to the Tremont School to pick up Wesley.

Wesley's teacher, Mrs. Hansen, looked up when Will cracked open the classroom door. All the children in the four grades of the *little room* looked over at Will, too, and a chorus of whispering rose up. Wesley remained seated and silent, his face perplexed.

"Children, be quiet. It's just Wesley's grandpa. Get back to your class work, and I'll see what Mr. O'Dell wants."

Mrs. Hansen walked over, and Will stepped back into the foyer. She stepped through the door and closed it behind her, leaving a crack open. "What brings you here Mr. O'Dell? I hope nothing is wrong."

"No, Wesley's mom made a dentist appointment for him in Birch View. She came by last night after he had gone to bed, and we forgot to tell him. We had a little excitement this morning—a cow got out and we were chasing her."

"Well, by all means, I'll excuse Wesley. Dentist appointments are hard to come by. I know how it is. Doc Jeffers is only in Birch View once a week, and then, if he has some emergencies, your appointment can get postponed." She stared directly into Will's eyes—the same way Will imagined she did at a student she suspected of not telling the truth.

Will was unsure of what to say, so he just nodded.

Mrs. Hansen continued, "That's happened to me two times."

Will nodded again, wondering if he was imagining the fact that her cheek looked a little swollen. He swallowed and shifted his weight to his left foot.

Finally, Mrs. Hansen opened the door and gestured for Wesley to come over. He got up slowly from his desk. The longer it took, the more Will felt like a criminal. *Get a move on here,* he thought.

"Get your coat, Wesley," Mrs. Hansen said. Wesley veered to the row of hooks on the wall for his jacket and then to the door.

"Wesley, your grandpa is going to take you to a dentist appointment," Mrs. Hansen said.

Wesley looked at his grandpa, confused.

"Wesley," Will said, "When the cow got out this morning, we forgot to tell you about the appointment." Wesley looked more confused, as if he were straining his memory and coming up blank.

Mrs. Hansen, who had vast experience dealing with boys telling fibs, narrowed her eyebrows in suspicion, but said nothing. Avoiding eye contact, Will thanked her and hustled Wesley to the car.

Wesley was quiet until they were in the car. "Am I really going to the dentist, Grandpa?"

Will's image of himself as an honest man would not let him carry the lie forward any further. His many proclamations of intolerance for liars and thieves echoed in his mind. "Well, I'm not sure, Wesley. Mostly, we need to go and see your mother."

"If Mrs. Hansen finds out that I didn't go to the dentist, I'll get in trouble."

The lies, particularly the one to Mrs. Hansen with her possible swollen cheek, and now, Wesley's concern gnawed at Will. "Well, the doc *is* in today, and you're overdue for a checkup. I'll talk to him and I expect he can squeeze you in. That ought to square things." Wesley looked relieved, but the lies still ate at Will.

"Wesley, the real reason we need to see your mom is that your dad is threatening to take you back to Iowa."

The color drained from Wesley's face. "But I don't want to go to Iowa. I want to stay here."

Steering with his stub, Will reached over and patted Wesley's knee. "Don't worry, son; we'll figure out something."

When Will and Wesley entered the door at the Cut & Curl, the shop was empty except for Eva. She saw them in the mirror and turned. "Well, this is a surprise. Rita's in back. Just a minute." She took a step toward the rear, and called out, "Rita, Wesley and your dad are up front."

Rita emerged from the back doorway, drying her hands on a shop towel, and rushed to the front. "What's going on, Dad?"

"You and I need to talk," Will said.

Rita put both hands on Wesley's shoulders and bent down to his eye level. "Are you OK, son?"

"Yes, Mama."

"Then, give your mama a hug." Wesley put his arms around his mother's neck. Rita kissed him on his head, then gently pushed him to arm's length and looked him in the eyes. "Wesley, I want you stay here with Eva and look at magazines. Grandpa and I have to talk. Don't worry; we're not going anywhere, and we'll be right back."

Rita and Will got in Will's car. "Dad, what's this all about? And why isn't Wesley in school?"

"I took him out on the way here. I told Mrs. Hansen that he had a dentist appointment, but let me start at the beginning. Last night after you left, the deputy sheriff came by and served Ray with the divorce papers. Ray hit the roof. I won't repeat all the stuff he said—and Mom was joining right in."

"I can imagine what he was like. I've seen his temper before, trust me. But what got you so concerned?"

"He said he was going to take Wesley back to Iowa and you and that damned lawyer would play hell getting him back."

"No! He couldn't do that. He's never taken care of Wesley."

"Don't put it past him. He's really hot, and he's got five hundred dollars and your car—"

"I should have never agreed to let him use it," Rita said.

"Anyway," Will continued, "as soon as they find out that Wesley is with you, all hell is going to break loose."

Rita looked panicked. "We've got to do something, Dad."

"What about your lawyer?"

"Eva and I saw him at the Owl Café this morning, and he's at the county seat all day. His mother, Mrs. Dalton, is watching the office today."

"Maybe we should contact the sheriff's office and have them send a deputy?" Will said.

"What good would that do? He hasn't committed any crime. You know Ray, old Smiling Ray; he'll act so innocent that they won't be able to do anything to him."

Will grunted in disgust.

"Let me go talk to Eva," Rita said. "I'll tell her what's going on. Maybe she can watch Wesley, and we can see if we can settle things down."

"All right," Will said, "I'll keep a lookout."

Inside the beauty shop, Rita told Wesley to stay put, and she and Eva went to the back room to talk. As Eva listened, her mouth dropped open. "This is terrible, Rita. You know I want to help, but I don't think this is the best place for Wesley to stay. If Ray comes looking for Wesley, this is the first place he'll try."

"You're right, but what else can we do?"

Eva paused to think. "I've got it. Let's ask Mrs. Dalton if Wesley can stay at J. Bob's office."

"Oh, Eva, he's already confused; he'll be scared to death staying with a stranger."

"No, he won't. He'll be fascinated by Mrs. Dalton. Don't forget that she raised J. Bob. I'm sure it will be OK. What are you and your dad going to do?"

"We thought we would try to reason with Ray."

"I don't think that's a good idea—he sounds crazy. You need to get J. Bob . . . or Sam."

"Not Sam," said Rita. "Somebody could get killed. I guess if Ray comes here, we could call the constable."

Eva rolled her eyes. "Stubby?" He's as worthless as tits on a tomcat. And like you said, what's the charge? He's the boy's father, and I don't think you can kidnap your own child."

Eva squinted her eyes like a child struggling with an arithmetic problem. After a brief moment she said, "We could have Mrs. Dalton call the courthouse and leave a message for J. Bob, but he's an hour away."

"Eva, I think I *will* go see Sam. Dad won't like his car parked in front of a tavern, but I can't think of anything else. Maybe he could call Speedo; Ray couldn't fool him."

Rita and Eva explained to Wesley that he was going to stay in J. Bob's office with Mrs. Dalton, and not to worry.

When Rita and Will got to Club 60, it was 10 a.m., and Sam's Buick wasn't there. The "Closed" sign was in the window. "What do we do now?" Will asked.

"I guess we wait," Rita said. Will's face grimaced, and Rita guessed what he was thinking. "We can pull around back; he should be here before too long."

On the way to J. Bob's office, Eva attempted to walk hand in hand with Wesley, but he told her he wasn't a little boy. "Well young man, you're right. A gentleman walks arm in arm with a lady." With her hand on his lower back, she guided him to her right. "And the gentleman always walks next to the street." She showed him how to hold his arm, bent at the elbow, and extended her arm in his.

After introductions and a brief explanation, with a few between-the-lines innuendos, it was agreed that Wesley could stay there. Mrs. Dalton told Wesley to sit in the client's chair in J. Bob's office while she and Eva talked for a moment. She gave Wesley a copy of *Missouri Conservationist* magazine to occupy him.

Mrs. Dalton closed the door between the reception area and the office. She looked Eva square in the eyes. "Now, what's really going on here?"

When Eva finished providing the details, Mrs. Dalton said, almost casually, "I don't anticipate any problem if this estranged husband shows up here."

Eva hadn't been back at her shop twenty minutes when Ray opened the door and filled the entrance. Eva was bent over the shampoo bowl rinsing a patron's hair. She had been keeping a watchful eye at the door, pretty much expecting Ray to show up.

"Where are Rita and my son?"

Eva wrapped a towel around the patron's head, assisted her upright in the shop chair, and calmly excused herself from the patron, whose interest was piqued.

Eva walked to the counter at the edge of the small waiting area where Ray was standing, still holding on to the door. She crossed her arms in front of her chest. "You can see they are not here."

"Well, where are they?"

"I don't know where Rita is. I assume Wesley is in school."

"No need to lie, Eva. I went by the school. His grandpa got him out of class to take him to the dentist here in Birch View. I'm sure that was a lie, too."

"I don't know where they are."

The two glared silently at one another. A moment passed. Ray broke the silence. "The lawyer!" Eva's face blanched. "I'm right, I can tell by your face. Where's his office—never mind—I'll find it."

"Ray, you're only going to get in trouble."

He turned and rushed out the door, slamming it behind him. With long determined steps he strode down the

First Street sidewalk looking from storefront to storefront until he saw the sign on the two-story brick building: J. Robert Dalton, Attorney-at-Law.

He opened the door and entered. A gray-haired older woman sitting at a receptionist's desk said, "May I help you?"

"I'm Ray Sanders and I'm looking for my wife and my son."

"I'm sorry, Mr. Sanders, but do you have an appointment? Mr. Dalton is not in. I'll be happy to tell him you came by."

Raising his voice, Ray said, "No, I don't have an appointment. I'm looking for my—"

"Mr. Sanders, I may be old but I'm not deaf. Furthermore, I'm sorry your mother didn't teach you better manners. I assure you that this office is not in the business of storing estranged wives and lost children. Mr. Dalton is not in. I'll tell him you came by; now please leave."

"I'm sorry ma'am, but I need to know if they are hiding here." With two steps, Ray was past her desk and had his hand on the door to J. Bob's office.

"Mr. Sanders, if you step in that office, I'll call the constable and have you arrested for trespass."

Ray opened the door and looked in. "Well, there's no one in here. What's upstairs?"

"It's a private residence. It's locked and I don't have a key."

"Well, you shouldn't mind if I check it out then."

"Mr. Sanders, I might be willing to let your rude behavior pass, but I swear by the grave of John Wesley that if you take one more step, I'll have you in jail by sundown."

The front door opened and Constable Stubby Davis entered. Eva was behind him looking over his shoulder. "What seems to be the problem, here?" Stubby said. "Eva told me that a man was disturbing the peace."

Ray stepped back from the door and gave the officer a big smile. "Officer, there's no peace disturbance. I was just looking for my wife and son. Eva, there, said they were down here."

"I said no such thing," Eva said.

"You two pipe down," Stubby said, looking first at Eva then back at Ray. "Mrs. Dalton, are you OK?"

"Stubby, I'm fine. I think Mr. Sanders was just about to leave. However, if that is not the case, would you escort him out? In fact, you might want to make sure that he doesn't get lost and finds his way outside the city limits."

"That won't be necessary. I was just leaving," Ray said.

As Ray started toward the door, Stubby, in a high-handed tone from the side of his mouth, said, "Son, wait just a minute. I'm giving you a warning: you best go straight out of town. I'll be watching you."

Ray glared at him. His smile was gone and his lips were stretched tight against his clenched teeth, but he said nothing and kept walking out the door to his car.

"Well, ladies," Stubby said, "if there's nothing else here, I'll go make sure Mr. Big Shot finds his way out of town."

As soon as Stubby left, Eva said, "Where's Wesley?"

"Oh, I expect we'll find him hiding under J. Bob's desk."

They went into the office. Eva called out, "Wesley, it's all right to come out." No answer. She looked under the desk. "He's not here. I wonder where he . . . What's wrong, Mrs. Dalton? Your face is white."

"The safe door, Eva. It's closed!"

They rushed to the door, and both pushed on the large handle. It would not budge. "Wesley, can you hear me?" Eva yelled. She put her ear against the cold steel. "I can't tell if I can hear anything or not. Maybe something muffled."

"I've got to call J. Bob," Mrs. Dalton said. She grabbed the receiver from the phone on his desk. The operator answered. "Sylvia, this is Mrs. Dalton. I need you to call the clerk's office at the county seat and have someone find J. Bob, and tell him to return to his office at once. This is an emergency—a life or death emergency!"

From behind Club 60, Rita and Will heard a car pull on to the driveway. Rita said she recognized the sound of Sam's car, and they drove around to meet him.

Because Sam and Will had never met, Rita made introductions and the men shook hands. Will was taciturn and tentative, as if he had just entered into a pact with the Prince of Darkness. Sam, conversely, and somewhat out of character, was a politician soliciting a vote. "What brings you two out this morning?"

"Sam, we've got a problem and didn't know where else to turn," Rita said. She was into the details of the situation and then stopped abruptly. "What's that? I hear a siren."

They looked eastward as the sound grew closer and louder. "Look," Rita said, "there's a highway patrol car with its light flashing."

"No," Sam said, "that's a sheriff's car—and J. Bob's car is hot on his tail." Both cars zoomed past.

"Wesley is at J. Bob's office! Something bad has happened!" Rita said.

"Both of you, get in my car," Sam said.

With Rita in the middle and Will riding shotgun, the Buick shot onto the pavement, throwing gravel and squealing tires. Within minutes they slid to a stop in front of the law office.

The office door was open. Will had barely opened the car door when Rita crawled over him and darted through the front door and into J. Bob's office. Will and Sam hurried behind her.

Breathless, Rita, asked, "What's wrong?"

210

Everyone started talking at once. "People, calm down," J. Bob yelled above the din. The voices stopped. He directed his attention to Rita. "We think Wesley is locked in the vault."

Rita's hands went to her mouth, and she whispered, "Oh my god." Her eyes welled with tears. Eva attempted to hug her, but Rita pushed her away. "We've got to get him out."

"That's the problem, Rita. Speedo and I tried to open the door, and we can't budge it."

Rita rushed to the vault door and put her face next to it. "Wesley, can you hear me, baby?"

"Rita, the door and walls are a foot thick of steel-reinforced concrete. It's dark and silent as a . . ." He stopped mid-sentence. "I mean, he can't hear you. And it's too dark for him to find the safety release—if it even works. But he should have plenty of air."

Rita gasped. This time, she offered no resistance as Eva embraced her.

"James Robert," Mrs. Dalton said, her voice betraying unusual fear, "I can't understand how he got that large door closed."

"Mother, unfortunately, as heavy as the door is, it's balanced so well on those hinges that a weakly bank teller could close it. I had a wedge in the latch mechanism, but he must have removed it."

"Don't you have the combination?" Sam asked.

"That was the first thing Speedo asked, but it's been lost for years."

"Maybe we could get a welder to cut in with an acetylene torch," Speedo said.

Sam said, "Mr. O'Dell, here, is a blacksmith." He looked over at Will and said, "Mr. O'Dell, what do you think?"

All eyes went to Will.

"Well, the door is so thick and the steel is most likely alloyed with copper and other material that I doubt you could cut through the door with a torch. Back in the thirties, and Mrs. Dalton will remember this, some bank robbers tried to breach the wall and couldn't do it. I remember because my dad, who was a deputy sheriff, arrested them."

"Dammit!" Rita snapped. "We've got to do something, and soon, or he's going to run out of air. J. Bob, you're the main cause of this, so you better start figuring something out quick."

"Rita, I'm so sorry. I'll think of something."

Everyone except J. Bob offered ideas, but all suggestions had fatal flaws. J. Bob sat at his desk with his head in his hands. Rita paced and sobbed as Mrs. Dalton and Eva tried to console her. Speedo and Sam looked at a drawing Will had made, and the three men discussed whether they could go through the floor or the roof.

"I've got it!" J. Bob sprang out of his chair. "Eva, come with me." He grabbed her hand and pulled her along as he headed for the door. "We'll be back in thirty minutes," he said over his shoulder.

Eva stumbled to stay on her feet. "Where are we going?"

"Get in my car. Hurry!"

A small crowd had gathered on the sidewalk. J. Bob saw Stubby approaching and told him to keep the people away from his office.

J. Bob wheeled his Ford from the curb, leaving a rubber strip on the pavement as he pealed out. He popped the clutch, shifting into second gear, and the tires squealed again.

"J. Bob, tell me where we are going. Now!"

He made eye contact with her. "Ethan's."

"What?" She practically screamed. "Are you out of your mind?"

"Listen, Eva, a bank combination is nothing but numbers. Ethan may be a wing nut, but he's a genius with numbers. He can do algebra and logarithms in his head and doesn't even know that's what he's doing. He can figure out stuff you'd have to have a ten-foot slide rule to calculate. And he can fix anything. I'm gambling that he can figure out that combination."

"And you're dragging me along as insurance in case he wouldn't go with you. You think if I ask him to do it, he will."

"That's right."

"God, I hope you're right."

"Eva, I don't think we have any choice. That vault is virtually indestructible. I read somewhere that a bank vault survived the atomic bomb blast in Japan. If we don't get that door open, that boy is going to die, and I couldn't live with myself."

J. Bob slowed and turned onto the road leading to Ethan's. The car hit the loose gravel, slid sideways, and J. Bob struggled for control.

"Slow down—we can't help anybody if we're in a ditch."

With the car headed straight, he sped on with both hands on the steering wheel and dust billowing in the car's wake.

"Eva, I once sued a man for leaving the door on an old ice box open when a child suffocated inside. In the trial I practically called the defendant a murderer. Now the chickens have come home to roost in my backyard."

When they returned to J. Bob's office with Ethan, the conversations in the room stopped abruptly. Sam's face looked to be in pain, as if he had just been dealt a joker. The rest were dumbstruck—except for Mrs. Dalton, who broke the silence. "Why, Ethan," she said, "it's good to see you again. It's been sometime. Did you come to open the lock for us?"

"I reckon so, Mrs. Dalton."

Ethan shuffled over to the vault. "I expect it has four numbers since it's a big lock." He leaned forward and sniffed

213

at the combination dial. He turned the dial back and forth. "It ain't rusted much." He stood up and stepped back rotating and stretching his neck as if he was relieving tension.

Gently, Eva said, "You need to hurry, Ethan."

"I already know one of the numbers, Eva."

"Now, how in the hell can he know one of the numbers?" Sam blurted.

"Sam, be quiet." Rita was hoping for a miracle and didn't want it jinxed.

Ethan put his ear next to the dial and slowly turned the knob. "Yes'm," he said as he kept turning the dial, apparently listening and feeling for tiny clicks. After about five minutes he stepped back, still facing the vault, and turned his head sideways, as if he were looking under a non-existent table, and made a grunting sound.

He moved back, turned the dial a quarter turn, and pulled the door lever down. The door opened. Cheers filled the room, but they didn't drown out Sam booming, "I'll be a son of a bitch."

Rita bee-lined into the vault. Wesley was sitting on the floor covering his eyes from the light that flooded the chamber. Rita dropped to her knees and put both arms around him. "Wesley, are you alright?"

"I'm OK, Mama. I fell asleep." Tears flowed down Rita's face, and laughter erupted in the room

Will came over and helped Wesley get up. "Son, were you scared?"

"No, Grandpa, you always told me if I got lost in the dark to just sit down and you'd find me, so that's what I did."

Ethan slinked to a corner as everyone huddled around Wesley. Eva broke away and went to him. "Ethan, I'm proud of you." She took his face in both hands and kissed him on the forehead. "Thank you."

Ethan smiled his simple closed-mouth smile and said, "Yes, Eva."

J. Bob drove Ethan home, mostly in silence, thinking. When he stopped in front of Ethan's place, he asked, "How did you know that first number? And what was it?"

"It was on the bank—an "8."

"On the bank?" J. Bob paused. "Oh, *Established in 1908.*"

"Yes'm. Four numbers is harder—three numbers is easy."

Chapter Nineteen

Doors Close

$\mathcal{A}$ few blocks east of the Missouri Capitol building, the state penitentiary in Jefferson City is a square fortress of dingy limestone blocks topped with guard towers and barbed wire. Sitting only a few hundred yards south of the Missouri River, it appears as a citadel of stone, excavated by prison labor from nearby quarries. But Ray did not have that view.

Ray had seen the Capitol earlier that morning, lit up against a black drizzly sky, as he looked out from the back seat of the Henderson County Sheriff's car. The statue on top the dome looked, to Ray, like a man peeing. In a different situation he might have laughed. Not then.

As the deputy pulled to a stop in front of a restaurant on High Street, Ray had known that this was his last stop before his freedom ended, even as he sat with his hands and feet chained to steel brackets bolted to the car frame.

From the passenger side in front, sheriff Speedo Green had turned toward Ray and said, "We're only a few blocks away, but I'm going let you use the restroom inside the café. You're going to be standing a lot getting checked in, and they won't cut you any slack. I saw a man piss on himself in the holding cell and then cry like a baby. That just didn't seem right to me."

When they were back in the car, Speedo had given Ray a paper cup half full of coffee and a glazed donut and said, "Son, this is the last coffee you're going to have for over a year that doesn't have saltpeter in it."

As two prison guards with night sticks marched Ray toward a monstrous steel door that led to the confinement area, the words "for over a year" echoed in his mind. The circuit judge had said, "I, hereby, sentence you to one year and a day, which is the minimum time for a felony conviction." And now, Ray had never been so afraid in his life. In spite of Speedo's kindness, he was fighting to control his bladder.

When the door clanged shut behind them, it sounded like two box cars coupling. Ray made a barely audible whimpering sound and felt as if he had just passed through the gate to hell.

As the younger guard unlocked Ray's leg chains, Ray thought how the man, blond and whiskerless, looked like a shavetail. Then both guards marched him down a corridor paved with brown tiles, polished to a high gloss, to the receiving unit.

They stopped at a shower room that smelled strongly of bleach, where he was stripped, searched, hosed, and disinfected. After the shower he was given prison-issue clothing: work-style oxfords, underwear, olive-drab shirt, and matching pants that had a black strip down the outside of each leg.

The shower shocked Ray to a state of dull alertness. He was acutely aware of his surroundings, yet at the same time, he felt numb as he was fingerprinted, photographed, and given a haircut.

After his processing, the two guards escorted Ray through a series of locked doors out into the prison yard. Ray had imagined the inside of the prison as a medieval courtyard full of jail cells. What he saw instead were several brick and stone dormitories, each three or four stories tall. They looked like big blocks deposited by giants.

Ray hesitated and stared ahead. "Move it," Shavetail said, and he pointed toward a building constructed of limestone blocks. "That's C-Hall, where we're taking you unless you've got some objection." Shavetail laughed at his own attempt at cleverness and added, "We could always put you in H-Hall . . . that's where we keep the black convicts."

"Knock it off," the older guard said.

The inside of C-Hall resembled the inside of a four-story warehouse. On the upper levels, walkways ran the entire length of the walls, passing rows of prisoner cells covered with vertical steel bars. *Like birdcages . . . cages for jailbirds,* Ray thought.

Shavetail and his partner directed Ray through the final door and into the cellblock area . . . and the noise. Inmates were banging metal cups on the bars, hooting, and jeering at him. Ray halted. The older guard pushed him forward with his billy club.

They stopped in front of a cell on the second tier midway down the row. Inside a man was lying on his side on the lower of two bunks that extended from the wall. Propped up on his elbow, he watched indifferently as Shave tail opened the door, while the older guard stood behind Ray.

"Collier, here's your new roommate. You two bunkies play nice," Shavetail said and motioned Ray inside.

Ray stepped inside. Shavetail locked the door, and both guards walked away beginning an unrelated conversation.

Ray and Elvin Collier stared at each other without speaking. Ray's stare was blank. Collier gave the acquired stare of a prison tough—aggressive and designed to intimidate.

After a moment, Collier stood up from his bunk. He was nearly as tall as Ray, but prison food had made him thinner. "I hear you're a paperhanger."

Ray mumbled, "A what?"

"A paperhanger—you write bad checks."

"Where'd you hear that?"

"Word gets around. There ain't no secrets in here."

219

"It wasn't really a hot check," Ray said. "It was a loan I couldn't pay back. I tried to explain that to that Judge Jenkins—"

"Judge Jenkins?" Elvin's face snapped to alertness. "The Circuit Judge in Henderson County?"

"Yeah," Ray said.

"Well, I'll be damned. That's the same son of a bitch that put me in here. What are the chances? Me, in here for sticking up a poker game, and you in for writing a hot check."

"It wasn't a hot check. I borrowed some money from this man my wife worked for at this tavern in Birch View."

"What tavern? Club 60?"

"That's it. His name was Sam Rockford. Do you know him?"

"Yeah, I know him. He's the lousy bastard that stole a pistol from me. He was supposed to be at that poker game, too. Man, I was going to fix his ass good."

Elvin began scratching the side of his face with long deliberate strokes and looked away. After a moment he stopped and refocused on Ray. "This is some kind of a sign— you and me ending up in the same cell—and I'm going to figure it out."

Three o'clock that same afternoon, Sam sat in Club 60 in a booth with a window view of the parking lot. The tavern was empty, and Sam was drinking coffee and smoking a Chesterfield as he skimmed the weekly *County Banner*.

A classified ad on the back page caught his eye: "Coon Dog For Sale (Blue Tick/Walker Mix)." That's the same as ol' Chappy, Sam thought. He heard a car slowing on the highway and looked out the window. J. Bob's Ford.

Sam started to get up when J. Bob came in.

"Sit down, Sam, I'll get a cup and join you."

"Help yourself, counselor."

J. Bob went behind the bar, poured himself a cup of coffee, and sat down in the booth opposite Sam. "Have you heard from Speedo? I figured he would stop by here on his way back to Hamilton."

"I expect he'll be another hour or so. When I went with him to witness an execution one time, it took us six hours to get back, and that was driving with his red light on part of the time."

"You witnessed an execution?" J. Bob's voice registered surprise.

"Yeah, I was back on leave after I got called back up for Korea, just before the *police action* started." He took a long drag on his cigarette and looked at the ceiling as he exhaled. "Counselor, it was the cruelest thing I've ever seen in my life. I've seen men killed in combat, but I have never seen anything as morbid as that man being executed in the gas chamber."

"Sam, you're giving me the chills. I didn't come to talk about morbid stuff. I wanted to talk to you about China."

"China?"

"Yes. I want to go to China."

"Why in the hell would you want to go there? If you want fish heads and rice, I'll cook you some here."

"Well, it's confidential. But I don't want to go on a luxury liner; I want to go on a tramp steamer."

"No, you don't. You have this romantic notion about adventure on the high seas. It's tough on merchant ships. With your smart mouth some seaman would run a knife through your ribs and throw you overboard. Now, cut the crap and tell me why you suddenly want to go to China."

J. Bob made the contorted face of a reluctant child being forced to tell the truth. "I want to go on a honeymoon."

Sam burst into loud laughter and then erupted in a coughing spree, spitting his cigarette on the table. He gained control of his breathing long enough to cough out, "Honeymoon," and then started laughing again.

J. Bob looked shocked. "Well, damn, Sam, it's not the most stupid thing that's ever been said about marriage in this joint." J. Bob picked up the smoldering cigarette and flipped it in the ashtray. "What about you and Rita? I got her divorced and her ex-old man locked up in the state pen, so when are you going to marry her?"

Sam's laughter subsided, and he retrieved a handkerchief from his back pocket and wiped his eyes. "Counselor, you're serious . . . about a honeymoon?"

"Yes, I am. Is that too unbelievable—J. Bob Dalton wanting to have a normal life? You know, sometimes I feel alone . . . incomplete and unaccomplished. Like I missed the train when I had a ticket. I don't feel that way when I'm with her."

"No, J. Bob, it's not unbelievable, and if you're serious, then I'm sorry. I just wasn't aware that your relationship with Eva—it is Eva?"

J. Bob nodded with a look of annoyance.

" . . . had progressed so far. Have you asked her?"

"Not yet."

"I see," Sam said, seeming to ponder the revelation. After a moment, he added, "If she says 'yes,' Rita and I will throw you a shindig."

"I appreciate that. However, you never responded to my question about you and Rita."

Sam reached for another cigarette, then put it down, and went over to the coffee maker. He returned with the glass carafe, topped off their cups, and put the pot on the window ledge as he sat down. He picked up the cigarette and reached for a book of matches. "There are some problems."

J. Bob moved forward to the edge of his seat. "What kind of problems?"

"She's worried about Wesley. His grandmother apparently told him that I'm the reason his father is in the pen."

J. Bob sat up straight, as if he were in court preparing to object. "Now, that's a hell of a thing for a grandma to say to her grandchild. You know, of course, that at one time she was sneaking around trying to become his legal guardian, no doubt, with an eye toward getting child support from his father or the government."

"Yeah, I know all about that. The problem is, now, he doesn't even want to see Rita. She's afraid if we get married, she'll lose him. I told her, regardless, she had to get out there to see him."

"Yes, she does, Sam."

Spot and Rags, a terrier and a hound-mix, greeted Rita as she got out of the car in her parents' driveway. It was the Saturday before Halloween. She carried an orange plastic pumpkin filled with Snickers and Three Musketeers bars, black jelly beans, bubble gum, two squirt guns, and a rubber Halloween mask.

Beulah met her at the kitchen door. "Well, we haven't seen you in some time." Her mother's tone was flat.

Rita hesitated at the step, trying to read her mother's attitude. "I brought Wesley a Halloween pumpkin."

"Have you, now?" Beulah said. Her voice was indifferent, but her lips tightened after she spoke. Rita knew it as a signature of disapproval.

Beulah opened the screen door and stepped sideways, holding it open with the back of her hand, providing an entrance for Rita. "Well, don't just stand there, come in." Motioning toward the kitchen table, she said, "Sit down; I'll get you a cup of coffee."

"OK, Mama. Where's Dad and Wesley?"

"Will is helping a neighbor build a gate. Wesley's upstairs." Beulah stepped to the adjacent living room and called toward the stairwell, "Wesley, come down. Your mother is here."

As Beulah poured coffee, Rita could hear Wesley's feet as he treaded down the wooden steps. When he arrived at the kitchen entrance, Rita pushed her chair back from the table and stood up. "Hi, Wesley, I brought you a Halloween mask and some goodies."

Wesley looked impassively at the pumpkin and then back at his mother. "Grandma already got me a mask. I'm going to dress up as a pirate."

"Well, now you have two masks. Come over and give your mama a hug."

Wesley began to step forward, and then his eyes averted to his grandmother.

Beulah smiled at the boy, and said, "It's OK, Wesley. Your mother drove all the way out here to bring you Halloween presents, and she's very busy."

Wesley walked to Rita's open arms and stood stiffly as she hugged him. Holding his shoulders, she turned him toward the table. "There's your Halloween pumpkin. It has squirt guns—you and your sidekick Ernie can have gunfights."

Wesley stepped away from his mother's grasp and looked at Beulah. "Grandma, where's the egg bucket? It's time for me to gather eggs."

"It's in the pantry, but your mother's here," Beulah said.

"Don't you want to spend some time with me?" Rita asked.

Looking at the door as he spoke, Wesley said, "I've got chores to do."

"Well, I could help you gather eggs—I used to be a pretty good egg-gatherer myself," Rita said.

"I'd better do it by myself. You might scare the hens; they're not used to strangers," Wesley said and went to the pantry.

Rita felt as if an invisible hand had reached inside her stomach and twisted it. Her throat constricted and she found

224

L. D. Whitaker

it hard to swallow. She bit her lip and breathed through her
nose to keep from crying as she watched her little boy march
toward the henhouse, bucket in hand.

She tried to compose herself before turning toward her
mother. When she turned, their eyes met but neither spoke.
Beulah looked defiant with her arms folded across her ample
breasts: a mother standing firm against an intruder.

Beulah broke the silence. "He's not been right since the
divorce and, you know, Ray's sentencing. Some of the kids at
school have been calling him names like Jailbird's Kid."

Thoughts of guilt, anger, and bitterness ran through
Rita's mind, but she only said, "I guess I better be going."

Rita was only a stone's throw away from the farm when
she burst into a full-blown crying jag, and the car slid off the
gravel road to an abrupt stop in a weedy ditch. She turned off
the key, put her head on the steering wheel and continued to
sob.

In the distance she heard the sound of an oncoming
car. She fumbled in her purse and found a tissue, wiped her
eyes, and saw a pickup approaching. The man in the truck
slowed to look but kept going when Rita waived at him. Rita
started the car and pulled back onto the road.

Chapter Twenty
Strange Bedfellows

Ray settled into the routine of prison life. He was given a job in the kitchen scraping plates that inmates shoved through a slot and then sliding them down a counter to a man who sprayed them with a hose before they were put on a washer conveyer. When he finished scraping plates, he went to a sink and washed pots and pans.

When Ray wasn't in the kitchen, other than periodic exercise in the yard, he was in his cell with Elvin. With Sam as a common enemy, a strange union had developed between Ray and Elvin. During the day they talked prison scuttlebutt: a rumored riot, fights, the screws, and inmates to avoid. But when the lights were turned off and they were lying in their bunks, as often as not, it was Sam they whispered about.

The spark of an idea had come to Elvin when Ray arrived. Elvin would have to do his full five-year term—no time off for good behavior on his part—but Ray would be out in a year.

On Ray's first night, Elvin had explored the subject. "Let me see if I've got this right, Ray. You borrowed money from your ex-old lady's boss, and then he got the law after you when the check bounced."

"Yeah, that's right." Ray's voice sounded tired, but the anger was clear. "They were trying to railroad me on the divorce, and when I showed up, I get slapped with a felony bad check rap."

Elvin could hear Ray flopping above as if he couldn't get comfortable. "Easy up there, big fellow, or you'll be coming through on top of me—and I ain't interested in having you in bed with me. You're not that kind, are you?"

"Hell, no, I ain't."

"That's good, a former married man like you. You did say you were divorced, didn't you?"

"Yeah. She got papers served on me the night I got the money from Rockford."

"Man, were you ever set up by your old lady and Rockford. They were playing house behind your back and wanted to get you out of the way, but you wouldn't play ball and give them a divorce, so they set you up."

"You think I don't know that? That's all I've been thinking about."

"Man, I thought *I* had reason to get back at Rockford. He's sleeping with your woman and probably raising your kid to hate you. If he had stolen my wife and got me put in the joint, I'd get that son of a bitch for sure."

"Dammit!" Ray pounded the mattress with his fists and started moaning and blubbering. "How could she do that to me?"

"Take it easy up there. I didn't mean to get you worked up; I just couldn't help but think that I'd get even with him. That's all."

In Tremont, the first week of May meant school would be closing for the summer. Country kids had to be available for plowing, planting, haying, and working in the timber. Even the youngest children worked in the vegetable gardens and truck patches that supplied vegetables for canning.

Now, on this the last day of school, Wesley was euphoric. The classroom session had been brief, and by ten o'clock, parents started arriving with a bounty of food for "dinner on the grounds."

Shortly after dinner, Wesley and two buddies, Ernie and Willie were biking to Crockett's Pond hoping to hook the lunker bass that could suck worms off hooks.

Crockett's Pond was located three miles from the school over a little-traveled dirt road. It was moss-covered, over an acre in size, and overgrown with willow and sassafras. It sat fifty yards behind a dilapidated farmhouse that had once been owned by Emory Crockett, but now, was owned by out-of-town relatives who rented the pasture land.

The boys hopped off their bikes in front of the farmhouse and climbed over a barbed wire fence that separated the house from the old barnyard. Wesley and Ernie led the way, bounding through waste-high weeds and blackberry briars, holding their rod and reels and coffee cans of worms above the bramble.

A briar nailed Wesley. "Ouch!" He glanced down instantly and saw a dark-colored snake fall from his right leg and slither into the underbrush. He was stunned in disbelief. *Was it really a snake? Did it bite me?* Then his leg felt as if it had been scorched with a match.

Ernie looked over his shoulder and saw Wesley bent over. "What's wrong?"

"I think a snake bit me."

Ernie rushed over to Wesley. "Where'd it bite you?"

"On my leg." Wesley pulled up the leg of his new jeans exposing two red puncture marks with bruising around them.

"That looks just like what Mrs. Hansen showed us on the blackboard. Did you see what kind of snake it was?"

"I couldn't tell. It looked dark brown, but I don't think it was a copperhead."

"I'll bet it was a cottonmouth. My dad told me to watch out for them."

Willie caught up with them. "What happened?"

"A snake bit Wesley—we think it was a cottonmouth. Look at the holes in his leg," Willie said.

Willie moved in for closer inspection. "That sure enough looks like a snakebite . . . look how puffed up it's getting. We better put a tourniquet on it and get some help."

Ernie pulled out his pocket knife. "Has anybody got any matches? We need to sterilize the knife and cut some "Xs" on the bite.

Willie, a grapevine smoker, pulled out a box of matches and handed them over. "Somebody's got to suck out the poison; I can't because I have cavities."

"I'll do it, then," Ernie said. "I don't have any. Willie you go get help."

In C-Hall at the state pen, a stooped old inmate who served as a "trustee" and pushed the library/mail cart stopped in front of Ray's cell and announced that he had a letter for Ray. The trustee examined the return address and said, "Looks like another one from Mrs. O'Dell." He flipped the envelope through the bars and it sailed in front of Ray's bunk and landed on the floor.

Not pausing for a reply, he plodded forward calling out, "Library man. Off your cots, I'm not waiting." Further down the row an inmate yelled, "Aw shut the hell up, library man, or I'll stick one of those books up your ass."

Ray picked up the envelope, which had been previously opened by prison personnel, and shook out the letter. A newspaper clipping fell out. He grabbed it and began reading.

Local Boy Suffers Snakebite

A Tremont boy was admitted to the hospital in Pine Grove Tuesday after apparently being bitten by a water moccasin. Wesley Sanders and two schoolmates were fishing at a rural pond after the end-of-term picnic at Tremont School when it happened.

The boys administered first aid, which they learned in school, and then summoned help. The victim was rushed by automobile to Dr. Benton's office in Pine Grove within two hours.

Dr. Benton said, "The boy was obviously bitten by a poisonous snake. Given the location (near a pond), I suspect it was a cottonmouth."

When interviewed the next day, young Mr. Sanders was resting comfortably and reading a book, "The Melted Coins," which had been given to him by a friend of the family, Sam Rockford of Ridgeview.

Young Sanders was released later that day and is expected to make a full recovery.

Ray wadded the clipping and threw it to the floor. "Dammit!"

"What's got you so ticked off?" Elvin asked.

Ray pointed at the clipping on the floor. "That."

Elvin got off his bunk, unfolded the crumpled newsprint, and began reading it.

Ray unfolded Beulah's letter.

June 14, 1958

Dear Son,

I hope this letter finds you well as can be expected under the circumstances. Just keep faith knowing that it is only a few more months until you get out. I would like for you to visit, of course, but Dad is against it. I think he fears you might get in more trouble.

We had quite a scare when Wesley was snake bit. He's OK, but some mornings he wakes up and will have an eye or his lip all swollen. I expect that the poison is working its way out. We didn't know how we were going to pay the hospital bill. It was $40. But that Sam Rockford paid it.

Maybe even he has a good side. I never thought I would say that.

We've already got tomatoes. Wish I could send you some.

Take care,
Mom

Ray wanted to cry, but had learned early on that it wasn't smart to cry in prison. He had watched a smallish, fearful man crying after being slapped around and ridiculed by a bully. Afterwards, the man was like a new chicken in a hen house—everyone began pecking at him. Unconsciously, Ray began shredding Beulah's letter into strips.

Elvin watched with a sarcastic smile. "This here newspaper story makes it look like Rockford's trying to be your boy's daddy, don't it?"

"Why don't you just shut up?" Ray said. The soft weakness he had felt in his stomach hardened, and his fists clinched.

"Now, no need to get all het up," Elvin said, "I just meant that Rockford's trying to move in, just like we been saying, and that he needs to be taught a lesson—that's all. Taking a man's woman is one thing, but trying to steal a man's son, now, it doesn't get any lower."

"That's not all he's trying to steal."

"What are you talking about?"

"My mother-in-law. We've always been like mother and son."

"How's that?" Elvin asked.

"In this letter," Ray said, nodding at the torn pieces of paper, "she says she didn't know how they were going to pay the hospital bill, and that Rockford paid it. Now, she thinks he's a hero. And if you read between the lines, she doesn't

232

want me to visit her when I get out. I can't believe that . . . it has to be because she is so hard-up for money."

"You're probably right," Elvin said, "but it might work out that when we take care of Rockford, you can get her some money, too. You'll need a gun."

"Where's an ex-con like me going to get a gun? Anyway, I wouldn't want to shoot him."

"There's ways of getting a gun, but maybe a paperhanger like you doesn't have enough ass in his pants to do a job like this."

"Yeah, maybe so, but the plan we been talking about has a lot of holes in it, and unless it's a lead pipe cinch, I'm not interested in a round-trip ticket back here . . . or worse."

Elvin seemed to ponder Ray's response, but then grinned as if he had answers that would never occur to Ray. "I haven't told you everything, and I still haven't heard back from my brother."

"The one who was in on the poker game stick-up?"

"No, my older brother, Enoch. Lives near my parents. He logs, hunts, and makes a little hooch. I expect to hear back from him shortly, saying he's coming for a visit."

A few days after Enoch's visit, Ray answered Beulah's letter.

July 18, 1958

Dear Mom,

I got your letter and was glad to hear from you. I guess that I won't be coming to visit for awhile when I get out. There's a fellow up north who says he'll give me work in his warehouse until I can get a job driving. That's what I want to do. As soon as I get a little money saved up, I'll try to send you some. Tell Wesley that I'm glad he is OK.

Love,

Ray

Ray's last night in prison, he barely slept. His mind prowled like a cat and kept reviewing the plan he and Elvin had concocted. During the planning it seemed so fool-proof, but in the pre-dawn darkness, Ray was not so sure.

By the time the guards started rousting prisoners that morning, Elvin was up, too. "Ray, don't worry, it'll work. You just make sure you're at the Highway 17 bridge tomorrow at dusk. Otherwise, he'll be there the next night. He'll only come for two nights; then all bets are off. If you get there early, hide out in the woods upstream of the bridge. He's got a '41 Chevy flatbed with a dark green cab and stock racks."

"I'll be there, but what if someone sees me hiding out?" Ray said.

"Just make sure you hide good."

"I mean later—after your brother picks me up. Four days is a long time to hide."

"Don't worry. Enoch knows places in them woods no one else does. Besides, they would just think you were hunting."

Shavetail ushered Ray through his out-processing. Ray exchanged his uniform for a suit of clothes from the prison tailor shop and received a train ticket to Rock Island and his wallet with the forty-five dollars that Speedo had originally taken from him.

Tugging at the lapel and admiring himself in the new suit, Ray said, "Guess I'm ready to go."

"Not yet, you ain't. You have to have your exit-interview," Shavetail said.

A few moments later, an assistant warden lectured Ray about staying on the *straight and narrow* and how it was a short road back to prison for those who didn't.

After they left the assistant warden's office, Shavetail said, "I'll be seeing you to the train station to make sure you get on that train. There's a local law that says ex-cons have to be out of town before sundown. It's only a few blocks away."

With Shavetail a step behind him, Ray stepped through the prison gate on a muggy September morning, his possessions in a brown paper bag, once again a free man. No probation. No parole. He'd done every day of his sentence, including the tagged-on ". . . and a day." Unlike in the movies Ray had seen, no one waited at the gate to greet him.

Outside the walls he suddenly felt nervous and unstable, as if parts of him were about to come loose and fly away. He saw that his hands were shaking and put his free hand in his pants pocket. He tried to whistle. His mouth was dry, but he continued blowing through his puckered lips, making a sound like a distant train whistle.

A voice in his head said, "What are you afraid of?" *Did I say that?* "You better get hold of yourself, old boy," Ray whispered.

Shavetail stayed several feet behind Ray.

A half-block away a woman walked hand in hand with a curly-haired little girl. As they approached, Ray's eyes met the woman's, and he started to speak, but the woman jerked the little girl's arm and hastened across the street. Ray's momentary joy at seeing the child crawled away, and the lowly, uncertain feeling returned.

They arrived at the station thirty minutes before the train was scheduled to depart at 1 p.m. Looking bored, Shavetail took a seat and began reading an advertising circular that had been left on the bench.

Ray's jitters made him crave a cigarette. Looking at Shavetail, he said, "Officer, I'm going to buy some smokes over there." Ray pointed to a cart vendor across the room.

"Go ahead, but I'll have my eye on you."

Ray bought a pack of Camels, three Hershey bars, and a *St. Louis Globe Democrat* newspaper and sat down at a bench across from Shave Tail so he could see out the window.

He lit up, took a deep inhale, and gazed at the cars and people outside. The cigarette made him dizzy and more nervous so he stubbed it out, stood up, and began pacing the room, always looking outside.

Ray heard the train approaching from the west and looked over at the clock on the station wall. *Thirty minutes goes by quickly when you're free,* he thought.

Without a word to Shavetail, Ray boarded the train and settled on a cushioned seat next to a window. As the train began moving, he could see Shavetail making his way back toward the prison. Farther in the background, he once again saw the statue peeing on the Capitol dome; this time he smiled. His nervousness passed, and he felt the euphoria of a long haul finished. He shut his eyes and dozed until the porter asked him for his ticket.

He was scheduled to change trains in St. Louis, but he had no intention of taking the second leg to Illinois, at least, not yet. He would save the ticket in case he needed it later.

Rita had spent Sunday night with Sam in Ridgeview, and on Monday morning they were in the Buick headed to Birch View. Sam had one hand on the steering wheel and the other wrapped around a pork and beans can that he had cleaned to use as a portable coffee cup. He took a mouthful of the lukewarm sludge that he had warmed from yesterday's pot. "Ah, that's better than good whiskey."

"How can you drink that stuff?" Rita said. "It's disgusting."

"In the navy you learned to drink strong coffee when you had to keep the late watch, and—"

"But, you're not in the navy now—you're a civilian—so why don't you drink civilized coffee?"

"I like coffee with some *beans* in it."

"Oh, never mind . . . I think you're full of *beans.*"

Sam looked out the window and started whistling "Anchors Away." Rita rolled her eyes and stared out the side window.

Sam quit whistling and glanced over at her. "Rita."

"What?"

"Speedo told J. Bob that Ray is getting out of prison today."

Attempting nonchalance, Rita said, "I knew it would be soon. A few weeks ago, my mother mentioned that he wrote her and said he was going to a job up north."

"Why didn't you tell me?"

Rita paused before answering. "I guess I didn't want to think about it. I have been afraid that he would come back here and do something crazy."

"Like what?"

"I don't know . . . possibly try to get even or something. After the divorce he said as far as he was concerned, I was still his wife."

In measured words Sam said, "If he knows what's good for him, he'll stay away."

"I don't think he would try to hurt Wesley or me. I've been more afraid that he might come after you."

"Don't worry, I can take care of myself."

"You've never seen him drunk, and if he got hold of a gun, who knows what he might try." Rita turned her head, looking out the side window.

"Well, Rita, if he comes looking for trouble, he may get more than he expected. I've got guns, too. What was it they said in the old west? Shoot first and ask questions later."

"Sam, I don't want to talk about this any longer."

"Rita, you ought to be glad you've got a good man like me that will protect you, and instead you dismiss me like I'm out of order."

"Sam, I don't to want fight. I'd just rather talk about something else."

237

Realizing they were on the brink of a fight that he didn't want either, Sam said, "All right, what do you want to talk about?"

"Let's talk about Eva and J. Bob's party."

"What's to talk about? We got the word out, and there should be a lot of folks showing up Saturday. We're going to have food set up in the back room; otherwise, it's business as usual."

"I know," Rita said. She edged closer to Sam and stroked the side of his face with her hand. "You missed a spot shaving . . . but, maybe, we could put up some decorations to make it like a real party. How about that?" She stopped stoking his face and began rubbing his neck.

The tension in his face relaxed. "Good old J. Bob. It still seems strange that he's getting married. If you want to decorate, I don't care."

When the train stopped at the Kirkwood station in the suburbs of St. Louis, Ray got off. The station was located a half block from U.S. Highway 67, which would intersect with U.S. Route 66 a couple miles south. From there he would thumb a ride to Rolla and hitch his way south on U.S. Highway 63 to Missouri 17. But for now, Ray had just one thing on his mind: a room for the night and a bottle.

The next morning he came to from a drunken sleep, thinking he was still in prison. In his undershirt and shorts, he sat on the edge of the bed and looked around the room trying to piece together the previous night. Wrappers from a couple hamburgers. Two empty Coke bottles. A mostly empty whiskey bottle—*just a pint . . . I guess I can't drink like I used to.*

His mouth tasted like stale onions. He picked up the glass from the floor, filled it half full of water, and poured in the rest of the whiskey. He took a drink, paused, and when it stayed down, he finished off the remainder in two swallows.

He made the growling sound of a roaring lion. "By God, I may live. Smiling Ray needs a toothbrush."

After ham and eggs at a diner, Ray stopped at a grocery store, salvaged a cardboard box, and borrowed a grease pencil from the butcher to make a sign: Trucker Headed To Rolla.

With his suit coat draped over his shoulder, and his shirt sleeves rolled to his elbows, he hoofed it to the intersection of Route 66 and Highway 67. He was there less than ten minutes when a tractor-tailor rig slowed to a stop.

The driver, a beefy man with stocky, tattooed forearms, leaned out the curbside window and motioned for Ray to come over. "Are you really a trucker?"

Ray gave his best smile. "Yes, I am. I've got to get to Rolla to pick up a load. There's no bus out until midnight and I thought I could hitch and be there by then. I'd sure appreciate a lift."

"Let me see your chauffeur's license."

Ray pulled it from his wallet and handed it to him.

The driver pulled his green-shaded sunglasses down on his nose and examined the license. "Iowa. This is going to expire in a little over a month."

"Yeah, I've been a little tied up lately, but I'll get it renewed."

The driver said, "I don't usually stop to pick up hitchers. It's strictly against company regulations, but since you're a trucker, I might make an exception. I've been up for eighteen hours, I'm dog-tired, and I've got to get to Springfield today. If you could drive this beast to Rolla and let me catch some sleep, I'll take a chance."

"You've got a deal."

"Get in behind the wheel so I can check you out."

Ray stepped up into the cab and the aroma inside was perfume to his senses. The mixture of diesel fumes and stale cigarette smoke evoked memories of his last truck.

The trucker extended his hand and said, "I'm Loren Miller. What's your name?"

"Ray Sanders."

"Well, let's get rolling, Ray."

Ray put his hand on the gearshift knob and engaged the clutch as easily as one would put on a comfortable old shoe. He checked for oncoming traffic in the side mirror and eased the rig on to the highway.

Ray went through the series of shifts, double-clutching each one without a jerk or grind and in a moment was cruising at forty-five miles an hour.

"Ray, you're a professional driver all right, but you haven't been driving much lately, have you?"

"What do you mean?"

"Well, unless you drive with your window closed, you haven't been in a truck cab lately or your left arm wouldn't be so white."

"Well, if the truth be known, Loren," I got highjacked by some Mexicans on a run to El Paso and had some trouble with my company. It wasn't my fault, and had nothing to do with my driving, but it's straightened out now."

"Well, you seem like a decent sort. You know how to get to Rolla?"

"Yeah, I know." Ray looked over and Loren had already closed his eyes.

Ray turned off Route 66 at the intersection with Highway 63 and pulled into the Mule Barn Truck Stop. "We're at Rolla."

Loren opened his eyes and looked at his watch. "Three o'clock—too early for supper—could I buy you a cup of coffee?"

"I wouldn't mind that at all, Loren."

After coffee and pie, the men shook hands and wished each other well. Loren drove west and Ray took the shoe leather express south on Highway 63.

At the outskirts of town, Ray stopped at a farm store and bought a pair of bib overalls. It had been Elvin's idea—to make hitchhiking easier south of Rolla. Ray changed in the feed room and headed back to the road.

In spite of a quick succession of rides, progress was slow over the winding, hilly roads that snaked through the pine and hardwood forests of the Ozarks. Ray feared he would miss the connection on the first night and have to sleep in the woods, but the last farmer who gave him a lift turned off Highway 17 only a couple of miles north of the bridge, still an hour before sundown. Even so, Ray noticed that it was already becoming shadowy in the valleys.

He trudged the final miles, scrambling to the woods with the sound of each approaching car, until he reached the steep decline of the river valley and saw the Jack's Fork Bridge. The overhead structure of the steel bridge below reflected the last rays of sunlight from over the hills. It spanned a hundred yards between limestone bluffs on one side and gorge on the other.

The Jack's Fork River below, a spring-fed stream of intermittent rapids and deep swimming holes, meandered through some of the most remote parts of the Ozarks Mountains. It was navigable only by canoe or johnboat.

Ray slid and stumbled his way down a steep path to the river's edge and grabbed a willow sapling to keep from tumbling face-first on a ledge at the bottom. After he secured his footing, he looked around and saw no floaters or fishermen. He sat on a rock outcropping and ate one of his Hershey bars.

As the darkness increased, the natural sounds of the river got louder and added to Ray's growing feeling of uneasiness. The rapids became waterfalls; the frogs were foghorns; and the locusts, grating in unison, were an annoying chorus in the background. Ray swatted at the whirring mosquitoes that swarmed around him, hoping that Elvin's brother would arrive soon.

Within the hour, the sound of a truck engine echoed in the river valley as the driver down-shifted to slow its speed on the steep highway. Ray's hopes were realized when he saw a truck pull onto a narrow access road on the other side and stop on the gravel bar at the bottom.

In the back glow from the headlights, Ray could tell it was an older flatbed with racks. Ray called across, "Collier, is that you?"

"Who wants to know?" a voice called back.

Hesitant to use his own name, Ray yelled, "A friend of your brother's."

"Sanders?"

"That's right."

"Well, get your ass over here. There's no place to turn around for a mile on the other side."

Ray climbed and crawled back to the highway and met his contact on the other side of the bridge. He opened the passenger door of the truck. The features of the gaunt man behind the wheel were dimly visible in the ambient light from the dashboard. His face was angular and bearded—a heavy, unintentional scruffy beard that resulted from a week without shaving. He smelled of cigarettes and sweat that had soured.

Ray said, "You must be Enoch," and started to step in.

"Now, just wait a minute," the man said. "Elvin said there was fifty dollars in this for me if I picked you up. You got the fifty dollars?"

"Not yet I don't. You'll have to wait, but you'll get it."

"You better make sure I do, because I know where you'll be staying. And another thing, it'll be ten dollars a day for the horse, and if I don't get my horse back, it'll be an extra hundred."

242

"Horse?"

"Yeah, the horse in back there. What's the matter—don't you see good?"

"What's a horse got to do with anything?"

"Where you're going to be staying, unless you want to walk, the only way to get around is with a logging horse or a mule. If you had one of my mules, it'd be five hundred dollars."

Ray got in and closed the door.

Enoch let out the clutch and the truck lugged forward up the steep incline.

Ray's feeling of adventure had waned. He felt tired and hungry and was filled with doubt. "Where is this place I'm going to be staying?"

Enoch bit off a hunk of chewing tobacco and put the remainder in the front pocket of his bib overalls. "It's a cabin down river near a place the old-timers called Rock Ridge. Nobody goes there anymore. It's on a strip of land my daddy bought at a tax sale years ago. It backs up to a thousand acres owned by some fellow out of St. Louis. We *grandma*—you know, *borrow*—a few logs off his property . . . he don't seem to mind—he never said anything." Enoch started laughing. It was a snorting laugh that came out in spurts.

After thirty minutes driving on blacktop, and intermittent spitting, Enoch turned on a gravel road and headed back north. Ray soon lost all sense of direction as the truck kept turning on smaller roads until finally they drove across a pasture and onto a rocky trail.

Enoch shifted into low gear and the engine revved as they descended a steep hill. The truck cleared protruding boulders that would have *high-centered* a pickup. Limbs from undergrowth scraped the sides of the cab and made screeching sounds. One slapped Ray on the side of his face. "Ouch!"

Enoch glanced over at Ray. "You best get used to the brush." He slowed the truck to a stop at the edge of a rippling creek. "Here's where we get out."

Enoch led the horse down a boarding plank that had half-inch slats running crosswise to provide footing. "This here's Brownie. She's as sure-footed as a goat. I got some feed in that tow-sack," he said, pointing at the truck bed. "Only give her two coffee cans a day—I don't want her foundering. A mule won't founder, but a horse will eat grain until it blows up. There's enough grass behind the cabin she can graze."

Brownie looked like a plow horse to Ray. "You got a saddle for her?"

Enoch contorted his face, and in the glow of a single red taillight, he looked like a gargoyle. "Saddle? You fixing to go to a rodeo? You need a saddle like a hog needs a sidesaddle. She knows these log trails so well she can bring you back to the cabin at night and never lose her footing. She'll always come back to where she was fed last."

Ray nodded and bit the inside of his lip. He was tired, hungry, and irritable, but he exercised his prison-learned patience. "I just wondered, that's all."

"In this other tow sack, I got you some supplies. Hey, do you have any money at all?"

Ray took a step back, ready to defend himself if necessary. "Yeah, I've got a little."

"Well, why don't you give me twenty dollars. That's ten for the supplies and ten for the first day for the horse."

"What kind of supplies?"

"I got you some coffee, a hunk of cured ham, a sack of beans, and some light bread. There's a lantern and a stove in the cabin. And I got you a twenty-two rifle and a box of shells—you might shoot a squirrel. You lose that rifle, and it'll cost you fifty dollars; it's a twelve-shot pump-action."

"I thought you were going to have a pistol for me."

244

"I don't know anything about that. If you don't want it, it's no sweat off by back," Enoch said.

"I'll take it," Ray said.

Enoch retrieved a kerosene lantern from the truck bed, struck a match, and lit it. With greater illumination, Enoch was still uncouth. He wasn't any taller than five-eight, but had a decidedly hard, mean look about him. Cleaned up, he would blend easily with the prison population.

"Tell you what, Enoch, I'll give you twenty dollars, but that'll be ten dollars for supplies and ten dollars for two day's rent of Brownie. I don't expect I'll be using her that much. And where the hell am I?"

"I'll take the twenty, but just remember, I know where you're staying. And I already told you, you're on Rock Ridge. This is still the Jack's Fork. By roads you're about five miles from Birch View. By the way the crow flies, over animal trails and log roads, you're only about three miles. I drew you a map."

A wet sputtering sound came from Enoch's lips as he spat tobacco juice on the ground. He wiped his mouth on his shirtsleeve, reached in his breast pocket, and pulled out a folded piece of tablet paper and spread it out on the truck bed next to the lantern. "Here's where you are now. This trail crosses the creek and if you follow it . . . . "

The map was crude, but understandable, including the destination. It ended in the woods across the highway from Club 60.

Enoch tied the two burlap sacks together and draped them over Brownie's withers. He raised the glass globe of the lantern and blew it out. "Get on Brownie, and I'll hand you the lantern and the rifle. Keep that hot lantern away from her or you'll end up on your ass. When I back the truck up, the headlights will shine on the river so you can cross. I got to go—I'm wasting time."

As Brownie plodded up the brush-covered rocky path, limbs slapped at Ray's face. He seemed to be going up a draw between two bluffs, but even with the beam of light from the truck, it was difficult to tell. He looked straight up at the sky, and the stars were brilliant and huge. He knew from his planning, there wouldn't be much of a moon.

He heard Enoch pulling away, just as he came to a clearing. His eyes had adjusted enough to make out the cabin. He got off Brownie, tethered her to a bush, and lit the lantern.

The cabin appeared to be a one-room shack with wooden shingles and two windows on either side of a center door. Ray checked the breach of the rifle—it was loaded. He hoisted the sacks over his shoulder and with the rifle in one hand and the lantern in the other marched toward the cabin. Over his shoulder he called, "Brownie, I'll be right back so don't go anywhere."

The door wasn't locked and creaked open on hinges that needed oil. A mouse scurried from the light across the plank floor. The place smelled like a rat's nest. Ray hoped there weren't any snakes inside. He chambered a round in the rifle just in case.

The light from the lantern filled the room with an eerie glow, revealing the sparse amenities. To Ray's right a table crafted from rough-sawn boards and two sawbucks was butted under a front window.

At the back wall a small potbelly stove sat on a base of ledge stone; a cast-iron skillet covered most of the stove top. A tarnished stove pipe vented the potbelly to an old stacked-stone flue that looked to have belonged to an original homestead dwelling. Two shelves on the windowless side wall held a few dishes, pots, and a bucket. A metal wash pan hung from a nail next to the shelves.

To his left an army cot, partially covered with a moth-eaten army blanket, was wedged kitty-corner between the other front window and the side wall, as if someone had positioned it to keep watch over the river.

Ray shook the blanket, and a brown wolf spider landed on the floor and scampered out of the light. "Aw, the hell with it." He spread the blanket over the bed and lay down. He blew out the lantern and lay with his eyes open, aching tired. *This is worse than prison.* Then he remembered Texas. *No, things could be worse.*

Ray awakened in the dawn light from a dream of a beaver chewing on a bass fiddle. As he reminded himself where he was, he realized that the chewing was an actual gnawing sound that seemed to be coming from below his bed—not inside the room, but under the house. He grabbed the rifle and went outside to inspect.

The cabin sat on the lower ledge of a towering bluff under a canopy of sycamore trees and surrounded by river willows and undergrowth. In front, through leaves and limbs, he could see the creek seventy-five yards below, but he doubted that a fisherman could see the cabin. Behind the cabin an overhanging ledge at treetop height formed a shallow cavern.

Ray no longer heard the gnawing, but he heard his own stomach growling and Brownie snorting. No doubt she was hungry, too.

Ray measured a coffee can full of the sweet-smelling feed, dumped it in the bucket, and took it to Brownie. She didn't raise her head out of the bucket until it was licked clean. He patted her on the flank and walked her down the path for a drink.

As Brownie sucked in the stream water, Ray looked up and down the river. He could see for fifty yards in either direction to bends with limestone bluffs on one side and gravel beaches on the other. The water was pristine and shining, reflecting the sun's rays peeking through trees on the ridgeline above. He rinsed the bucket, filled it with creek water, and trudged back to the cabin.

Inside, he rummaged through the burlap bag of supplies and found a sack of brown beans and dumped them in the bucket. Thinking that he couldn't cook until after dark, he decided to let the beans soak in water all day. If he could find a wild onion, he'd throw it in with a hunk of ham and simmer the beans over a slow fire that night. He was famished and could almost taste them already.

Ray spent the next couple of days exploring and riding, orienting himself with the map. Enoch had been right; Brownie was surefooted and could manage the unmarked trails without much assistance from him.

On his first day, he discovered a spring in the cave behind the cabin where Enoch made moonshine. He also uncovered some of Enoch's work product in a crock jug that proved to be drinkable when mixed with spring water.

It seemed to Ray that living alone in the woods made his senses keen. He imagined it was like being behind enemy lines during the war, living off the land, fording the stream at night, and reconnoitering the enemy.

On the second night he watched Sam leave Club 60 around ten o'clock.

Chapter Twenty-one

Showdown

On Saturday night J. Bob picked up Eva and headed to their party. As they approached Club 60, J. Bob began braking the Ford. "Eva, will you look at that? There must be fifty cars parked. Well, I'll be; there's Speedo's car. Now, that's a site—a sheriff's car in front of a honky-tonk on Saturday night. He'll keep things from getting too rowdy."

"You know, James, I've never—"

"Eva, you're the only one who uses my given name. Everybody else, except my mother, calls me J. Bob."

"Well, I'm not *everybody else*. We're engaged and I want to refer to you in a way that's special to me."

"Then it's special to me, too. Maybe I should have a special name for you." J. Bob paused. "How about *Evangeline?*"

"James, you're impossible."

"Look," J. Bob said, "they reserved a parking place for us." He pointed to a cardboard sign: Reserved for Eva and J. Bob.

Across the highway, Ray watched from his hiding place in the brush. *This could be quite a reunion,* Ray thought. *First the sheriff that took me to prison shows up, and now Rita's lawyer and her smartass girlfriend.*

By half-past midnight only two cars remained in the Club 60 parking lot: the Ford Ray used to own and Rockford's Buick.

The exterior neon lights went out, and Sam and Rita stepped out the front door, silhouetted against the light from the pinball machine and beer signs inside the tavern.

249

When they got to the Ford, Rita turned and faced Sam. On tiptoes she met his lips, threw both arms around his neck, and her body closed with his.

Ray moaned and jerked his head toward the rifle lying on the ground. *I ought to shoot that son of a bitch now and be done with it.* But his eyes again fixed on Rita and Sam. What he saw was less than he had imagined while in prison, but the actual sight of them together spiked his anger. He reached into the burlap sack at his feet, pulled out the Mason jar, and gulped a swallow of the moonshine and then another.

Rita drove away and Sam went back inside. Shortly after, the tavern light went out. It was just as Elvin had said; Rockford was going to sleep there with the till.

Ray waited until he was sure Sam was not coming back out and then sprinted across the highway to the right of the parking lot and dove in the weeds. He tried to brace his fall with the butt of the rifle, but the stock went sideways, and he landed hard on his stomach. Booze rushed up the back of his throat and burned a path out his nose. Ray struggled to his knees, coughing, and trying to breath.

When Ray caught his breath, he low-crawled through the weeds until he was behind the tavern. He stood up and could see Sam through a lighted window spreading a blanket on a cot.

Thoughts blurred through Ray's mind so quickly that they sounded like gibberish. From the mental din, one voice kept surfacing louder than the others—Elvin's sneering taunts. *He's sleeping with your woman and probably raising your kid to hate you . . . but maybe a paperhanger doesn't have enough ass in his pants for a job like this.*

Ray bent to a crouch and advanced toward the building. His hands shook as he wiped the sweat that was dripping into his eyes. His sweat had a musky smell and his mouth had gone dry. Ray pumped a round into the chamber.

Chappy started barking. Ray froze. Chappy was now howling. *Paperhanger doesn't have enough ass . . . .*

Ray shifted the rifle to port and moved into the light cast from the window. Inside, Sam stood motionless with a revolver pointed directly at the window. Their eyes locked on each other. Sam's faced showed recognition but no fear.

Ray darted out of the light and slammed himself against the side of the building. A shot from inside exploded and shattered the window. The light inside went out. Chappy was going crazy.

Ray's mind, which had been so cluttered with thoughts, was now focused only on escaping. He bolted past the outhouses through the brush behind the tavern, hoping to make it to the woods beyond. No going back to the front— he'd be shot for sure.

Brush and briars whipped his face as he ran in the darkness, dodging low-hanging limbs, until after fifty yards, he tripped over a trampled-down barbed wire fence and stumbled face-first into a trickling branch-run. He lay there panting and felt sick as a poisoned dog, with no strength to go forward.

Ray's next awareness were men's voices and a hound warbling from behind the tavern.

"Speedo, over there's where he went through the brush," Sam said, pointing his flashlight. He redirected the beam. "And look over there where Chappy is sniffing. He must have been lying in wait there."

Speedo inspected the spot with his own flashlight. "Looks like he took a piss while he was waiting. Can your dog follow a trail?"

Sam snatched the hound by the scruff of his neck and pointed him southward. "Come on, Chappy, follow that scent."

"Take it easy, Sam. He could be waiting to ambush us." Looking toward the direction of the getaway, Speedo yelled,

"Sanders, this is Sheriff Green. If you're out there, give yourself up before you get in more trouble."

Ray forced himself to all-fours. *The rifle. Where was the rifle?* He felt around with an outstretched hand until he found it half-submerged in muck.

His senses were now fully alert. He could hear the sheriff behind him, but he also heard another sound coming from the east: a train, and it was coming closer and slowing as it headed toward town. Ray scrambled up an embankment and fled toward the sound.

As the train passed, Ray hunkered in the brush at the edge of the track waiting for anything to grab on to. There it was—a wide open box car. He sprang from his cover, threw the rifle in the boxcar, and pulled himself up.

Onboard and breathless, he looked around, but it was too dark to tell if the car was empty. "Anybody here?"

A voice from the rear said, "Just another 'bo."

Sam and Speedo gave up the chase at the railroad tracks and returned to the tavern, where Sam poured them each a shot of Jim Beam.

Sipping his whiskey, Speedo said, "Sam, so you're sure it was Sanders?"

"No doubt in my mind."

"Any chance you hit him when you shot through the window?"

"No, he had already dodged to the side when I fired. At that point, I wasn't trying to hit him. I was like a rattlesnake sending a deadly warning."

"Well, I'd say it worked. Was he armed?"

Sam thought for a moment. "I couldn't swear to it, but he must have been; he was standing like a soldier at port-arms. Mostly, I looked at his eyes."

"You might have been better off if you *had* shot him."

"Why do you say that?"

252

"If you'd shot him, you'd at least know where he is now. Even if he didn't have a weapon, the prosecutor could have brought some criminal charge against him and sent him back to the slammer."

"I don't trust Chester Martin. If I had shot Sanders, that bastard Martin would have prosecuted *me*. And there's another issue; it would put me in a hell of a position if I were the one that shot or killed Wesley's father."

Speedo nodded in understanding but did not speak for a moment. "Well, Sam, as I see it, there are only two courses of action: Call the sheriff in Winn County and have him stop the train in case Sanders hopped on it, or try to track him after daylight."

Speedo's face looked skeptical, and Sam said, "But what else, Speedo?"

"Sam, all we have is your statement that you saw some man in the dark for, maybe, two seconds that you claim was Sanders. And you can't say whether or not he was armed. I don't think Chester would bring window-peeping charges with that evidence. And if I stopped a train or got out a posse based on that information, he'd have my ass. He'd have to wake the judge up to get an order signed. You're right, he's a bastard, but I have to work with him."

"Well, what should I do?" Sam asked.

"First, install a damned flood light out back like I've told you and make sure the doors and windows are locked. If you're going to sleep here at night, change the location of your cot and put up some shades. I'll put out an alert with the area law enforcement and have a deputy check your place periodically at night."

"Speedo, I don't expect he will be back, and between you and me, I don't know how much longer I'm going to keep Club 60. I've got other ports that are calling."

Two weeks later, Ray knocked on the door of the little house on Vaquero Street in Fort Worth. The door opened. "Ray, welcome back; I always hoped to see you again," Padre said.

Chapter Twenty-two
Beulah Land

*W*esley coasted full-bore on his bicycle down the hill from the schoolhouse, navigating between the parallel tire ruts etched in the dirt lane. The fall air chilled as it blew underneath his unbuttoned denim jacket. He pedaled backwards to apply the brakes and slowed near the bottom turning right on the gravel road to the farm.

This would be Wesley's last year at the Tremont School. The next year, 1958, it would be absorbed into the Birch View school system. And in something of a truce between Rita and Beulah, Rita acquiesced to allow Wesley to live with Beulah and Will and stay enrolled at the Tremont school until it closed.

It was a fall-back position for Beulah, but, as she saw it, her only move. Beulah expected that Rita would marry Sam, move to Ridgeview, and take Wesley with them. With Ray's whereabouts unknown, her plans for custody and support payments had vanished, and the thought of losing Wesley forever was overwhelming.

Moreover, Rita did not want to pull Wesley away from his teachers and friends and enroll him at Birch View, only to move him again in a year if she and Sam got married.

Wesley had ridden his bike to school that day in order to come straight home because his grandpa was sick and Beulah needed help with chores. The concern on her face had worried Wesley all day. He had seen his grandma upset before, but never afraid.

He leaned over the handle bars and pumped furiously until his wind gave out a quarter-mile later as he passed the old Webster place. No matter what, Wesley always stared up the tree-lined way to the hilltop house. It was fronted with a double-deck porch, and sat on who-knows-how-many acres. It also boasted the best bluegill pond in the county, according to his grandpa.

With a half-mile to go, he leaned left and banked the curve at Railroad Hill trying to get a run at it. Cruising out of the curve, he stood up to pedal. It was a mark of accomplishment and local status if a boy could pump Railroad Hill without getting off to walk his bike.

Just before the crest his legs ached and he was short of breath. Over the summit he saw a dust cloud from an approaching car or truck. Probably a car he thought—too quiet for a truck—but it was coming fast. He hopped off his bike and walked it to the top.

A hundred yards away, he could tell it was Sam's Buick. Sam was driving and his grandpa was on the passenger's side.

The car slowed and stopped next to Wesley. Will looked half asleep, slumped on the passenger's side with his head drooped and his chin resting on his chest.

Sam rolled down the window. "I'm taking your grandpa to the doctor's. You need to get home and help your grandma."

Wesley peered past Sam at Will. Fear sucked at his gut. "Hi, Grandpa," he said tentatively.

Will looked over with a tight-lipped smile and raised his stub. It was simply a lame recognition of Wesley's presence. It wasn't his normal gesture. It wasn't the stub that when armored with a mechanical hook could still, at his age, hoist a seventy-pound oat bale. It was the stub of a marionette whose string had gone slack as Will let it fall back to the car seat. His right arm was braced against the seat as if it were propping him upright.

Sam began rolling up the window and with a hard look, said, "We've got to go. Get on home, Wesley." Wesley moved back, and Sam eased his car forward.

With a sinking feeling still in his stomach, Wesley watched as the Buick went down Railroad Hill and around the curve. Before his next conscious thought, he was back on his bike speeding home.

He barely slowed as he turned onto the driveway and skidded next to the house. He threw his right leg over the mid-section of the frame and hopped off, pony express-style, letting his bike fall to the ground.

Rushing through the kitchen door, he found Beulah and his mom sitting at the table with cups of coffee between them. "Is Grandpa going to be—" He stopped mid-sentence. His mother was smoking a cigarette . . . but so was his grandma.

His bewildered stare was not lost on either woman. Beulah glanced at him and then back at her coffee cup, as if she had been caught in a worldly act by the preacher.

Rita returned his stare and held it. "Wesley, I gave your grandma a cigarette to help calm her nerves, so don't get excited. She used to smoke during the war when Grandpa and I worked late shifts."

"Is he going to be OK?" Wesley asked.

"Well, we hope so," Rita said. "He may have that Asian flu that's going around. His cough and fever got worse today, and we're afraid it might go into pneumonia."

Beulah added, "He nearly died when he got pneumonia when you were a baby. So when Fred Morgan delivered feed this morning, I asked him to call your mother so she could take him to Doc Benton in Pine Grove."

Wesley sat on a three-legged stool milking Bessie, while Beulah bucked a bale of hay from the hayloft to feed calves in the barnyard.

Will usually fed the calves, and when Wesley had volunteered to do it, Beulah had said, "You start the milking; I'll do my husband's job."

257

With the smell of milk, three panhandling barn cats showed up at the door meowing for a handout. Normally, Wesley would have pointed a teat in their direction and squirted them from six feet away to watch them bite at the stream of milk. Today, he paid little mind to the cats.

Halfway through his milking duties, Beulah nudged Wesley on the shoulder. "Let me finish up here; you won't be able to get the last milk stripped out. Go to the henhouse and get some eggs for supper."

The ammonia smell of the chicken house always burned Wesley's nose; gathering eggs was a chore he rushed through. Even so, by the time he finished and darted out, he saw his grandmother trudging toward the house.

With her left arm extended to counter balance the nearly full three-gallon bucket, she swayed from left to right with each step. Wesley thought of bandy-legged old Mr. Webster, who wobbled when he walked.

When Wesley got back to the house, his mother was at the stove frying bacon in a cast-iron skillet, and Beulah was sitting at the kitchen table looking exhausted and breathing short, shallow breaths.

"Grandma, you shouldn't have gotten the hay out of the loft," Wesley said.

Rita jerked her head toward Wesley. "You let your grandma go up in the barn loft?"

"Oh, you two dry up," Beulah said. "I'll be fine as soon as I catch my breath."

Wesley said nothing more, but his plaintive expression protested innocence. Rita's face softened. "Did you get enough eggs for supper?"

"I got ten," Wesley said.

"Good, that'll be enough. Sam can eat three by himself, and maybe Dad will feel like eating something."

"I hear a car," Wesley said.

"That'll be them," Beulah said and went to the door and opened it. "Will's not with him." She rushed out and met Sam as he was getting out of the car.

Rita and Wesley followed close behind.

"The doc put him in the hospital," Sam said. "Will was dehydrated from the nausea and needed to have intravenous fluids."

"I need to be with him," Beulah said.

"The doc said no visitors until tomorrow, and then, no one under twelve," Sam said, glancing at Wesley.

As they ate dinner, Beulah pressed Sam for details concerning Will's condition. What exactly had the doctor said? Did he have a nurse or a nun attending him? Beulah didn't like the fact that the hospital had nuns working there who knelt and prayed in front of a statue of Mary, which Beulah thought was idol worship.

Sam stopped chewing and said, "You know Beulah, I share your concern, because when Wesley was in there, they made him wear a pendent of the Apostle Paul around his neck because Paul was the patron saint of snakebite victims."

Beulah's mouth dropped open, suddenly speechless, and her eyes gaped wide. "Wesley never—"

"No they didn't, Grandma," Wesley said.

Rita burst into laughter.

Sam swallowed and started laughing, too. The contagion spread to Wesley, who joined in the mirth. A guilty grin came to Beulah's face as if she had heard a recording of her voice and didn't much like the sound.

The laughter settled and the conversation around the table gradually got smaller. Sam, the last to finish eating, wiped his mouth with a napkin, pushed his chair back a tad, and shook a cigarette from his pack of Chesterfields.

Rita lit up one and extended the pack to her mother.

"Oh, no thanks," Beulah said, "I don't want to get started again. It was too hard quitting. To this day when someone lights up, I still want one."

"You're right about that, Beulah," Sam said, as he took a full-breath inhale. "It's a disgusting, filthy habit." Sam tilted his head upward and exhaled a cloud of smoke and resumed talking.

"Beulah, tell me how Will lost his hand. Rita says he never talks about it. He reminds me of men coming back from the war who never talk about their experiences. Is it too painful for him to broach?"

Beulah's face waned and her eyes adjusted upward as she seemed to recall other dark days. She released a long sigh and uttered, "We've been through a lot together."

"Mama, go ahead and tell them," Rita said.

Beulah began. "Well, Rita had just turned six and we were living near the oil fields at Gladewater, Texas. Will and his brother-in-law, Irvin Duffer, had a blacksmith shop. They shoed horses on one side, and on the other side, they made trailers and hammered out 'fishtail' bits for drills."

"What kind of trailers did they make?" Sam asked.

"They made trailers to haul pipes and equipment to rigs in the oil fields."

Beulah paused and took a sip of coffee before resuming her story. "One of their metal-cutting machines had a part missing, and they needed go to Dallas to replace it. It was over a hundred miles to Dallas, and they were so busy they kept putting off the trip and using the older machine.

"That older machine didn't have a safety guard. Will always said, 'somebody is going to get hurt, and hurt bad.' It turned out to be him."

"He was operating the old machine when the rotating cutter caught his sleeve and jerked his left hand into the teeth. By the time he hit the trip switch the contraption had chewed his hand up.

260

"When it finally stopped, his arm had been cut off six inches up from his wrist. Blood was spurting from the severed arteries. The bone had been pulverized. All that was left hanging was shredded skin and sinew."

"Oh my God," Sam said.

Wesley had never heard the details of the accident and looked stunned.

Rita and Beulah exchanged knowing looks, and Beulah continued. "With a presence of mind I cannot fathom today, he took off his belt and strapped it around the stump to staunch the bleeding. Then he walked a block to our little shanty.

"I was outside with Rita and saw him coming up the road. I made Rita go inside and told her to stay, and then I ran to meet him. I knew it was that old machine. When I got to him, tears were streaming down his face and he said, 'Beulah, I've ruined myself.' It was so pitiful."

Beulah took a deep breath and let it out slowly. Her eyes were flooded. She removed her glasses and dabbed her tears with a napkin.

Rita intervened. "I remember him coming up the street and sensed something was wrong, but I didn't know what. He wasn't wearing a shirt; I remember that."

"So, Beulah, what happened next?" Sam asked.

"He had wrapped his shirt around his arm. I pulled the shirt back and it looked like a butchered calf's leg. I nearly fainted. All I said was 'Oh Jesus, Will. We have to get you to the hospital.'"

"Irv was right behind in the truck. He had been at the other end of the shop when he heard Will scream. He ran toward him, and Will yelled at him to get the truck. I was afraid he'd die before we got him to the hospital.

When we arrived, the doctor said Will was in shock and should have been lying down in an ambulance. I thought Irv was going to punch that young doc. Heavens and earth, we did the best we could!" Her eyes filled with tears again.

"Go on, Mama," Rita said, "I think it's good to get some of this out."

Beulah took a deep breath and sighed. "Back then, all the doctor could do was cauterize the stub and pull some skin down and stitch it up. The big fear was infection because they didn't have penicillin then. The pain was just awful. They kept him doped up with morphine, or I don't know how he would have gotten through it."

Beulah paused, and Rita said, "How long was he in the hospital? I just remember when you and Uncle Irvin brought him home."

"He was there most of a week, and then we brought him home. He should have stayed longer, but we didn't know how we would pay for it with Will not working. The doctor showed me how to dress the stub and gave me pain pills to give him—and that's another story—he was getting hooked on them. He kept saying he could still feel his hand."

"Mama," Rita said, ". . . are you going to tell them about that *other thing*?" Her eyes met Beulah's directly.

Beulah's face was drawn and dreadful as if she were being asked to open a door that had been locked years before. She sat silently staring at her coffee cup.

"What thing, Grandma?" Wesley asked.

"Be quiet, Wesley," Sam said, and Wesley eased back in his chair.

Beulah took another swallow of coffee. "Each night around sundown, I'd dress his arm and give him two of the pain pills so he could go to sleep. His sleep was always so fitful; he would sweat through the sheets and moan and talk— you'd swear he was talking to someone.

"I had fixed little Rita a pallet out of quilts on the floor so she could be in the room with us. She was so worried about her daddy.

"One night after they both were asleep, I finally dozed off. I couldn't have been asleep for more than a few minutes when I felt the mattress sink on either side of me. It felt as if someone had leaned over me and pressed down with both hands.

"For some reason it didn't startle me—it just struck me as odd. I opened my eyes and there was Will's sister, Lillie, at the foot of the bed. Lillie had been dead five years."

Wesley's eyes got wide and Sam's narrowed, but neither said anything.

"She was just standing there: a specter, but not like I had imagined a ghost—her form was solid. She had features like an old daguerreotype, gray and charcoal, but her hair was white instead of bleached. Then Lillie, or *it*, said, 'I've come for Will.'

"I tried to speak, but it was as if someone's hand was around my throat and nothing came out. Suddenly, I heard my voice saying, 'You can't have him!' And then little Rita started crying, 'Mama, who's that woman?' And I said, 'It's your aunt, but she's leaving.'

"I wanted to scream at this thing . . . at Lillie, but she looked sad, so I just said in a normal voice, 'Lillie, go on back where you came from,' and she turned around and faded into the wall.

"The next morning Will's fever broke and he was able to sit up and drink some tea . . . and I never saw Lillie again."

Nobody spoke for a moment, and then Sam, weighing his words, said, "Beulah, if someone from the *other side* was making an appearance, why was it Lillie?"

"She was Will's favorite sister. He was heartbroken when she died and was convinced that the guy she married had smothered her with a pillow for the insurance money. She died in Oklahoma, and her husband quickly shipped her body back here on the train. I do believe if the man hadn't left

Tremont the day after the funeral, Will might have killed him."

Beulah's face was less drawn, as if telling the story had been cathartic. She focused on Sam. "Well, there you have it. . . a wild yarn from a crazy old woman." Beulah continued looking directly at Sam with a stare that beckoned a response—an affirmation or a rejection.

Following Beulah's lead, Rita and Wesley looked at Sam, too, as if he was the arbiter of fact and they were waiting on his judgment.

Sam's military bearing and rational mind were clearly being tested, but his poker face gave no hint of his thoughts.

If Rita had told the story, he would have dismissed it outright. But this older woman, seasoned by life, and hesitant to tell the story in the first place, had no reason to try to impress anyone. No, she wasn't crazy, and he knew she didn't give a damn if he believed her or not. She was like a soldier finally reporting the details of an old battle, long suppressed.

The small kitchen was becoming smoke-filled. Although Sam was immune to smoky rooms, he got up, raised the window a smidgen, and cracked open the door.

Still standing, he lit another cigarette and said, "Beulah, on a battlefield soldiers sometimes see phantoms in the shadows, but they are hesitant to report it, so I'm not shocked at your story. But what strikes me most is how hard it must have been for Will to recover in his head. I mean, a one-armed man who made his living with his hands suddenly becoming a cripple."

Beulah's eyes became watery again. "I didn't mean to suggest that it got easy after that night. He was an angry man. I was afraid he might go crazy. He kept having these imaginary pains. He said that his missing hand still hurt, but there was nothing left of it; that machine had chewed it up. All we found was his thumb, and we put it in a jar of alcohol.

Somebody told us we needed to bury it for his pain to stop. So we put it in a match box and buried it behind the shop."

"Grandma, did that make the pain go away?" Wesley asked.

"No, it didn't go away for years, until he went to this Mennonite chiropractor when his back got out of place."

"I remember that, Mama," Rita said. "We thought it was a miracle."

"What happened then?" Sam asked.

"Well, as I said, he went to this chiropractor for his back, and as he was examining Will, he said, 'Mr. O'Dell, where you lost your hand, does it feel like you still have a clinched fist?' And Will, said, 'Oh my yes. I feel like if I could just straighten those fingers, it would quit hurting.'"

Beulah's mood, obviously improved, paused dramatically as if she were telling a bedtime story to a child.

"So what happened?" Sam asked.

"The chiropractor told him that when the muscle in the arm was severed, a message was sent to his brain that the fist was closed. The muscle is extended when the hand is open. When it is contracted, the hand is closed. When Will's arm was severed, the muscle was shortened and his brain thought his hand was closed."

Sam looked at his forearm, opening and closing his fist. "Well, that makes sense, Beulah, but what did this Mennonite chiropractor do?"

"I don't know exactly. Will said he manipulated his neck and told him to look in his mind's eye and imagine he could see his missing hand clinched and then see it open. He told Will to imagine that every night before he went to bed, and as soon as he awoke in the morning to do it again for at least five minutes." Beulah hesitated and stared upward as if she was recalling more details.

Wesley was on the edge of his chair leaning on the table with his eyes locked on his grandmother.

Rita focused on Sam and his apparent interest in Beulah's story.

"Well?" Sam asked.

Beulah refocused and continued. "He kept doing what the chiropractor had said, and about a week later, he woke me up, all excited, and said, 'Beulah, it's gone. My fist isn't clinched anymore.'"

"That's remarkable, Beulah," Sam said, "a real example of mind over matter."

"Don't get me wrong, Sam, we still had some tough times, but that morning was a real turning point."

The next evening after dark, Sam and Rita drove Beulah to Pine Grove to visit Will in the hospital. They had dropped Wesley off at Morgan's store. Vivian had volunteered that he could stay with her.

On the way, Beulah's mind sorted through the countless times she had traveled this same route with Will. It seemed ominous to be riding without him. The cold drizzle splashing on the windshield did nothing to lift her mood. Sam and Rita's chit-chat sounded to Beulah like the background noise of a radio—she heard it, but she paid no attention to what was being said.

The Pine Grove hospital, technically, St. Luke's Hospital of the Ozarks, was a one-story red brick structure. It was only five years old and located at the site of the old Pine Grove Clinic, which had burned down.

It had been a remarkable blessing when the bishop in Springfield had announced Pine Grove as the location for a new hospital. Pine Grove was not a Catholic town, but the bishop for the region recognized it was a community in need, and one that served a much larger surrounding area.

A cast-stone statue of St. Francis of Assisi wearing a monk's robe and cowl flanked the entrance. His hands were folded and his head bowed in prayerful adoration of stone birds gathered at his feet.

As they walked from the car toward the entrance, Sam unconsciously flipped a cigarette butt that flew five feet in the air and landed next to the stone saint. "It looks like he's feeding chickens," Sam said.

"Sam!" Beulah said and scurried over to pick up the butt. She glared back at Sam. "I'm not Catholic, but that might be blasphemous, and we can't take any chances."

"You're probably right, Beulah," Sam said in an apologetic tone. He opened the glass entrance door for the women and followed them into the reception foyer.

They were greeted by the open arms of a life-size statue of the Blessed Virgin Mary standing in an alcove. The Holy Mother was adorned in a pink robe and illuminated by two alabaster wall sconces on either side. Looking at the statue, Beulah whispered to Rita, "She does look peaceful and kind."

Rita grinned and then partially covered her mouth with her hand and leaned closer to Beulah. "You're just trying to make amends for Sam."

"No, I'm not," Beulah said.

As they walked down the hallway to Will's room, Beulah's senses were on full alert: the hospital smelled of alcohol and medicine, which heightened her worry; an officious nurse, probably a nun, was snapping instructions at a man as she pushed his wheelchair; and the hushed tones of conversation from the rooms they passed reminded her of gossipy church women.

Will was sleeping when they entered his room. An IV tube ran to his right arm from a bottle suspended from a movable stand. He was curled up on his side covered by a white cotton blanket. His mouth was open, but he hardly seemed to be breathing. *He looks so small,* Beulah thought. *My strong man looks so weak.*

A curtain partitioned the room, and on the other side she could hear the murmured laughter of folks visiting the other patient in the room. Beulah bristled. More gossipy people. There was nothing to laugh about in her mind.

"Do you think we should wake him?" Rita asked.

Without turning her head from Will, Beulah said, "No, he needs to rest."

Sam, who had said nothing since coming inside the hospital said, "Let him rest in—" He stopped abruptly to modify his comment. "He needs to rest."

Will opened his eyes and blinked a couple times. "Mom, is that you?"

"Yes, Will. Sam and Rita are here, too."

Will fumbled on the bed stand for his glasses and knocked them off on to the floor. He frowned in frustration. Sam picked them up and placed them in Will's hand.

Will put on his glasses. "Now, I can see. Glad y'all could come." His tone was a faulty attempt to sound well.

Beulah leaned over the bed and kissed him on the forehead. His head felt hot and damp. She took his stub in her hand. "Are you feeling any better?"

"Maybe, a little . . . I'm just so tired and achy." A cough erupted with a rattling echo in his chest.

Beulah grabbed a tissue and covered his mouth as he spit up mucus.

Rita moved to the foot of the bed and touched Will's leg. "Hi, Daddy. You better get well soon before old Mr. Webster comes courting."

Will nodded his head and managed a thin smile but then appeared ready to doze off again, and Beulah said, "The doctor told us to only stay for a short time, so we're going to leave so you can get your rest. But we'll be back tomorrow."

Will opened his eyes wider and said to Beulah, "Come closer; I need to tell you something."

268

Beulah bent forward until her ear was in front of his lips. "What do you want to tell me?"

Will whispered in her ear.

Beulah's face turned ashen. She drew a quick, short breath and stood erect.

"Mama, are you OK? You look like a goose walked over your grave."

Beulah didn't reply for a moment. "I'm fine, I just got a chill. We need to get going." She tapped Will's stub and said, "Get some rest. We'll be back tomorrow."

Will was already asleep.

On the way home from the hospital, Sam had the car heater on high, and Rita tried to make conversation with Beulah, who was sitting in the back seat. Neither effort removed the chill that seemed to linger with Beulah, who sat without responding.

They had been on the road for nearly ten minutes, when Rita, gazing straight ahead, said, "Mama, what did Daddy say to you just before we left the hospital?"

Beulah had obviously anticipated the question and answered with measured rhythm. "It's between your dad and me, and I'd rather not say."

Rita turned around and looked at her mother over the seatback. "Mama, please tell me. It may do us both some good. You used to say 'a problem shared is one half-repaired.'"

The headlight beam from an oncoming car gave Beulah a shadowy appearance. She sat buttoned up in her winter coat, wrapped in her own arms, and clutching her purse against her bosom as a child might cling to a doll. Barely audible over the noise of the heater fan, she said, "He saw Lillie last night."

Chapter Twenty-three
Who Are You Going to Tell?

Sam sauntered from the front door of the three-bedroom ranch house that was now home for Rita, Wesley, and him. It sat on five acres just outside Ridgeview. He had been in dry-dock there for nearly a year, but it was beginning to feel like a home port.

The early fall morning had unfurled with military precision. Wesley made the school bus on time, and by the time Sam had shaved, showered, and had his first cup of coffee, Rita had ham and eggs on the table. Now, it was only half-past ten, and he was on schedule to be in Tremont before noon.

A 1956 Pontiac Chieftain sat in the driveway: a green and white two-toned V-8 with an automatic transmission. The dealer had said, "Sam, it's only three years old, and it's a dandy!" Sam had traded his Buick for it the previous day.

He reached in his pocket for the keys. The different feel of the Pontiac keys gave him a bit of nostalgic remorse. Remembering the sales pitch, Sam thought it may be a dandy, but he was skeptical that it could match his Buick, which he had paid cash for when he mustered out of the navy.

This Chieftain carried a promissory note and a chattel mortgage. *A car note, now that's a hell of a note.* It was unsettling, but he supposed he would get used to that, as he had the other changes of the past year: Selling Club 60 and getting married.

He got behind the wheel and pulled onto the county blacktop for the trip to Tremont. His stated purpose for the trip was to road-test the new car, but in fact, he wanted to see how Beulah was doing and take her some groceries.

He turned left when he got to Main Street and stopped at the Sinclair station on the east side of Ridgeview. Hoary-headed old Carl Tilton, the owner, emerged from the garage wearing a station cap that resembled a military officer's dress cover. He wiped his hands on an oil rag as he approached. "Fill her up with ethyl, Sam?"

"No, Carl, that's too rich for me until I get the restaurant open. Fill it with regular. I want to check the mileage and see if the dealer took me to the cleaners on this heap."

"Regular it is, then." Carl inserted the nozzle and peered through the side window. "I suspect this is a pretty good car. Generally, if a car is as clean on the inside as this one, the previous owner has taken care of the engine, too."

"Well, I hope you're right."

"Say, Sam, when are you going to get your new restaurant open? I'll bet you're not going to miss that drive back and forth to Birch View."

"In a few weeks, I hope. And you're right; I won't miss the drive. I'll tell you something else. Running a tavern is a hard life, and after Rita and I got married, we decided that it wasn't a life we wanted for Wesley."

"I know what you mean. All the goody-two-shoes in town could make it rough on a kid."

"That's for sure." Sam didn't tell Carl that he had recently donated a hundred dollars to the First Baptist Building Fund as a preemptory strike.

"You know what else, Sam?" Carl didn't wait for an answer. "By the time he got in high school, all his buddies would want him to steal beer for them."

"Oh, that's great news, Carl. I'd have to put my old buddy J. Robert Dalton on retainer."

"Well, from what I hear, if you need a good lawyer, he's the one to get."

Sam pondered Carl's observation for a moment. "Well, if you need his services you'll have to wait a few months. He and his new bride are on an ocean cruise to China. We got a postcard from Hawaii a few weeks ago."

"All the way to China," Carl murmured, as he returned the nozzle to the pump. "That'll be two-fifty. You want the oil checked?"

"Nah, I already checked it." Sam handed him the money.

"Thanks, Sam. See you later."

"You bet, Carl." Sam's tone was upbeat, but a wave of nostalgia had come over him. It seemed odd that J. Bob was the one at sea, and the real sailor was on land.

On the road, the Pontiac cruised along without the rattles the old Buick had developed. All those back-and-forth miles between Ridgeview and Birch View had taken a toll. The Pontiac smelled newer, too. The previous owner had installed seat covers that left the seats show-room perfect when Sam purchased it. He hoped old Carl was right about its maintenance history.

He turned on the radio. "Well neighbors, it's Thursday," a female announcer said. "Time for our weekly program, 'Gone but Not Forgotten.'" Sam frowned and said out loud, "Oh, crap, that's the sob sister Beulah never misses to find out who died." He changed stations to one playing music, but he couldn't help being reminded of Will.

Will's death had not been anticipated by his family. Sam had not appreciated that Will was the gravity that kept Rita's two worlds coexisting in close orbits. Sam's epiphany had come that last night in the hospital. He had seen the future as well as any stargazer: when one of the worlds breaks apart, the survivor inherits the pieces.

And Sam was a survivor. But he had always been a lone survivor, a sailor. And a sailor knew that survival often meant swimming away from other victims. They might pull you

273

down, or more likely, in a misguided attempt at heroism, you'd try to save them and end up drowning, too.

His initial thought had been to pack his sea bag, set sail, and jump ship at some port of call and hide out. But that fanciful notion only lasted until he saw Beulah, Rita, and Wesley looking like shipwreck castaways. At that moment, he knew in his gut he would be dropping anchor.

Sam's thoughts returned to the road, and to his surprise, the Tremont crossroads were just ahead. He applied the brakes and flipped the turning signal lever—another change—no more hand signals.

Fred Morgan was in front of his store loading a sack of feed onto his Tremont Grocery pickup. He looked over his shoulder to see who was turning off the blacktop. Sam waived, and Fred nodded in return, but his look was suspicious; it was clear he didn't recognize Sam in the Pontiac.

Beulah's new house was on the same gravel road as the old farm and only a quarter-mile from Morgan's. She had insisted on staying in the area after she sold the farm.

An early fifties black Chevy sedan, which Sam didn't recognize, was parked in Beulah's driveway. He hadn't anticipated her having company.

Sam hoisted two sacks of groceries from the back seat and closed the car door with his knee. The sacks contained supplies that Sam thought were essential: bread, eggs, bacon, coffee, toilet paper, and dishwashing detergent. The loaf of Holsum bread at the top of one sack smelled just-off-the-truck fresh.

Beulah met him at the door and ushered him inside. At her kitchen table, a fleshy man, not more than forty, sat with a coffee cup and a "have-I-got-a-deal-for-you" smile. He wore a white dress shirt, unbuttoned at the collar, with the sleeves rolled up to his forearms. *An insurance salesman?*

"Sam, I'd like you to meet Brother Melvin Wilson. He's the pastor at Pilgrim's Way, the new church I've been attending.

A preacher.

"Brother Melvin," Beulah said, "I'd like you to meet my son-in-law, Sam Rockford."

Melvin moved his chair back to stand up.

"Don't get up, Reverend." Sam sat the groceries on the table and extended his hand.

Still seated, Melvin gripped Sam's hand and said, "I'm glad to finally meet you, Sam; I've heard so much about you." Still holding Sam's hand, Melvin stood upright and said, "We were just talking about how nice it would be to see you at our services some Sunday."

Sam retrieved his hand from a clutch that had just gotten too warm. Turning to Beulah, he said, "Got any more coffee?"

"Sit down and I'll get you a cup."

Sam took a seat opposite Melvin but kept facing Beulah. "It sure smells good in here, Beulah."

"I baked cookies this morning."

"I can tell, but there's something else in the background. Sam surveyed the large country kitchen, and his nose focused on the scent coming from a table in the corner. Bunches of sage, dill, and lavender were drying in the sunlight that filtered through blue gingham check curtains. Several jars of home-canned green beans and blackberry jam highlighted the colorful palette.

"That's what I smell; those dried plants over in the corner. It reminds me of a little town I was in outside of Marseilles, France."

Beulah sat a cup of coffee in front of Sam and a plate of oatmeal cookies between the two men on the round oak table. "Brother Melvin, Sam was a navy man, and has been all over the world."

Reaching for a cookie, Melvin said, "Myself, I've never been overseas."

Sam had been assessing Melvin since he arrived. "Reverend, weren't you in the service during the war?"

Melvin, reaching for his second cookie, while part of the first still lingered in his mouth, said, "I have flat feet."

"Sam," Beulah said, "before Brother Melvin arrived, I was listening to 'Gone but Not Forgotten' on the radio. I couldn't believe the number of men who had died that were no older than you. There were two that I knew: Frank Nicholson and Tom Hays. Frank was only—"

"Jesus Christ, Beulah, doesn't anything good ever happen around here?"

"Sam, I wish you wouldn't use the Lord's name in vain," Beulah said. She gave him a sideways glance that practically said, *Especially with the preacher here.*

"Excuse me, Beulah," Sam said, but his face showed no trace of embarrassment.

He shifted his view to Melvin and was surprised that his irreverence hadn't prompted a reaction. Melvin had not risen in righteous indignation to rebuke Sam's sinful nature or to counsel him concerning his salvation. *Maybe I preempted his cue to jump in.* Melvin just kept slurping coffee, eating cookies, and smiling. It was a smile that came too easily to suit Sam.

"Parson, how long have you been a preacher?"

After washing down his last bite with a swallow of coffee, Melvin said "Well, I made a profession of faith at a revival in Pine Grove five years ago, and then two years later I got the call to preach."

"Where were you ordained?" Sam's tone was matter of fact, but he was reading Melvin's face as if they were playing poker. He saw a brief squint of anger around the edges of his eyes that was replaced in an instant with the smile. From the corner of his eye he could see Beulah glaring at him.

Still smiling, Melvin said, "I was ordained at this little church near the Arkansas border . . . I doubt you've heard of the town."

"Oh, maybe I have," Sam said with just a hint of curiosity."

"Sam," Beulah said, "Brother Melvin came highly recommended to the deacons of our church."

"I'm sure he did, Beulah."

Melvin pushed his chair backwards and stood up. "Well, Beulah, I need to move along. I have several other visits to make. Sam, it was nice meeting you."

"The pleasure was mine, Reverend," Sam said.

"Brother Melvin, before you go, I have a few things for you. I need to get a bag. Oh, I'll use one of these," Beulah said, nodding at the two sacks of groceries Sam had brought.

She emptied the sack with the loaf of bread and toilet paper and replaced them with two quarts of green beans and two jars of jam from the corner table.

Looking at the bread Beulah smiled. "You know, I just got a loaf of bread, and I'm afraid this one will be stale before I finish the other, so I'll just give it to you, Brother Melvin."

She put the loaf in the sack without looking at Sam. If she had, she would have seen his inscrutable face flinch. "Would you like some cookies, too, Brother Melvin?"

"Man can't live on bread alone," Melvin said and then chuckled at his own wit.

Beulah saw Melvin to the door and then sat back down at the table with Sam. "Well, what did you think of Brother Melvin?" Her voice was proud like a mother speaking of a favorite child and daring criticism.

"I think he's a freeloader. I thought preachers were supposed to help the poor, not make people poor."

"Oh, really." Beulah's mouth was a twitching thin line. "Well, Sam, just what do *you* believe in?"

"I believe in Sam's Code."

"And just what is that?"

"It means everybody pays his own way."

"Brother Melvin does a lot of good. He—"

"Ought to get a job of real work," Sam interrupted.

"He doesn't have time for another job. During the week he has to make home visits, and then—"

"Yeah, and I'll just bet his pastoral visits always coincide with dinner and supper."

"That's not true. As I was going to say before you interrupted me, he raises a few chickens to help make ends meet, and he's over at the church, late, several nights a week refinishing the basement. He won't let anyone help him either. It's going to be real nice when he finishes."

Silence followed, the subject was changed, and after awhile Sam indicated that he, too, had to go home.

As he stood up from the table, Beulah said, "Sam, tell Wesley that we're having a singing in two weeks at Pilgrim's Way, and we'd like him to bring his quartet. Tell him Frank Miller and I will be singing a duet. Maybe you could drive them. There will be dinner on the grounds."

Sam thought *drive him my ass*, but mumbled that he would tell Wesley, even though he had no intention of attending Pilgrim's Way, or any church for that matter. He didn't mind if his stepson went, but Rita would have to do the driving. He had no interest in seeing that preacher again.

As Sam motored home to Ridgeview, thoughts of Brother Melvin kept plaguing him. He had driven twenty miles to bring Beulah ten bucks worth of groceries only to have her give them to Melvin the Mooch. He lit another Chesterfield, inhaled deeply, and stared at the road.

When he arrived home, Rita was standing at the kitchen counter in a cobbler's apron dredging chicken pieces in seasoned flour and putting them on wax paper. On the wall in front of her, three ceramic geese were forever flying away across an orange wallpaper sky of coffee cups and saucers.

278

Sam wondered if he had made any more genuine headway today than those geese.

Rita turned her head, keeping her flour-covered hands over the counter. She flashed the smile of a wife who knew her husband would be pleased with the meal she was preparing. "We're having fried chicken tonight."

Sam slipped behind her and put an arm around her shoulder. "You're the best cook and the prettiest woman in town."

Rita leaned into his hug. "You say that to all the girls. How were things at my mother's?"

"Her preacher was there. What a freeloader. He sat there eating cookies like a truck driver eating peanuts. Then he left grubstaked with an armload of groceries, including a loaf of bread I took her."

"Well, he probably needed the food, Sam. You know preachers don't make much money."

"Ah, preachers always have their hands out. I spent twenty years in the by-god United States Navy, and that psalm-singing bastard isn't even a veteran. And I'll tell you another thing, the way he clutched on me when Beulah introduced us, I thought he was going to start the laying-on-of-hands right there."

Rita wiped her hands with a towel and faced Sam. "You just don't like preachers."

"That's not true. I liked old Reverend Love."

"It was *Dove* not *Love*, and that's just because he used to come to the backdoor of Club 60 for a six-pack so none of his flock would see him."

"Is the coffee ready?"

"Not quite. Go in the living room, and I'll bring you a cup in a minute."

Sam turned on the TV and sat down at his usual place on the couch. It was his habit to sit on the forward part of the seat cushion, which made it easier to reach the hubcap-sized ashtray on the coffee table. With time the cushion foam lost all memory, and no longer had a front edge. Neither Wesley nor Rita sat there because the backs of their thighs would rest on the frame.

Rita brought in the coffee and sat down at the other end of the sofa to watch the Huntley-Brinkley newscast.

A half-hour later, Wesley came home from school and sat down in a chair near his mother. "Wesley, Sam tells me that Grandma wants you to bring your quartet to the singing at her church next month."

Wesley frowned. "Jeez, I don't want to do that. None of the guys will want to go to a country church with a bunch of hillbilly singers. Anyway, we don't know any church songs. We're a folk group."

"Now, Wesley," Rita said, "if you tell them there will be plenty of good food and homemade pies, they'll want to go. Tell them a bunch of cute girls will be there—they'll go."

"Nah, I don't want to do it."

Sam shifted his view to Wesley. "Look, pal, you seem to have forgotten something. You're only twelve years old, and you're not making the rules around here. Don't worry about your buddies; I can talk to their parents."

The following week Sam was at the Ridgeview Drugstore drinking coffee at the soda fountain and talking to one of the regulars, Pooch Simpson. Pooch owned a small dairy farm and made deliveries to a dozen homes in town, including Sam's. He was complaining that he was routinely short of milk jars because his customers didn't return them.

"Pooch, a jar can't cost that much," Sam said.

"Maybe not, but what really pisses me off are all the cockeyed things they do with my jars. They use them to catch drips from leaky faucets, fill them with crankcase oil, or leave them full of water next to a dog's bowl."

Pooch stopped talking to refill the bent-stemmed briar that was hanging from his protruding lower lip. The pipe was practically a fixture in his mouth. Years of smoke had cured his face to a poochy, puckery droop. He was only sixty, but he looked ten years older.

Sam began telling Pooch about the preacher and the groceries. He was only about a minute into the story when Pooch interrupted him.

"Hell, Sam, I know who Melvin Wilson is. He used to drive a truck for the Farmers' Exchange in Pine Grove before he got religion. I think he got fired. As a matter of fact, I saw him the other day at White Plains buying corn. He bought a hundred pounds. Said he had chickens."

"I wonder why he would drive to the next county to buy chicken feed," Sam said. "I didn't think he paid for anything, anyway."

"Maybe he's got a little something on the side," Pooch said out of the side of his mouth as he puffed on his pipe.

On the morning of the singing, Rita and Wesley looked at each other in disbelief when Sam announced that he was going to drive everyone. Rita thought that at the last moment he would find some excuse to change his mind, but an hour later, the Pilgrim's Way Church came into view with Sam behind the wheel, Wesley and Rita up front, and three boy singers in the back.

From a half-mile away the white steeple of the church could be seen on a hill beyond dried-out hayfields. Mature oak trees shaded the church and adjacent cemetery, creating an image worthy of a bank calendar.

After Sam stopped the car in the parking area, Rita said, "Now, boys have fun, but behave and remember this is like being at church."

The boys promised good behavior and scrambled out of the car.

281

Sam peered through the open side window at the folks gathered about the church yard. "Well, there's Beulah, and she's with the preacher. Rita, why don't you let your mother know we're here and meet Brother Melvin."

"Aren't you going to come over, too?"

"I've already had the pleasure of meeting the blessed reverend, and I better go ride herd on the boys," he said as he took stock of the picnic area. "Man, will you look at all that food."

A veritable feast was being spread on tablecloths that covered sawhorse tables. Women in Sunday dresses arranged crockery bowls, heaped with potato salad and golden-brown fried chicken, among platters of fresh tomatoes, cucumbers, pickled beets, and deviled eggs. A sugar-cured ham that must have weighed twenty pounds anchored the end of one table; the other end held a multitude of pies, cakes, and cookies.

The spread did not disappoint Sam and the boys, who took places elbow to elbow and ate with the enthusiasm of threshers.

Jimmy, the quartet's tubby, bass singer, said he had never tasted anything so good as he gobbled his second piece of blackberry cobbler.

Rita hoped to persuade a Pentecostal lady wearing an old-fashioned sunbonnet to share a molasses cookie recipe with her.

When the singing was about to start, Beulah informed Rita and Sam that she and Frank Miller would be singing first and that the boys would be next to last.

"Well, Beulah," Sam said, "I'll slip in the back to hear you and the boys, but meanwhile, I'm just going to loaf around outside."

Brother Melvin, looking full and important, assumed the pulpit to welcome the gathering. He still had on the suit and tie he had worn for his sermon that morning. He glanced at his wristwatch and then squared his gaze to the audience. He paused until it was silent.

"Welcome everyone. I'm Melvin Wilson, the pastor here at Pilgrim's Way. As you all can see, we're an ecumenical gathering: Pentecostals, Baptists, Methodists, and non-denominational. But we have set aside our doctrinal differences and are here to make a joyful sound unto the Lord. We must have nearly seventy here. Amen!"

A few "Amen's" resounded from the congregation.

"Frank Miller, our song leader here at Pilgrim's Way, will start things off by leading us in 'I'll Fly Away.'"

Frank, a banty rooster of a man, strutted to the front with a guitar strapped over his shoulder. He thumbed through the dog-eared pages of his paperback hymnal and found the selection. "Turn to number thirty-three in your hymnals."

Without aid of his guitar, he began to croon, "Some glad morning when this life is over," and in response to his beckoning arms, the congregation joined as a chorus.

As he continued to sing, Frank sat his song book aside and began strumming his old Silvertone archtop guitar. It was strung with Black Diamond strings, and the tinny sound resonating from those strings was a perfect match for the nasal intonation and pitch of Frank's singing voice. It was the same voice that called his hogs. It was the voice of a backwoods musician and reflected his seventy-two years.

At the close of the last stanza, Frank quit playing and basked in the group's enthusiasm. After a moment, he said, "I'd like for Beulah O'Dell to come up and help me with a special number this afternoon." Beulah dutifully got up and assumed her position to his left.

"We're going to sing 'Love Lifted Me,'" Frank said. He strummed their starting pitch and they began. Beulah's alto harmony softened Frank's thin tenor, and Frank echoed the after-time refrains. They sang without aid of a songbook.

283

Beulah couldn't read music, and Frank was a shaped-note singer.

Sam could hear the singing inside as he roamed in the cemetery, nursing a cup of coffee and smoking a cigarette. The late September sun had warmed the breezeless day to the mid-eighties, and after fifteen minutes, he moved to the shade of a post oak tree at the side of the church.

He lit another cigarette and rested back against the tree. Gazing at the church, he concluded it needed a coat of paint. Rita once said, "After twenty years in the navy, if something doesn't speak or salute, Sam is liable to paint it."

The peeling paint on the basement window frame had his attention, but a nagging suspicion about the preacher made him want to investigate.

He walked over for a closer look and scraped loose chips from the frame with his pocketknife. *Needs linseed oil,* he thought. As he picked at the glazing around the pane, he peered into a window to the basement. His view was the inside of a closet.

"Well, I'll be a son of a bitch," he said under his breath. A shaft of sunlight lit a section of coiled copper tubing that protruded from underneath a canvas tarp. *A copper worm.*

When Wesley's group was announced, the boys sidled from their pew to the front. They had attempted to dress alike in black slacks and white short sleeve shirts, but with various rumples and poorly tucked shirt tails from playing tag after dinner, their appearance was still motley. Only their haircuts were in tune: flattops, short and plastered with Butchwax.

Wesley blew the starting note from a pitch pipe and tried to hum the tone, but missed the mark and started a half-step flat on "Michael Row the Boat Ashore."

By the end of "Michael," it seemed to Wesley that a chill was coming from the audience. Nothing joyful was evident in the swarm of grimaces and beady eyes in the pews.

It was the card-trick-at-school feeling all over again. Then, like a cloud passing to reveal the sun, he saw his grandma, who was mouthing encouragement for him to continue. The boys regained a musical ear for their second selection, "Kumbaya," but the audience was already lost.

From the front row, Esther Eyepock, a gray-haired Pentecostal woman, with the beadiest eyes of all, furrowed her brow and glared at the boys. Then, too loudly, like a person hard of hearing, she leaned sideways and said to her two sisters sitting next to her, "Those songs are too worldly." Her sisters took up the vigil and began glaring at the boys, too.

Esther was their leader. She was a maiden lady committed to the strictness of her religion. With a fair complexion and facial veins close to the surface, her parchment skin had the powdery blush of a persimmon. Like her sisters, she was a tall, bony woman who did not suffer foolishness—particularly from children.

The boys returned to their pew, but they could feel the continued scowls of the Eyepock sisters.

The sisters were next to perform. Wesley gawked at them as they strode forward. He nudged Jimmy and said, "They look like they ought to be on a covered wagon."

"No, I think they look like witches," Jimmy whispered back.

A stern look from Beulah silenced the two boys.

Esther nodded to Brother Melvin, and the sisters began singing, "There were ninety and nine . . ." Their voices were cacophonous and shrill. Wesley could see out of the corner of his eye that Jimmy was trying not to laugh. Wesley hoped Jimmy wouldn't start; he was prone to giggle-fits.

As the Eyepock sisters sang, a flash of gold from Esther's mouth caught Wesley's eye. By Jimmy's facial expression, he had seen it, too. It was a capped tooth with gold around the edges. It was catching on her lower lip.

"Looks pretty worldly to me," Wesley said out of the side of his mouth.

Jimmy was unable to contain himself. He snorted and burst out in laughter. He put his hand over his mouth and strained to keep it in, but the giggle bug had him. Wesley became infected and started laughing, too. The situation might not have reached critical mass, but Jimmy farted. It was a blunderbuss, and the rest of the quartet erupted in laughter. Gabriel's trumpet at the Second Coming couldn't have been more disruptive.

Beulah elbowed Wesley, glared, and shushed at the boys with little effect. They were out of control. Just when it seemed the laughter had stopped, an aftershock rumbled.

Nearly everyone in the audience had their eyes on the commotion in the third row. Those in the back leaned forward for better views, and those in the front turned around.

The incident may have only lasted a minute, but the effect was insufferable to the Eyepock sisters. They were in the middle of their second verse when the blasphemy occurred. They continued singing but did not start the third verse as intended. Their eyes were riveted on the boys as they went back to their seats.

Brother Melvin rushed to the pulpit and the room became quiet. He ignored the incident, concluded the day's celebration with elaborate praise for the participants, and invited everyone to stay for fellowship and coffee.

Beulah and Rita wasted no time marching the boys over to the Eyepock sisters to apologize. The boys' attempt at redemption was ignored. Esther eyeballed Beulah and Rita, as if the boys did not exist, and reproached them that the boys should be taught manners. Without further word, she walked away with her sisters.

The ride home was mostly without conversation.

286

That evening, after Wesley had gone to bed, Sam and Rita were sitting in the living room. Sam said, "You know, I think I'll pay a visit to my old buddy, Sheriff Green."

"Are you planning on going coon hunting and drinking whiskey with Speedo all night in the woods again? You'll get bursitis if you do."

Sam didn't respond.

"What are you up to?"

"Oh nothing."

At one o'clock in the morning the following Thursday, Speedo Green didn't expect to find anyone stirring at the Pilgrim's Way Church. To be sure, he surveyed the premises with the spotlight that was mounted on the left door of the patrol car. The church and the cemetery were stark and white in the beam.

"Well, it looks empty," he said to Sam, who was riding shotgun. "Are you sure it's in there?"

"I'd bet a hundred bucks on it."

Speedo parked behind the church. The padlock on the basement door was little challenge for Speedo. The second selection from a ring of keys he had brought opened the door. Another skeleton key worked on the closet door inside. Twenty minutes later, Sam and Speedo were back on the road with two copper moonshine stills in the trunk of the cruiser: a twenty-five-gallon square still and a five-gallon pot still.

"Sam, I have to tell you, this is the first time I ever confiscated a still and felt like a burglar."

"You were just avoiding the red tape," Sam said. "I can just see that preacher's face when he discovers his stills are gone. He'll be lucky if he doesn't get struck by lightning, the way I expect he'll be cussing."

Later that morning, Sam confessed to Rita that he hadn't gone coon hunting and showed her the stills he had stashed in the utility room. "Isn't that little one a cutie."

Rita put her hands on her waist and frowned. "Now, let me get this straight. Mama's preacher had moonshine stills in the church basement, and you and the county sheriff stole them from him."

"We didn't *steal* them from him. Anyway, who's he going to tell?"

"And just what are you going to do with them . . . go into the moonshine business?"

"No, I just want to make some for personal use. I could save five bucks a bottle."

"I remember when you tried to save money by making your own potato chips for the tavern. This won't turn out any better. At least you couldn't go blind from bad potato chips."

"Nobody is going to go blind from these stills—they're copper," Sam said.

"Just where do you plan on keeping them?"

"The big one can be hidden in the attic—the only entrance is from our bedroom. And I'll lock the little cutie in the closet in the utility room; anyway, you can hardly get to it with all the junk stored from Club 60. In fact, I'm going to use that old electric range to cook it off."

Over the next week, Sam assembled the equipment he would need. He followed Brother Melvin's example and bought small amounts of corn, sugar, and yeast in different counties to avoid suspicion.

Sam had never made moonshine before, but he had a recipe and fair understanding of the process. He combined the ingredients with warm water in a stone crock, covered it with a sheet, and locked it in the utility closet. Four days later the corn had sprouted—the mash was working.

A week later Sam announced to Rita that the mash was ready and that he was going to cook a batch that night as a proficiency run.

"Well, wait until Wesley has gone to bed . . . and don't blow up the house."

L. D. Whitaker

By midnight the utility room was organized like the staging area for a military operation. The still, a gallon glass jar, a meat thermometer, an electric fan, a sprinkle can with ice water, and a pint Mason jar filled with a flour and water paste mixture were lined up in a row by the stove.

He filled the pot still two-thirds full with the mash and sat it on the largest burner of the stove. On the side of the still, above the level of the mash, he inserted a meat thermometer in a small hole he had punched. He wouldn't heat the mash much past 175 degrees—the point of vaporization.

Rita's cautionary words weren't lost on Sam. He sealed the cap of the still and the opening around the thermometer with the paste mixture to act as a pressure valve. The gallon jar, which he was using as a catch-container, was positioned away from the stove. Alcohol and fire did not mix.

As the mash warmed, the room was saturated with the aroma of green wood and yeast; Sam opened the window and turned on the fan. He got a cup of coffee, fired up a cigarette, and sat in an old rocking chair, as focused as an alchemist on the brink of a discovery.

An hour and six Chesterfields later he saw the first condensation on the coiled tubing. He stubbed out a half-finished butt and began sprinkling the copper worm with ice water.

Minutes later, the first drops of translucent liquid fell into the jar. In another hour he had collected nearly a gallon of *singlings*—what moonshiners called the first run.

The second run was quicker. Before the sun came up, Sam had over a half-gallon of fairly high-proof ethyl alcohol. He lifted the jar and sniffed the contents. *Doesn't smell like much.* He dabbed his index finger into the brew and licked it. It wasn't bad. He sat the jar back on the floor and sighed. White lightning. Mountain Dew. Moonshine. Stump water. And, he had made it.

He crept into the bedroom and touched Rita on the arm. "Hey, Rita," he whispered, "get up. It's ready for tasting."

She raised her head, not fully awake, and looked at the clock. "It's four o'clock!"

"Yeah, I know, but we need to sample it. "

"I'm not going to taste your hooch on an empty stomach," she said.

"Ah, hell, eat a piece of bread, first." Sam said, vexed at Rita's lack of shared enthusiasm.

A few moments later Rita was in the kitchen wearing a robe and a look of annoyance. Sam didn't look up as he dipped a coffee cup into the jar and pulled it back half-full. His face was glowing and his eyes wide, not the mug of a man who had been up all night.

From his cup, he poured two fingers' worth into a glass, formerly a two-ounce pimento spread jar, and presented it to Rita.

Rita sniffed the glass. "It doesn't smell like anything."

"Pure alcohol has almost no smell," Sam said, "and this is probably about 140-proof, or 70 percent alcohol. It's the flavoring that's added that gives gin and whiskey the smell."

Sam raised his cup toward Rita in the gesture of a toast. "Here's to Brother Melvin—may his water always turn to wine."

"That's cruel," Rita said, but she tapped his cup with her pimento glass and brought it to her lips with the hesitance of a man about to taste breast milk.

"Come on, Rita, you hardly tasted it."

Rita took a swallow. At first her face registered nothing, then it contorted as she coughed and gasped for air. "It didn't burn going down. It burned from the bottom back up," she said, watery-eyed, and sat the glass on the table.

"Yeah, but it stayed down," Sam said, as if that were the measure of a distiller's success. "But how did it taste?"

Rita wiped her eyes with her hands, "It has kind of an oily taste."

"That's the fusel oil; this was only the second run. After the third and fourth runs, the alcohol content will get higher—maybe a 190 proof—then I'll filter it through charcoal to remove the last trace of the oil."

"Well, Sam, I have to say, I am surprised that you pulled this off. It's actually remarkable." Rita patted him on the head. "But let's go to bed."

"I've got to clean up the mess first."

"Well, I'm going back to bed."

Sam put a lid on the jar and stored it in the cabinet under the kitchen sink. He pushed it back to the side, out of view. He locked the door to the utility room and tiptoed to the bedroom—he didn't want to wake Rita a second time.

Just after sunrise that morning, Pooch Bailey knocked on the front door. He was there to deliver milk and pick up a return jar. There was no return jar on the porch. When no one answered, he stepped to Wesley's front bedroom window and tapped on it with his pipe.

"Hey, Wesley, wake up. I need a jar."

With a few more taps, Wesley went to the front door still half-asleep, and Pooch told him again that he needed a jar. Wesley clomped to the kitchen, but didn't see a jar on the counter. Then he looked under the sink. At first he didn't see one, but when he got on his knees and craned his neck to the side, he saw a jar filled with water. He poured out the clear liquid, gave the jar to Pooch, and went back to bed.

Later that morning after Sam quit cussing, and he and Rita deduced what had happened to the moonshine, a wry smile came to Rita's mouth.

"What's so funny, Rita?"

"Well, Sam, it looks like you're in the same boat as Brother Melvin."

"How's that?"

"Who are you going to tell?"

Sam frowned and then paused. "Do you think Wesley can keep a secret?"

"I expect he can if *you* ask him.

A thoughtful look came to Sam's face, as if a latent feeling had become lucid. "You know, baby, we've been through a lot the past few years. It seems like yesterday when you brought Wesley to Club 60 the first time, and he was so shy. Now, he's almost a teenager, but I think you're right that if I asked him, he could keep a secret."

"Sam, I never told you this, but when Mom found out that I had gotten a job at Club 60, she told me I was driving my geese to a poor market—she was wrong. And I don't think she believes that, now."

"That's nice to hear, but she's changed since you first came back. She gets along much better with you. It must seem like she went away, but has come back."

"It does seem that way, but it's funny that the religious woman's path home went through a barkeep. Or should I say *moonshiner*?

Lonnie Whitaker grew up in the Missouri Ozarks and attended a two-room country school; managed to survive the sixties and Missouri University Law School; and is now district counsel for a federal agency. He lives with his wife, two standard poodles, and a tomcat in Jefferson County, Missouri. On Missouri Tiger games days, they all wear black and gold.

His writing credits include articles in magazines and literary journals; awards in nationally advertised fiction contests; a residency fellowship at the Writers Colony at Dairy Hollow; and serving as associate editor for an Hourglass Books anthology, *Peculiar Pilgrims: Stories from the Left Hand of God*.